HUCKLEBERRY SPRING

"Do you like Adam Wengerd?" Ben asked.

Emma swallowed hard. "I . . . I don't know."

"I don't think you should date him anymore."

"You don't?" Through the fog, she latched on to one thought. Had Lizzie's plan worked? Was he jealous enough to get back together with her?

Of course not. How could she dare open her heart to such a possibility?

Instead of pulling away like he absolutely, positively should have, Ben traced his finger down the side of her cheek and rubbed his thumb along her jawline.

"Adam can't take care of you the way you need to be taken care of," he said in a low, rumbly tone that might have made her swoon if she had been prone to fainting.

She couldn't read the emotion in his eyes as he grew breathlessly still and stared at her mouth.

Oh, no. Oh, no.

Without warning, he wrapped his free hand around her waist, pulled her closer than she would ever have dared hope, and kissed her. . . .

Books by Jennifer Beckstrand

HUCKLEBERRY HILL

HUCKLEBERRY SUMMER

HUCKLEBERRY CHRISTMAS

HUCKLEBERRY SPRING

Published by Kensington Publishing Corporation

Huckleberry Spring

JENNIFER BECKSTRAND

ZEBRA BOOKS
KENSINGTON PUBLISHING CORP.

http://www.kensingtonbooks.com

ZEBRA BOOKS are published by

Kensington Publishing Corp.
119 West 40th Street
New York, NY 10018

All Kensington titles, imprints, and distributed lines are avail-
able at special quantity discounts for bulk purchases for sales
promotion, premiums, fund-raising, educational, or institu-
tional use.

Special book excerpts or customized printings can also
be created to fit specific needs. For details, write or
phone the office of the Kensington Special Sales Manager:
Attn.: Special Sales Department. Kensington Publishing
Corp., 119 West 40th Street, New York, NY 10018. Phone:
1-800-221-2647.

Zebra and the Z logo Reg. U.S. Pat. & TM Off.

First Printing: February 2015
ISBN-13: 978-1-4201-3649-4
ISBN-10: 1-4201-3649-6

First Electronic Edition: February 2015
eISBN-13: 978-1-4201-3650-0
eISBN-10: 1-4201-3650-X

10 9 8 7 6 5 4 3 2 1

Printed in the United States of America

Chapter 1

Felty's eyes did not stray from his newspaper as Anna Helmuth laid a four-inch stack of brochures on the table next to his recliner.

"Take your pick, Felty," Anna said sweetly, plopping herself into her rocker and scooping up her knitting. "What kind of surgery would you like to get?"

"Hmm," Felty said, not paying attention as he perused the death notices.

"Sometimes you squint. Maybe you'd like to get Lasik."

Felty lowered *The Budget* so he could spy his wife over the top of it. "What are you saying, Annie Banannie? You think I squint?"

Rocking back and forth, Anna inclined her head toward the thick stack of papers without missing a beat in her knitting. "It's that purple brochure on the top. I don't know. You might be too old for Lasik."

"I'm only eighty-four—not too old for anything." The newspaper crunched as Felty set it in his lap. He stared curiously at Anna's potpourri of brightly colored brochures. "What is Lasik, and why do you have a brochure about it?"

"I already told you, dear. You need to pick what kind of surgery you want. Lasik is just one of many choices."

"Do I need surgery?"

"Of course you do, dear. Spring is the busiest time of the year on a farm, and I need you laid up and unable to work for at least a month."

Felty took off his glasses and cleaned them with his handkerchief as if this would help him decipher what Anna was talking about. "You want me laid up for the spring work?"

"You're squinting, dear. You need Lasik."

"What will become of the chickens?"

Anna lifted her eyebrows, pursed her lips, and nodded as a gesture of reassurance. "I've got it all worked out. Our grandson Ben will take over the farm while you're indisposed. And look after the chickens."

Felty furrowed his brow as if someone had taken a plow to his forehead. "You're not still scheming to get Ben and Emma Nelson back together, are you? It's a lost cause, Banannie. A lost cause."

"Lost causes are my specialty," Anna insisted as her fingers and knitting needles seemed to meld together in a blur of fuzzy pink yarn. "Ben and Emma belong together, and if anybody can make it happen, we can. We've never missed yet."

"I don't know if I'd say we've never missed."

"Then what would you call our amazing success matching up our grandchildren?" Anna asked, tilting her head to one side and peering at her husband over her glasses.

"Lucky guesses."

Anna shook her head. "No such thing."

"It doesn't matter," Felty said, smoothing his paper to get a better look at the story about pike fishing in North Dakota. "It would take a miracle to get Emma to set foot on Huckleberry Hill ever again."

"Leave that to me. I have a few tricks up my sleeve."

Felty frowned as if he'd already lost this debate. "But Ben lives in Florida. What young man in his right mind would trade Florida for Wisconsin?"

"Ben would, if he knew his *dawdi* needed him. If he knew the farm would fall to pieces without his help."

"Ben's got twenty cousins living in Bonduel who could help with the garden and the animals. He'd wonder why we couldn't use one of the other grandchildren."

Anna's ball of yarn tumbled off her lap. "Don't you worry. I'll see to it that all of the other grandchildren are excessively busy on their own farms."

"And how will you see to that?"

"Now, Felty. They all want Ben to come home.

If I tell them we're going to lure Ben with your surgery, the cousins will be perfectly happy to neglect their grandparents. Ben has such a tender heart. He'll come back when he knows we need him desperately, especially when you're going to be feeling so poorly after your operation."

Felty leaned back in his recliner and raised his arms in surrender. "I'm feeling worse already."

"That's the spirit!"

Chapter 2

Emma Nelson plopped herself down on a chubby tree stump, glanced around to make sure no one lurked in the woods, and burst into tears. After months of hiding her deepest emotions, she deserved to wallow in a little self-pity today. Despite her aching heart, she had refrained from blubbering all winter long.

Of course, her stiff-upper-lip act hadn't fooled her brother Mahlon. Only when she made a point to burn the bread and "accidentally" let the chickens into the house did he suspect the worst was over.

She shouldn't have strayed from the lane, but she had been unable to resist when her curiosity pulled her in the direction of the white aspen tree. She wanted to see if it was still there. Not that the tree would have uprooted itself and walked away, but maybe, by the hand of Providence, it had been struck by lightning or smitten with a disease and toppled over sometime during the long winter.

But *nae*. The gnarled old aspen hadn't moved. Even though it dripped with fuzzy springtime buds instead of silvery green summertime leaves, it could have been yesterday that she had sat on this very stump and watched Ben carve her name into the bark.

Ben loves Emma.

After seeing her loss so plainly etched into the tree, her carefully guarded composure had disintegrated, and here she sat, bawling like a baby over a stale memory. Why had she not ignored her heart and continued marching up Huckleberry Hill without a sideways glance? Why had she not taken an axe to that tree last autumn or rather, asked her brother Mahlon to take an axe to that tree? Mahlon forbade her from picking up sharp objects. He had definitely overreacted to that incident in the haymow three years ago.

Emma swiped the tears from her cheeks. They were quickly replaced with new ones. She had exactly five more minutes to cry before her appointment with Anna Helmuth. Time to quit wallowing.

With a sigh, she stood and brushed off her dress. She dabbed at her face with her apron and pinched her cheeks. Crying made her complexion pasty.

Dry leaves crunched beneath her feet as she found her way back to the lane and trudged up the hill. Despite her reluctance, she had promised Anna she would come, and she didn't want to be late.

Anna's request for a visit had surprised Emma. Didn't the entire Helmuth family despise her? Why would Anna want help from Emma, the girl who had somehow impelled Anna's grandson to flee to Florida?

The thought of seeing Anna almost called forth fresh tears. Before their broken engagement, Emma had spent many happy hours on Huckleberry Hill with Ben and his adorable grandparents. Once Ben moved to Florida, Emma had avoided his entire family. She wasn't in the same district as Anna and Felty, so she hadn't been forced to see them at church, and she kept away from the places that Anna and Felty and the rest of Ben's family might frequent. The associations and memories were too painful to bear.

After a brief pause to collect herself, Emma squared her shoulders, ambled around the last bend in the lane, and came within sight of the house. Anna, looking like springtime in a peach sweater, stood on her covered porch grinning with anticipation and clutching the railing as if she might float away if she let go. No doubt Anna had knitted the sweater she wore. She loved to knit, and no one had the heart to tell her that Amish sweaters and coats were supposed to be black. Only black.

Anna clapped her hands in delight, which was the same greeting just about everyone got when they came to Huckleberry Hill. Anna had a way of making each person feel as if they were her favorite. Emma thought it was an invaluable talent for a *mammi*, a grandmother, to possess.

"Lo and behold, it's Emma Nelson," Anna squealed.

She skipped down the porch steps as if she walked on twenty-year-old knees and drew Emma into her embrace. "It's been ages, absolutely ages since you've set foot on Huckleberry Hill. We've missed you something wonderful."

Emma pulled away and blinked rapidly to keep the tears from forming. She cleared her throat and gave Anna a warm but guarded smile. "How have you been, Anna?"

"Right as rain, except for not seeing you as much as I would like."

"And how is Felty?"

"You know how badly he snores at night."

Emma shook her head and sprouted a half smile. "I didn't know."

"Well, he's getting his deviated septum fixed next week. We're hoping he's off his feet for at least a month, maybe longer. But they say it's a pretty routine surgery." Anna looked a little concerned at the possible ease of Felty's recovery. She patted Emma's arm. "We'll hope it gives us enough time."

For the better part of a year, Emma had been pretending that she didn't care for Ben Helmuth. If she could convince Anna of that fact, she could probably convince anybody. "And how is Ben?" she said, lacing her tone with casual interest and unaffected cheerfulness so she sounded like a polite friend asking about the grandchildren in general. A twinge of pain twisted her stomach into a knot. She hadn't said his name out loud for months.

Anna tugged her sweater more tightly around

herself. "Oh, we've no time to talk about Ben just yet. Come out of the chill."

Anna led the way up the porch steps and into the great room where her husband Felty filled the stove with wood and sang at the top of his lungs. *"Time has made a change since my younger days, Many of my friends have drifted away, Some I never more in my days will see. Time has made a change in me."*

"Felty," Anna said with a smile as wide as the Wisconsin River, "look who's here."

Emma loved Felty like he was her own dawdi. He had always been so kind and nothing seemed to ruffle his feathers, even Anna's cooking. He stopped singing and turned his gaze in Emma's direction. His eyebrows rose in unison. "Annie, I don't know how you do it, but you are a wonder."

Emma wasn't quite sure what to make of his reaction. "It's nice to see you again, Felty."

He straightened, stroked his beard, and studied Emma's face with a twinkle in his eye. "Are you ready for all this rigmarole?"

She still couldn't make heads or tails of what Felty talked about. Maybe he was finally beginning to show his age.

Going to her husband, Anna giggled uncomfortably and nudged Felty in the direction of the hallway. "What a silly notion, Felty. There'll be no such thing as a rigmarole here. There won't even be a kerfuffle. Emma is here to help me with my vegetables. Everyone knows the Nelsons have the most beautiful produce in Bonduel."

Shaking his head, Felty shuffled down the hall. "If I were Emma, I'd buckle my seat belt, just the same," he called over his shoulder.

Dear Felty. His mind was definitely going.

A knot formed in Emma's stomach as she glanced around the room. The massive cast-iron cookstove and the gas-powered fridge stood against the far wall. A counter holding the sink jutted from the wall at her right and cut the kitchen in half. A round kitchen table sat on Emma's side of the counter. She and Ben and his grandparents had spent many an evening playing Bananagrams at that table. Anna would invent wild spellings, and Emma would sneak all her *Z*'s and *X*'s into Ben's pile when he wasn't looking. He would protest in mock indignation and then come up with outrageous words like *zyzzyx*. Ben was the smartest boy she knew.

The great room looked as if not even a newspaper had been moved since last summer. She and Ben had often sat on the sofa talking late into the night. Once he'd even dared hold her hand. Emma caught her breath and stuffed her fist into her pocket. After all these months, she could still feel the tingle of Ben's calloused skin against hers.

Maybe this wasn't such a *gute* idea after all.

She took a deep breath and did what she always did. She pretended that nothing could possibly be wrong.

She smiled as if she'd be delighted to spend the entire summer on Huckleberry Hill playing Banana-grams with Anna. "Are you ready to get started?"

Anna glanced at the bird clock on the wall before bustling to the counter and retrieving a box of supplies. "*Jah.* I got a jar, scissors, some tape, and newspapers, just like you said."

She laid the box on the table, and Emma picked up the medium-sized jar and separated a sheet of newspaper. "You want the newspaper to be two widths the size of your jar." She showed Anna how to measure the paper using the jar as a guide and handed Anna the scissors. "Now we cut off the extra paper."

"Oh, dear. I don't think I can make it perfectly straight," Anna said.

"No need to worry about that. It can be crooked and still work fine."

With more uncertainty than was required, Anna slowly trimmed the newspaper to the proper size.

"Gute," Emma said. "Now fold the paper two-thirds of the way down. Jah, like that."

Anna grinned. "I'm gute at folding. I folded plenty of diapers in my day."

"Now lay the jar on its side and roll it up in the newspaper."

Anna followed directions well. Emma taped down the edge of the newspaper and showed Anna how to fold it over the bottom of the jar and tape it again. "Now pull the jar out of the paper, and you have a seedling pot for your pumpkin plant."

Anna worked the jar carefully from the newspaper and balanced her creation in the palm of her hand. "I never thought I'd see the day."

"How many pumpkins plants do you want to grow this year, Anna?"

"Just one."

"One?"

"And I desperately need your help."

Emma curled the corners of her mouth. "Pumpkins aren't hard to grow. They just need plenty of water and sunshine."

Anna's eyes danced as if they held a thousand eager secrets. She looked at the clock again. Did she have somewhere to go? "I want a giant pumpkin, like the one you grew last summer."

Emma's heart did a little flip-flop. The eight-hundred-pound pumpkin. Ben had been so proud of her. Even though they weren't supposed to flaunt their talents, he had called the local paper to take a picture and then found a buyer who paid her three hundred dollars for her pumpkin. Ben was even more excited than Emma had been. He told her he thought she was the most wonderful, smartest girl in the world to grow such a thing. Oh, how she loved him for that!

Or rather, *used to* love him. That's what she wanted everyone to believe. None of her family should spend a single day worrying about how she got along without Ben.

"Giant pumpkins take a lot of work. You need to tend to them every day."

Anna nodded vigorously, as if Emma had guessed a riddle. "That is why I insist on paying you for your trouble."

"You want to pay me to grow a pumpkin?"

"It would mean so much to my great-great-grandson Toby. I promised him a giant pumpkin this summer."

Emma regarded Anna doubtfully. Toby was barely two years old. He wasn't likely to have begged Anna for a giant pumpkin. Even if he had, anything over fifty pounds would be plenty giant for him.

Growing a giant pumpkin for Anna was sure to be a strain on Emma's carefully guarded emotions. Memories of Ben would permeate the very air of Huckleberry Hill. She'd see his shadow everywhere she went and in every pumpkin that sprouted from the stem.

Inwardly, she chastised herself. She had to be strong for *Dat* and Mahlon and all the other people who fretted about her. What better way to prove to everyone that she wasn't suffering than to keep company with Ben's grandparents without so much as thinking twice about the grandson?

Her mother had admonished her months ago. *Emma, get over the boy. You're as mopey as an old cat.*

As far as *Mamm* knew, Emma's heart had moved way down the road from Ben. She couldn't abide *Mamm*'s irritation any more than she could bear Mahlon's fretting.

Anna waited for an answer. Was she holding her breath?

"Are you sure you want *me*?" Emma said. The girl who'd accidentally burned down Zimmerman's chicken coop last year? The girl their grandson found so unworthy?

"I won't settle for anyone else."

Anna's adamant response took Emma aback. What could Anna possibly see of value in Emma's help? Anna certainly didn't act as if she felt any ill will toward her grandson's ex-fiancée. Had she forgotten about the chicken coop?

Emma pursed her lips. If Anna didn't object to Emma's tending pumpkins on Huckleberry Hill, then Emma would do her best to help. Perhaps Ben's family would not think so badly of her if Ben's mammi accepted her with open arms. "Okay," Emma said. "I'll do my best."

Anna all but burst with laughter. "That is wonderful gute. Felty will feel so much better knowing you are watching out for our pumpkin."

As long as the chickens didn't protest. Every hen in the county was probably terrified of Emma Nelson, even if Anna wasn't. No doubt Emma had a dangerous reputation among the chickens.

She took a deep breath. "I can come three days a week to tend the pumpkin, and maybe I should plant some other vegetables for you too, so you'll have plenty for canning come autumn."

Anna's eyes strayed to the clock once again. "I love peas and beans."

"Okay. And some cucumbers?"

"I love dill pickles," Anna said, gushing like a newly drilled well.

Emma couldn't help but crack a smile. Anna's

enthusiasm rubbed off on everybody who came within ten feet. "I will go to the market and buy special pumpkin seeds and bring them back tomorrow so you can plant one in your pot."

Anna's face lit up. "Tomorrow? That would be better than my wildest dreams."

Emma giggled. Sometimes the enthusiasm went a little overboard.

A firm knock at the door caught their attention. Anna glided across the room and opened it.

Emma's throat constricted, rendering her unable to breathe while her heart hammered against her chest, making it all the more likely that she would suffocate.

Ben Helmuth, looking as handsome and formidable as ever, stood on Anna's doorstep with a suitcase in one hand and his straw hat in the other. His tousled golden hair framed his face like a halo, and the cleft of his chin made his jaw look as if it were chiseled out of stone.

Their eyes locked, and Emma found it impossible to look away. A mixture of utter astonishment and undiluted pain flashed across his face. He was as shocked to see her as she was to see him. What was he doing here?

"Emma," he said, so softly it felt like a caress. She wanted to melt at the sound of that low, beautiful voice, even though he spoke as if it were torture to say her name.

How she managed to talk, she would never know. "I . . . Anna . . . I've got to go look at your dirt." Her sentence made little sense, but Emma wasn't about to hang around to explain herself. Keeping her head down, she snatched her sweater from the hook and practically ran out the door, trying to ignore Ben completely even as she stumbled over his foot when she rushed past him. She couldn't have helped it, even though he tried to step out of her way. He was so tall and broad that he left little room for her to pass.

Halfway to Anna's vegetable patch, she heard Anna call out cheerfully, "After you look at my dirt, you must stay for supper."

Stay for supper? If Anna thought for one minute that Emma would set foot in that house while Ben was there, she truly didn't understand anything.

Why, oh why had she ever agreed to come today? Horrible, horrible mistake.

A groan tore from her lips as she tromped to the garden, scattering Felty's chickens in her wake. Ben Helmuth was back. She might never feel happy again.

Ben stood frozen in Mammi's doorway while the great room spun around and around him as if he sat on a merry-go-round. At the barn raising seven years ago, he'd cracked his thumb so hard with the hammer that he'd actually seen stars. Seeing Emma felt much worse.

What was she doing on Huckleberry Hill? And

how would his heart go on beating now that he'd seen her?

His gut clenched violently. All that time in Florida and nothing had changed. After a glimpse of Emma, he felt less in control of his emotions than ever, as if a tidal wave had swept him off his feet and sucked him into the depths of the sea.

With her yellow hair and eyes the color of the ocean at sunrise, she had haunted his dreams every night since he'd left Wisconsin. If anything, she was more beautiful than he remembered. With that ten-second look at her, he realized that his absence had made him long for her even more.

"Oh, dear," he heard Mammi say, as if from a great distance.

With his suitcase clutched tightly in his fist, Ben found that his legs would not support him. He stumbled to one of the kitchen chairs, dropped his suitcase with a thud, and buried his face in his hands.

"Did you have a taxing journey?" Mammi asked, seemingly oblivious to what had passed between him and Emma.

Emma had blanched white as a sheet when she'd seen him, and she tended to stumble over things when she was embarrassed. Well, not really. She tended to stumble over things no matter what state she was in. Surely she had gotten over him by now. At least that's what his sister Lizzie had written in her letters. But maybe Lizzie had been mistaken. Ben kneaded his forehead to clear his thoughts. "Is she okay?"

Mammi patted him on the shoulder and took his hat. "She didn't come specifically to see you, if that's what you're asking. We're growing pumpkins together."

Dear Mammi. She never saw anything amiss with the entire world. "But the way she ran out of here, do you think she was upset?"

Mammi hung his hat on the hook where Emma's sweater had been. "She was quite eager to take a look at my dirt."

Ben couldn't be satisfied with that answer. Of course he'd upset Emma. They hadn't seen or heard from each other since they'd broken their engagement. He had to go out there. No matter how hard it would be to talk to her again, he had to make sure she was okay.

Ben stood up, put his arms around Mammi, and kissed the top of her head, glad he'd gotten his height from Dawdi. Mammi was a puny little thing. "It's so good to see you."

Mammi hugged him back with the affection of a hundred mammis. "For a year I've prayed that you'd come back to us."

In spite of his heavy heart, Ben smiled. According to Mammi, she'd been praying for his return before he'd even left. He'd been gone exactly seven months and twenty-seven days. It wasn't hard keeping track when every hour seemed like a year away from Bonduel. "I need to make sure Emma's okay," he said. He took Mammi's hand and squeezed it reassuringly. "And then I want to hear all about

Dawdi's surgery. I don't want you to worry. I will take care of the farm, and we're going to do everything we can to get Dawdi better."

Mammi's eyes twinkled. At the moment, she didn't seem all that concerned about Dawdi's condition, even though her letter had brimmed with anxiety. "You'll never know what a blessing you are to us."

Setting aside his own serious misgivings about coming home, Ben had hopped on a bus the minute he'd received Mammi's letter. Dawdi needed him. That's all that mattered. Not even his feelings for Emma or his pain at seeing her again mattered. "I'm going to go check on Emma," he said, patting Mammi on the arm. "I'll be right back."

"Tell her I made something special for supper."

Ben closed the door behind him. If he wanted Emma to stay for supper, he'd better not tell her that Mammi had done the cooking.

Emma tripped out to the garden as fast as her trembling legs would take her. Ben looked as straight and sturdy as a maple, and so handsome. The emotions rushed at her like a runaway horse, stronger and more devastating than ever. Her voice cracked as the hitch in her throat turned into a gut-wrenching sob.

She loved Ben Helmuth. She loved him so much. And it hurt so bad.

A torrent of tears flowed unchecked down her

cheeks as she marched past the bare garden plot, dodged Felty's peach trees, and ran into the safety of the woods.

Just get over it, Emma. He doesn't love you.

He had been so repulsed by her that he had moved all the way to Florida so he wouldn't be forced to lay eyes on her again.

When she ran far enough to be assured that no one would hear her crying, she stopped to catch her breath, pulled a tissue from her pocket, and blew her nose loudly. Ben would probably find that repulsive too.

She growled in self-condemnation. She'd worked so hard to bury her emotions and stifle the insistent tears. She usually cried over Ben in private, and now she'd done it out in the open twice in one day.

The look of anxiety and concern she had seen on his face was the same one he had worn the day he broke off their engagement. Ben was so kind and so sensitive to other people's feelings that she was sure it pained him to hurt her, even if he didn't love her. The bitter truth was that she didn't deserve him, and he pitied her for it.

Her heart sped to a trot when she heard shuffling through the underbrush behind her. She turned to see Anna's little dog, Sparky, waddling toward her. She must have followed Emma out of the house. Emma bent over and scooped Sparky into her arms. She rested her cheek against Sparky's fur and scratched behind her floppy ears. Even if Ben didn't like Emma, Sparky would always be her friend.

She cried her last tears and wiped her eyes. Taking a deep, hiccupping breath, she played Mamm's voice in her head.

Buck up, Emma. It's not the end of the world.

Sparky had settled comfortably into her arms. "Sorry, Sparky," Emma said as she placed Anna's dog on the ground. With her handkerchief, Emma dabbed at her nose in a way that not even Ben would have found repulsive. She would go back into the house and show Ben how happy she was and how hard she was trying to be a girl worthy of a gute Amish man. And she would not trip over her feet, no matter what.

"Emma?"

Her heart all but somersaulted in her chest, and she thought she might be sick. She couldn't face him, not looking like this. Ducking behind a tree, she did her best to gather up the pieces of her heart she'd strewn about the forest floor. She could just make out Ben's tall frame through the budding trees as he stood in the garden plot and called her name. He didn't know where she was. It gave her a few seconds to talk herself into being brave. Ben would admire someone with courage. She smoothed her dress, did up the buttons of her black sweater, and despite everything, pinched her cheeks.

Mustn't look pasty and pale for her reunion with Ben Helmuth.

She snapped her fingers to bid Sparky to follow her and decided on a leisurely stroll out of the woods. Ben would assume she had taken a walk and never guess she'd been crying.

Whom was she fooling? He'd know exactly what she'd been doing. Her eyes and nose were probably bright red and as puffy as Mamm's special dinner rolls. Maybe she should rub a little mud on her face just in case.

Ben didn't love her. What did it matter how homely or disheveled she looked?

"Emma?" he called again, the apprehension growing in his voice. He was always more concerned about other people than the other people were about themselves.

Her foot caught on a lumpy tree root, and she stumbled noisily but managed to maintain her balance. "Oomph," she grunted as leaves and pine needles crackled thunderously beneath her feet.

"Emma?"

Righting herself, she pasted a smile on her face. "Coming," she sang, as if she were an irritating little bird chirping her way through the forest.

He turned around and started walking in her direction, no doubt bent on helping her navigate through the thicket. She quickened her pace and met him at the edge of the woods.

The moment she looked into those eyes, she recalled a thousand lovely memories, and her best intentions nearly crumbled. How could she pretend to be happy when Ben stood before her in all his wonderfulness?

Hoping Ben wouldn't see her hands shaking,

Emma bent down and picked up Sparky, the only ally she had at the moment. She wished Mahlon were here, or better yet, twenty of her friends. No boy could break through the defenses of a gaggle of giggly, silly girls. A boy usually gave up on any girl if she was surrounded by a wall of friends.

They stared at each other briefly, Emma reliving every moment of the last time she had seen him. The memories were overpowering.

"I . . . I wanted to check on you and make sure you were okay," he said, breathing heavier than he needed to for only having walked to the garden. His expression brimmed with sympathy. Of course it did. He felt sorry for her. "I know it must have been a shock to see me after so long. I didn't expect to see you."

She used to love it when he looked at her like that, as if he understood everything about her—her fears, her sorrows, her lack of balance—and cared about her more than he cared for himself. Today she couldn't bear to see that look of pity, as if she were beneath his notice but he was giving it to her anyway. His expression made her whole body ache.

Averting her eyes, she smoothed Sparky's fur and checked the dog collar to make sure it was securely fastened. She squared her shoulders and smiled until she thought she might grind her teeth into powder. "Anna wants me to help her grow a giant pumpkin, like the one I did last summer." Her voice cracked, but Sparky yipped at exactly the same time and covered Emma's blunder. Sparky was proving to be a valuable friend after all.

By the look on his face, she could tell he was thinking about last summer's giant pumpkin too. Was it a good memory or just one more reason he had left her?

"I am glad to see you're out doing things you enjoy and helping my mammi in the process. You were always so thoughtful."

"Anna didn't tell me you were planning a visit."

"I wasn't, until she wrote about Dawdi's surgery."

"His deviated section? For his nose?" Emma couldn't remember the word. Was that what Anna had told her?

"I'm not even sure what kind of surgery. All I know is that Dawdi is very sick and needs my help."

That was Ben to a fault. He would drop everything to help someone else.

She clamped her lips together so nothing remotely close to a sob would escape. Why did her thoughts attack her like that, making her remember all the things she loved about him? If she ever wanted to feel normal again, she would have to shove those memories aside. But, oh, it was so hard to do.

Emma expelled a deep breath and walked among the peach trees to the garden plot. She finally gained control of her voice. "Will you be here long?"

"Only as long as Dawdi needs me. Maybe a month. No longer."

Of course he wouldn't care to stay any longer

than he had to. Eight months ago, he had wanted nothing more than to be as far away from her as possible. She cleared her throat. "I told Anna I'd help with the garden, but if you would be more comfortable, I don't have to come back."

His expression darkened, and for a brief moment he looked truly stricken. Then he masked whatever emotion had been there and replaced it with concern. "Emma, I'm truly sorry for hurting you the way I did."

The compassion in his voice brought her a hair's breadth away from tears. She couldn't reply for fear the dam would break. She managed a slight twist of her lips and a dismissive wave of her hand, as if she were swatting mosquitoes.

He raised his eyebrows and nodded encouragingly. "Lizzie kept me up to date."

Lizzie Helmuth. Ben's sister. Another precious relationship Emma had lost in the aftermath of Ben's rejection. When Ben left his family and moved to Florida, Lizzie had blamed Emma. They hadn't spoken since August.

"Lizzie wrote and told me you were doing well." He studied her face for confirmation. She forced the corners of her lips upward and nodded.

Ben seemed relieved, as if a huge burden had been lifted from his shoulders.

His reaction stung like a thousand yellow jackets.

She wanted to lash out at him, to tell him how devastated she had been when he left her, how she still cried into her pillow several times a week. How the very mention of his name made her want to double over in pain.

If she wanted to hurt him as badly as she was hurting, all she had to do was tell Ben how terribly she suffered. He had always been attuned to other people's feelings. During *rumschpringe*, he couldn't see a sad movie without being depressed for days. He'd quit going to movies even before he was baptized.

Since she couldn't speak, she tried to make her expression as serene and reassuring as possible.

"Since it looks like you're going to be spending a lot of time here," he said, "I hope we can put the past aside and be friends again, even if it's just for a few weeks." He suddenly looked uncomfortable, as if he wasn't really sure he wanted what he said he wanted. He gave lip service to an amicable relationship, but Emma could tell friendship was out of the question.

She couldn't look him in the eye. Kneeling down, she let Sparky slip from her arms and then picked up a handful of dirt and sifted it through her fingers. "Gute soil for pumpkins."

Unfortunately, he squatted beside her so his icy green eyes were level with hers. "I don't think we should avoid each other, but I don't want you to think . . ." He cleared his throat. "I mean, I'm going back to Florida, no matter what."

Emma swallowed his words and tried not to choke on them. He thought that poor, desperate Emma would get her hopes up if he was nice to her, which wasn't altogether unlikely since Ben Helmuth was the most desirable boy in the world. Who wouldn't hope for him every minute of every day?

Still on her knees, she coughed and sputtered as if she'd eaten a bug. "Oh, no need to worry about that. I'm just here to grow vegetables." She couldn't help herself. "I'm sure there's lots of suitable Amish girls in Florida."

His frown deepened. "Jah. Plenty."

Probably hundreds of beautiful, tan girls who had never tripped over their own feet or even had a clue what fire extinguisher foam smelled like.

This forced conversation, this fake friendliness between them, was infinitely more painful to Emma than Ben's surprising appearance at Anna's front door. He acted as if he'd completely forgotten what they'd been to each other. She leaped to her feet and marched toward the house before she lost her precarious self-control.

Curse those long legs. He caught up to her in about three strides. "Emma, all I want is for you to be happy."

What a lie. He'd rather be far away than see her happy. He wanted Florida girls more than he wanted her happiness. She quickened her pace. The exertion kept tears from forming in her eyes. It also made her voice bounce up and down like a rubber ball. "Well. I will. Be fine. Just fine." In about twenty years or so.

That answer didn't satisfy him. His frown was

about as deep as it could go without cutting into the back of his head.

She walked even faster until she practically ran. She was taking a big risk. She didn't usually keep her balance when she ran. But Ben wouldn't let her pull away, determining to reach the porch at the same time she did. "I would feel so much better if—"

"I have to go to the bathroom," she blurted out, which was technically true. She needed a long piece of toilet paper to mop up the tears that were about to burst forth.

Ben stopped as if he'd run into a brick wall. He knew better than to get between a girl and her toilet needs. It was a dirty trick, but at least he stopped following her.

She jogged into the house without saying a word to Anna or Felty, ran to the bathroom, and locked the door behind her. She let a silent sob escape her lips as she tugged a piece of toilet paper off the roll.

There was only one thing to do. She'd hole up in the bathroom until she could slip away from the house without being seen. And yes, she'd square her shoulders, get control of herself, and return tomorrow. Ben's appearance had taken her by surprise. Now that the shock was over, she was perfectly capable of being around him without dissolving into a puddle of tears. Ben would be satisfied, Mahlon wouldn't have to worry, and Anna would get her pumpkin.

As long as everyone else was happy, her feelings didn't matter one whit.

She looked down. Without meaning to, she had managed to unroll the entire roll of toilet paper. It sat in a fluffy white heap at her feet. Sighing, she slowly started to roll it back onto the cardboard. She hoped Ben didn't need to shave or anything. She'd be here for a while.

Chapter 3

Mahlon pounded his fist against the table and made her jump. "I can't stand it."

Emma set the jam on the table and studied her twin brother doubtfully. "What's the matter?"

"This bread is golden brown," he said, as if that explained everything.

"I thought I did a gute job on it. You should eat it while it's still warm. The rest of the family will be home soon enough. You might not get another piece."

"You didn't burn the bread, and not one egg is cracked. Not one."

Emma felt herself get warm. "I don't always burn the bread."

"No, you don't. You only burn the bread when you're having a gute day. The eggs get cracked when you waltz around the coop with your basket. You haven't waltzed for months."

Emma pretended not to know anything was different. "That's ridiculous, Mahlon. Maybe I'm becoming less clumsy because I'm not a teenager anymore."

"Only last month you started burning the bread again. You spilled potting soil on Mamm's rug last week. I thought you were doing better. What happened?"

Emma averted her eyes and spread jam on her bread. After Ben had left for Florida, Emma had kept to her room for three days while Dat took up the habit of pacing back and forth in front of her door and Mahlon had stomped around the house slamming doors and growling like a bear, which he only did when he was deeply troubled about something.

That's when Emma realized she had to stop wallowing so Mahlon and Dat would stop worrying.

August twenty-fifth, a week after Ben decamped for Florida, Emma had pasted a smile on her face and attended every gathering, singing, and frolic she could get to. Her cheeks got sore from grinning. Her throat wore raw from laughing. She encouraged every young man who seemed interested. She canned spaghetti sauce and peaches and made three quilts for the mission fund and hadn't pricked her finger once.

It had been exhausting, but Dat had stopped worrying and surely Ben's family saw a quick recovery. Only Mamm and Mahlon had suspected the truth—that on the inside she had shriveled up like a daisy in the winter. Mamm admonished her again and again to "cancel the pity party." Mahlon had been excessively concerned about her. He was her twin brother, after all.

After her embarrassing morning on Huckleberry Hill, she had come home and baked two loaves of bread. Unfortunately, Mahlon knew that since Ben had broken up with her, she had been concentrating very hard on fixing her many flaws. That was why she hadn't cracked eggs or accidentally set anything on fire for months.

"When you won't look at me, that's when I know it's really bad," he said. She immediately lifted her gaze to meet his, and he smirked. "You can't hide anything from me, Em. I can tell when you've had a hard day."

"It wouldn't have anything to do with the fact that my eyes are puffy and red?"

"A dead giveaway." He scowled. "I knew you shouldn't have gone to the Helmuths' today. It's too soon to be keeping company with the enemy."

"The Helmuths aren't my enemies."

"Their grandson broke your heart. They're my enemies."

Emma looked daggers at her brother. "Don't ever say such a terrible thing, Mahlon. We should feel only forgiveness in our hearts."

He slumped his shoulders. "I know. You're right. But I get so mad for you, and you won't get mad for yourself. For him to dump you like that after you got engaged—it was heartless."

She lowered her eyes and studied the crisscross pattern of the tablecloth. "He had his reasons."

"Which I can't understand."

"The wonder is that he ever wanted to marry me in the first place."

"How can you say that? Any boy would consider himself doubly blessed to marry you."

"Not someone as smart and as good as Ben," Emma said. "I know how lacking I am compared to him."

Mahlon scowled and shook his head. "That's the stupidest thing I've ever heard."

Emma sighed from deep in her throat, frustrated that Mahlon refused to see it. She counted her faults on her fingers. "I have skinny legs and unruly hair. I'm a mediocre cook, a bad quilter, and although Ben never saw me change a diaper, he must have guessed deep in his heart that I'm not good at it."

"As usual, you are talking nonsense."

"Admit it, Mahlon. I'm always getting myself into trouble. Ben pulled me through more than one scrape last summer. He must have decided he didn't want to be babysitting me for the rest of his life."

"So you've been trying hard all winter on not having one mishap." Mahlon frowned until his eyes were mere slits on his face.

"I'm maturing."

"You're hoping Ben will take you back if you never have an accident again."

Emma caught her breath in surprise. "Ben is

never taking me back. I simply want to prove that I'm not hopeless, like everyone thinks I am."

"The nonsense is flowing like a river out of that mouth of yours."

Emma grabbed a knife from the drawer and sat next to Mahlon. "I lost one of the cows once. What if I lost one of my own children? No man wants to marry into trouble like that."

Mahlon shook his head and grinned reluctantly. "I don't think so, Em."

"I'm a mess," she said, buttering a slice of bread for Mahlon. Maybe she could distract him into forgetting this whole conversation.

"Just because you don't let the small details bog you down doesn't mean you're a mess. There's no one more fun to be with."

The words crowded in her throat before tripping clumsily out. "Ben doesn't think so."

Mahlon pounded on the table again. His anger always manifested itself noisily. "Then forget him."

Emma's lips drooped. Mahlon was grumpy enough, but he would be even more unhappy with what she was about to tell him. "That is going to be impossible."

"No, it's not. He's gone. Pretend he doesn't exist."

She stood up and busied herself at the counter. "I can't," she said, in a matter-of-fact tone sure to raise Mahlon's blood pressure. "He's back."

His mouth dropped open. "Back in Bonduel?"

"He is helping his grandparents on the farm while Felty recovers from surgery."

Mahlon scooted his chair from the table and stood up. "I'm going over there right now."

"No, you're not."

"Yes, I am. I'm going to tell him to get himself back to Florida on the next bus and leave my sister alone. After what he did, he's got no right to show his face here ever again."

Emma put her hands on Mahlon's shoulders and pushed him to sit. "You'll do no such thing. Ben's being here is none of your business."

"What did he say to you? Did he make you cry?" Realization leaped into his eyes, and he pounded the table yet again. "Of course he made you cry. I should have connected the puffy eyes."

Mahlon, who was fiercely loyal to the people he loved, tended to get carried away with his affection. He might have made a lot of noise and blustered like a summertime cloudburst, but he never meant any harm to anyone, even Ben. He simply wanted to be sure Emma knew how indignant he felt for her sake.

Emma shaped her lips into a scold and let her eyes flash with reproof. "You can take a deep breath and control your temper."

Mahlon unclenched his jaw and wilted beneath her gaze. "Okay, okay, I'm sorry. You know I don't mean it. I'm venting."

"Venting is not a very Christian thing to do."

"What about throwing eggs at him? I could probably get away with that."

She shook her head with what she hoped was an unbelievably stern expression on her face.

He raised both hands. "Just kidding. Mostly."

"It's not nice, Mahlon."

"I know, but if he saw how devastated you were, he would ask me to throw eggs at him."

Emma huffed a defeated sigh. "Jah. He would."

"You can still avoid him while he's in town. If he's here to help while Felty has surgery, he won't be around long. You don't have to go to Huckleberry Hill, and you won't see him at *gmay*. It will be like he's not even in Wisconsin."

"I'm seeing him tomorrow."

Mahlon scrunched his face as if he'd popped a dandelion into his mouth and chewed it up. "What for?"

"I promised Anna I'd help her plant pumpkins yet."

He lifted his fist to pound the table.

"Don't," she warned, almost laughing at the look of annoyance that traveled across his face.

He pulled back and folded his arms across his chest. "Are you trying to kill me or what?"

"If I truly want to get over Ben Helmuth, don't you think it would be better if I faced the problem head-on instead of avoiding it?"

"Nope. Not better at all."

"Then look at it this way. You know what kind of

a person Ben is. He would be upset if he knew I still grieve over him."

"So? You shouldn't be the only one suffering. He broke off an engagement, Em. That's not a small thing."

"Believe me, he wasn't smiling when he did it."

This didn't seem to make Mahlon feel better. His eyebrows were still almost touching. "I don't see why you need to go up there. Pretend you're over it from a distance."

"I promised Anna."

"Then I'm coming with you."

"Nae, you're not." He opened his mouth to speak. She stopped him. "And I refuse to take any eggs with me."

"It's just an idea. You don't feel like taking them right now, but you might get up there and get the urge to hurl a few at him."

Emma giggled. "I won't."

"If you won't give Ben what for, I'll have to take matters into my own hands."

She glared at him in mock displeasure. "You behave yourself."

"Of course I'll behave myself. I'm only venting."

"Venting is unchristian."

The rest of the family burst into the house and interrupted the relative calm. Andy and Perry each had several plastic Walmart bags slung over their arms.

"Hullo, Emma and Mahlon," ten-year-old Andy

said, straining to lift his armload of bags onto the counter.

"Your arms are going to fall off," Mahlon said. "Are you too lazy to make two trips?"

Percy slid his bags onto the counter. "We had to do it all in one trip. We knew you'd be too lazy to help us unload."

Emma had three brothers and two sisters. She and Mahlon were the oldest. Their brother Percy was fifteen, Rose had turned thirteen last month, and Lisa and Andy were both still in primary school. Dat hired a van every two weeks to take the family into town to Walmart for shopping. Emma usually stayed home, but the younger ones found it to be a great adventure.

Lisa and Rose came in the house with one bag each, put them on the counter, and started putting groceries away while Dat lugged in a battery for the new light. In addition to propane floor lamps, the bishop had approved floor lamps that used a regular bulb powered by a large battery. The new lights were much safer than propane lanterns and didn't hiss like the propane did. Many folks liked the quiet of the new lights, but Emma found the propane-lantern hiss quite comforting on a dark winter's evening.

"It smells like fresh bread," Dat said, passing through the kitchen with his armload. "Mahlon, go help your *mater*."

"Don't need it," Mamm said, coming into the house with as many bags slung over her arms as either Andy or Percy had. "Rose, leave the hamburger out. I'm making spaghetti."

Emma busied herself helping Rose and Lisa put groceries away. Lord willing, Mamm wouldn't notice the puffy eyes.

"How was Walmart?" Emma asked.

"Busy as ever," Mamm said. "How did the bread turn out? It doesn't smell burned this time."

"It's perfect, Mamm," Mahlon said, with just a hint of disgust in his voice.

Mamm didn't seem to notice. "Gute." She slipped a new bottle of cinnamon into the spice rack. "What did Anna Helmuth want this morning?"

"Oh," Emma said. Why did her voice betray her like that? She covered the catch in her throat with a cough. "She wants me to help her grow a giant pumpkin for her grandson."

The ploy didn't work. "Look at me," Mamm said, propping a hand on her hip.

Ach, how she wished she had tried cucumber slices instead of plain cold water on her eyes. Edna Fern said cucumber slices made everyone's eyes look five years younger and completely erased any signs of uncontrollable weeping.

"Emma, look at me."

Hoping to look poised and perky, Emma raised her eyebrows, stretched a smile across her teeth, and turned to face Mamm.

Insincerity never fooled Mamm, especially not in one of her children. "You've been crying," she said, as if Emma's feelings were the biggest nuisance of her life.

"I'm not crying now," she said weakly.

Mamm waved away the excuse. "I'm not surprised. When you left for Huckleberry Hill this morning, I knew you'd come back like this."

"Like what?"

"Like your whole life is over." She shook her head and looked away, as if she were too vexed to give her daughter the time of day. "I won't put up with the wallowing, Emma. Your dat was like to worry himself sick."

Emma found Mahlon's anger vastly more bearable than Mamm's disgust. Mahlon wanted her to be happy again. Mamm seemed to find Emma's heartbreak inconvenient to the entire family.

She didn't need a lecture, not when her emotions threatened to burst like a dam right here on the kitchen floor. "I'm sorry, Mamm. I'm doing much better. Today was just one of those bad days."

"If you ever manage to become someone's wife, you won't be able to afford the luxury of a bad day. You have to make every day what you can of it without wallowing."

If you ever manage to become someone's wife. Mamm's words stung as if she'd been smacked in the arm with a wet towel, the way Mahlon used to do when they dried dishes together as children. Even her own mamm had doubts that Emma would ever marry. As flawed as she was, who would have her?

"I won't ever wallow again," Emma said, which

was a hopelessly ridiculous statement but exactly what Mamm wanted to hear.

"Gute, because wallowing makes your face wrinkly. Boys want someone young and fresh to marry. It won't help your cause to look old before your time."

"Yes, Mamm."

"Ben Helmuth is not the only fish in the lake. Be happy he's gone to Florida."

Emma glanced at Mahlon. How would Mamm react if she knew Ben was back? Perhaps it would be better to give her that piece of information when her irritation simmered. Mahlon frowned and raised an eyebrow. He might not like her planting pumpkins on Huckleberry Hill, but he knew better than to say anything like that in front of Mamm.

Instead, he rescued her. "Mamm, Emma said she'd help me milk the cows before dinner."

"Then go," Mamm said, as if she had closed the door on all of Emma's problems. That's how it worked with Mamm. She'd persistently beat a dead horse unless somebody sidetracked her.

"*Denki* for pulling me away," Emma said as they went outside and Mahlon closed the door behind them. "You know how much I irritate Mamm."

"I'm sorry she's so hard on you, but she's right about one thing."

"That I'll never manage to get a husband?"

"Don't be ridiculous, Emma. Of course you'll get a husband, if you want one. Ben isn't the only fish in the lake. Maybe you should consider other fish."

"I hate fishing."

Mahlon linked elbows with her and steered her in the direction of the chicken coop. "There is something you can do that will help you not be so sad."

"What's that?"

"Let's go get some eggs."

She yanked her arm from his. "Forget it, Mahlon."

"I'm just venting," he protested in mock confusion. "Can't I vent without you getting all huffy?"

"Venting is unchristian."

"So I've been told."

The gravel crackled beneath the wheels as Ben drove Dawdi's buggy up the lane. His sister Lizzie and his mamm, in thick black jackets, hung clothes on the line. Lizzie's hands were mottled red. Hanging laundry was still chilly in April.

Lizzie turned her head to see who drove down the lane, and her eyes almost popped out of her head. He hadn't told them he was coming. They'd be thrilled. And uselessly hopeful that he was home to stay.

Mamm sprinted to the buggy with her arms outstretched as Lizzie ducked into the house, no doubt to alert the rest of the family to his return. Ben jumped from the seat and caught Mamm as she threw herself into his arms.

"My boy, my boy," she squealed. "Wonderful gute." She laid a kiss on his cheek and held on tight. "You've come back."

He squeezed his mamm tightly, savoring every fleeting moment he had with her. Titus Junior, Ben's younger brother, raced out the door with Lizzie and Dat close behind.

Mamm let go, and Titus took her place, being careful not to poke Ben with the toothpick he had sticking out of his mouth. Dat wrapped his arms around both of them, and they laughed with pure joy. Waiting for her turn, Lizzie embraced Mamm and tears sprang into both of their eyes.

"Ben," Titus said through his tears, "I've missed you something wonderful yet."

Ben couldn't help it. He shed a few tears himself. It felt so gute to be home.

Dat put a hand to Ben's cheek. "Your mammi told us you would be coming. We're so happy."

"Mammi told you? I didn't even know myself until three days ago."

Dat shrugged. "My mamm has a sense about these things. I've learned not to dismiss what she tells me."

Ben reached over and took Lizzie's hand. "You've grown even prettier since last August. I didn't think it was possible."

Lizzie grinned. "Quit your teasing." She stepped into his arms. She had definitely gotten her height from Mammi Helmuth. Lizzie stood more than half a foot shorter than Ben. "I'm glad you've come back, even if it's just for Dawdi."

When Ben shot Mamm a curious look, she

nodded. "Mammi warned us. You're only here for Dawdi's surgery."

Ben's heart sank. Only for Dawdi's surgery. It wasn't long enough, and yet it would be too much. He didn't know where he would find the strength to pull away again. "How bad is Dawdi, really? Mammi sounded so frantic in her letter, but when I asked her about it, she says it's nasal surgery, which doesn't sound all that serious. Is she trying to keep me from worrying?"

Dat cleared his throat. "You know Mammi. She likes to keep all of us guessing. We're glad you came and that you can help Dawdi in his time of need."

Mamm was already halfway to the house. "I know you'll be staying at Mammi and Dawdi's, but I'll move some beds around in case you want to lay your head here a night or two." She glanced at Dat. "I need a strong man to move that furniture."

Dat puffed out his chest and followed Mamm.

"Titus, help Lizzie and Ben finish hanging laundry," Mamm added, over her shoulder, "and then, Titus, muck out before dinner." Ben often wondered if all mamms were as bossy as his.

Dat and Mamm marched into the house while Ben, Titus, and Lizzie ambled to the clothesline.

Lizzie didn't take her eyes from his face. "You look terrible."

Ben didn't know whether to laugh or wince. Not only did he look terrible, he felt terrible, but he had hoped that nobody would notice. Leave it to Lizzie to be observant. He decided to smile teasingly at his baby sister. "Okay, thanks for that encouragement."

"I think he looks fine," Titus interjected, though Lizzie wasn't interested in his opinion.

"You're still not over her," Lizzie said. "If anything, you seem worse than before. Being away has taken its toll on you."

Ben picked up a pair of trousers. "That's not so. You haven't seen me for eight months. I'm doing much better."

Lizzie handed him two clothespins. "I don't think so."

Titus tossed his toothpick and grabbed a blue shirt from the basket. "Maybe the Florida winter made you go soft."

Lizzie dragged the line through the pulley. "What will you do if you run into her?"

Ben's gut sank to his toes. "I already have."

This news didn't seem to trouble Titus, who worked very hard at turning the shirt right side out, but Lizzie's eyes couldn't have gotten any bigger. "You've seen Emma?"

"She was the first person I laid eyes on when I got here. She's helping Mammi grow pumpkins on Huckleberry Hill."

Lizzie's reply almost sounded like she was crying. "Ach, Ben. Are you okay?"

Her sympathy weakened his defenses. "No."

Lizzie pulled hard on the line and catapulted the hanging clothes into the air just as Titus was attempting to get the shirt on the line. He nearly lost his balance.

"Emma doesn't have to grow pumpkins for Mammi," Lizzie said. "Titus and I will go up there and do it."

"We will?" Titus said, working on a knot that had formed in the sleeves of the blue shirt when Lizzie had sent the clothes flying.

Ben pinned some trousers to the line. "She's very unhappy, Lizzie. Your letters gave me hope that she might be doing better."

Lizzie waved her hand dismissively. "She's doing fine. Last fall, she made all these quilts and such. I see her at gatherings and benefits, and she smiles all the time. She's not sitting home pining for you, that's for sure." Lizzie sounded almost bitter.

"I don't want her to."

"She's fine," Lizzie insisted.

Ben looked at Titus. "What do you think?"

"I don't know," Titus said. "She goes to lots of gatherings. Seems okay, I guess."

"See?" said Lizzie, as if Titus's halfhearted opinion confirmed the truth.

Ben hung a shirt. "But has she set fire to anything lately or fallen into any rivers?"

Mamm stuck her head out of the back door. "Titus, come fix this table. It's wobbling something wonderful."

Titus threw down the damp shirt, which he had managed to tangle beyond recognition. "I heard her foot went through the ice while skating last winter," he called as he jogged toward the house. Titus always tried to be helpful.

Ben rubbed the side of his face. "That's something, I guess."

"I don't care how Emma feels, Ben. I'm worried about you. Someone so sensitive as you must be downright miserable."

Ben hung a handkerchief while Lizzie finished with an apron. "But what has Emma told you?" he said. "She's your best friend. How is she really feeling?"

The question seemed to suck all the wind out of her. She lowered her eyes and picked up the laundry basket. "We haven't spoken since you broke up."

She might as well have smacked him upside the head with a flyswatter. "What do you mean you haven't spoken?"

Lizzie fingered the basket and twitched her lips guiltily. "I couldn't do it, Ben. I couldn't look her in the eye and pretend that everything was okay. Because of her, I lost you."

With rising agitation, Ben took Lizzie's basket, laid it on the ground, and wrapped his hands around her upper arms. "Nae, Lizzie. Don't you ever believe that. Everything was my fault."

She shook her head. "I knew you'd defend her, but someone needs to stick up for you, Ben."

"I don't want anybody to stick up for me."

"I will whether you want it or not, even if I'm just the little sister nobody cares about."

Ben cracked a smile. "Nobody? You're the sun,

and Mamm and Dat revolve around you. You've always been the favorite."

Amused indignation sparkled in her eyes. "Everybody says that because I'm the youngest. Someone's got to soak up all the attention when the other siblings move out, although I really don't get much. I might as well be invisible when the grandchildren come over."

Ben thought of Emma, and a fifty-pound lump of coal parked on his chest. "You've got to make things right with her, Lizzie."

"Why should I be the one to make things right? Emma could have come to me whenever she wanted to."

"Do you really think Emma would do that? She blames herself for everything, including the weather. She probably thought you never wanted to see her again." He pressed his lips into a rigid line.

"Maybe I *didn't* want to see her again."

Ben clenched his jaw. How could things have gotten this bad, when all he wanted to do eight months ago was make things better? "Emma has done nothing wrong."

"I don't see it that way. Why did you go to Florida if she didn't drive you away? You should quit trying to make things better for her and focus on yourself, like how your family needs you and wants you to come home."

The weight of Lizzie's longing squeezed him like a clamp. The battle between two choices raged within him, like it always did. He didn't know which way was up anymore.

He led Lizzie to the porch steps, where they sat and he took her hand. "Lizzie," he said, pinning her with an earnest gaze. "I know you wouldn't purposefully hurt a fly."

She scooted a few inches away from him but didn't try to reclaim her hand. "I kill flies all the time," she said sullenly. She must have known what was coming.

"Please patch things up with Emma. She needs you."

"She has plenty of friends."

"But you were her best friend. It's the reason she and I got so close in the first place."

"That doesn't change how I feel," Lizzie said.

Ben wrapped his arms around his kid sister. "Try to understand how important it is that Emma be happy again. Don't do it because it's a commandment to forgive or because this has been nagging at you for months—"

"How do you know?"

"Do it because I am your favorite brother, and it would mean the world to me."

Lizzie pulled away from him and sighed as if expelling all the air in her lungs. One corner of her mouth curled upward. "Titus is my favorite brother."

"Do I at least come in second place?"

"Fifth, after Titus, Paul, Norman, and Dan."

"Hey, that's last place." He poked her side, and she squealed and jumped to her feet. He grabbed her hand before she could move too far from him. "I'll settle for a consolation prize. Will you do it because I'm your favorite brother who lives in Florida?"

Lizzie slumped to sit on the step again. "You're asking a lot of the girl who used to throw snowballs at the boys who were mean to her. I'm quite resentful when I want to be. Remember, I'm the one who put a mouse in Teacher's boots because she scolded my penmanship."

"You were always a fighter."

Lizzie twitched an eyebrow. "You used to tell me I was stubborn."

"Same thing."

He stared at her until she gave in to a smile. "Okay. I will see if she would like me to help her plant artichokes or asparagus or something horrible like that in her garden."

Ben felt lighter by about three tons. "Denki. I love asparagus."

Lizzie stood and propped her hands on her hips. "And if she refuses to be friends with me? What then?"

"Emma has a gute heart. She won't turn you down."

Lizzie narrowed her eyes while a grin played at her lips. "So Emma has a gute heart, and I'm the stubborn one?"

"Jah, that's it."

"I'm beginning to think I'm not your favorite sister."

"You're in last place," Ben said.

She offered her hand and pulled Ben to stand. "How can I be in last place? I'm the only sister you've got."

"I think you can figure it out."

With her smile firmly in place and a bag of potting soil in her fist, Emma knocked on Anna's door. The crying was over, the blubbering was finished, and nobody, not even Mahlon, would suspect that she'd only gotten four and a half hours of sleep last night. It was hard to sleep on a soggy pillow when your little sister hogged the blankets and poked her knees into your back.

Even with her heart fluttering like a hummingbird's wings, she was determined to be painfully cheerful and studiously unclumsy in Ben's presence. She'd be preparing the soil today, and if she could manage to avoid his spring-green eyes and not smack her foot with the hoe, things would be fine.

Anna opened the door and invited her in. Emma placed her bag on the table and let her gaze travel around the room. Ben was nowhere to be seen. It was already turning out to be a wonderful-gute day, probably because she had prayed extra hard this morning.

"Did you bring the seeds?" Anna asked.

"Jah," Emma said. "Did you get the fertilizer?"

Anna nodded.

Emma pulled the seed packets and the potting soil from her bag. "I thought maybe we could make a few more newspaper pots and start some tomatoes and a cantaloupe in addition to the pumpkin. And we can plant peas outside in about two weeks."

Anna carefully read the seed packets. "This is too good to be true. With all you've got planned, you'll be spending hours here every week."

Emma felt a little silly telling Anna otherwise. Certainly she wouldn't be spending more than four or five hours on Huckleberry Hill weekly. She hoped not. There was a limit to her restraint. More time spent here would mean more interaction with Ben, and more interaction with Ben meant more crying.

How did Anna know Emma was thinking about her grandson at that moment? "Ben is pruning peach trees, but he's been given strict instructions to help you with the hoeing."

Emma thought it would be hard to hoe and bawl like a baby at the same time. "He can finish the peaches. I'll hoe by myself."

"Nonsense," Anna said. "Hard work like that takes muscles. And don't worry about the fertilizer. Ben can heft a hundred pounds of potatoes without working up a sweat. Unless it's July. Everybody sweats in July. I work up a sweat in July when I knit.

Felty is tending to the chickens, and he's been given strict instructions not to help with the hoeing."

Once she and Anna made a dozen little pots, filled them with dirt, and planted seeds in them, Emma set their pots on the windowsill to soak up some sun. "Water them every day, but not too much."

"I'll be careful."

Emma knew about watering too much. She used to do it all the time last summer when Ben still loved her. She daydreamed about him and the pots often ended up saturated because she mooned over her boyfriend instead of concentrating on horticulture.

Anna went to her closet and pulled out twelve knitted . . . somethings, each a different neon color. They looked like little woven bags. She slipped one of the newspaper seedling pots into one of her knitted containers. It fit like a sock around a tin can. "This will keep them nice and warm, and they look cheery lined up on my windowsill."

"Lovely," Emma said, taken aback but delighted all the same. The shabby newspaper pots looked almost charming when encased in bright pink yarn. Maybe when she felt like crying, she could think of the knitted pot holders sitting on Anna's windowsill. Anna didn't hesitate to give hours to her knitting when she thought it would make someone happy.

Once outside, Emma practically sneaked to the toolshed for a hoe. If Ben didn't know she was here, she could hoe in peace. He wouldn't be the wiser, and she wouldn't have to lay eyes on him all morning.

Donning her leather gardening gloves, she found the wheelbarrow in the shed next to a seriously large bag of Pumpkin Pro. She studied the label. Fifty pounds. She'd have to summon Ben to lift it for her. Anna said he wouldn't even work up a sweat.

Emma took a deep breath and wondered how puffy her eyes would get if she cried two days in a row. On second thought, there was no need to bother Ben. She had a wheelbarrow and two strong arms. She was perfectly capable of moving the bag of Pumpkin Pro by herself.

After scooting some garden tools and terra-cotta pots out of the way, she maneuvered the wheelbarrow closer to the fertilizer bag and tipped the clumsy thing onto its side. The bag stood firmly against the wall as if propping it up. If she scooted it just right, the bag would tumble into the sideways wheelbarrow, and with very little effort, she would be able to right the wheelbarrow with the Pumpkin Pro inside. Probably.

She clutched the heavy brown bag at the corners and pulled with all her might. The bag creaked and groaned, as if complaining that it didn't want to move. It fell over, but not in the direction she wanted it to. It ended up flat on the ground parallel to the wheelbarrow but not inside it.

Emma puffed the air from her lungs, bent over,

and tried to scoot the lazy bag into the wheelbarrow. It proved even heavier flat on the ground like that. It felt as if she were trying to move a . . . well, a bag of fertilizer that wouldn't lift a finger to help her.

She stepped back to gain some leverage, as if that were going to make any difference, and her foot found the handle of a rake. The rake must have sneaked up behind her at the bag's request. Obviously the bag of Pumpkin Pro would stoop to anything to keep Emma from moving it.

She wasn't quite sure how it happened, but she stepped on the rake and her feet slipped out from under her. She stumbled backward and tumbled into the sideways wheelbarrow, which by some inexplicable law of balance righted itsclf with Emma in it. With a squeak of alarm, she came to rest on her back, gazing at the ceiling of the shed with feet and arms pointing in every direction like an upside-down potato bug. She waved her hand in surrender. That was one clever bag of Pumpkin Pro. A worthy opponent indeed.

"Emma, are you okay?"

Upon hearing that low, beautiful, why-did-he-have-to-come-into-the-shed-at-this-very-moment voice, Emma winced and clamped her eyes shut as if playing a game of toddler hide-and-seek, pretending that if she couldn't see him, then he couldn't see her.

Wrong thing to do. Concern tinged his next words, and she could hear him move closer. "Emma, are you hurt?"

She opened her eyes to see Ben standing over her, looking handsome enough to charm the bees out of their hives. She'd seen that look he gave her a hundred times before when they were courting. Every time she had made a fool of herself or tripped over the neighbor's cat or set fire to something, compassion would flood his expression as if he felt her pain. When he had made sure she was all right, the amusement would always twinkle in his eyes, and he would act as if he thought her mishaps adorable.

Well, she knew better now. He didn't think her clumsiness was adorable. He had moved to Florida to get away from it.

For the second time, she squeezed her eyes shut and pressed her lips together. She would not cry.

She would not cry.

Ben's voice grew deep and rough as he laid a hand on her arm. "Emma, can you hear me?"

Still attempting to gain control over the pesky tears, Emma didn't trust her voice. Without opening her eyes, she nodded emphatically.

"Do you think you can stand up? Let's get you into the house, and then I can run to the neighbors and call a doctor."

All thoughts of crying fled. She immediately opened her eyes and with a jerk, tried to sit up. The wheelbarrow sucked her back into its depths. She growled in exasperation. "I'm fine. I thought I'd see if the wheelbarrow would be a gute place to take a nap later on."

A grin played at his lips as he reached out his hand. With only a moment's hesitation, she took it. The wheelbarrow suddenly felt as deep as a bathtub. With nowhere for her feet to gain purchase, she managed to sit up, but couldn't touch the ground. Ben took her other hand and pulled.

She grimaced as she sort of scooted her hinter part to the edge and searched for the ground with her toes. There was no graceful way to exit a wheel-barrow. Ben gave a firm tug. Finally locating solid earth, she stumbled forward and ended up in his arms. The world seemed to stand still for a brief moment as she looked at him and he stared back at her as if a best-forgotten memory attacked both of them at the same time. Emma held her breath and wished for the thousandth time that she didn't love him so much.

Regaining her balance and her wits, she jumped back as if he were on fire. He frowned and almost made her believe that her pulling away had hurt his feelings.

He cleared his throat and tried to smile. "Are you okay?"

She pointed to the supine Pumpkin Pro. "He tried to kill me."

Ben smiled, a genuine smile this time, bent over, and hefted the bag over his shoulder, just like she knew he could. His shoulders were so broad, she could have parked a buggy on them. "Where do you want it?"

Emma turned her face to the great outdoors to

keep from staring, but that didn't stop her heart from jerking around her chest like a skater bug. She ground her teeth together.

She would not cry.

"Put it in this handy wheelbarrow," she finally managed to say. "I can take it to the garden myself. Denki for your help."

A hint of teasing flashed in his eyes, and he strolled out of the shed as if he were going to church. With a fifty-pound bag slung over his shoulder. "Seeing as how it tried to kill you, I'm not letting it out of my sight."

He was always thoughtful like that, seeing a job through to the end. She loaded the rake and hoe and a few other supplies into the wheelbarrow and pushed it out to the garden plot. She tried to move deftly over the grass to show Ben that no wheelbarrow would ever get the better of her again. She only stumbled once.

Ben laid the bag of Pumpkin Pro at the edge of the dirt and gazed at the garden plot. Anna had been right. Not one drop of sweat appeared on his forehead.

He hadn't even been looking to see how well she pushed the wheelbarrow. Perhaps she should push it in a circle around him just once. She decided against that idea. With her history, she'd trip on a clod of dirt and end up facedown in the wheelbarrow.

She tried not to notice how tall and straight he

stood or how he seemed to command the very air he breathed.

She pursed her lips and cleared her throat. Ben had nice posture. Lots of boys had gute posture. Ben's wasn't anything remarkable, even if he did have broad shoulders.

"What are you going to plant?" Ben asked without looking at her.

"Peas first. Then tomatoes and beans. The pumpkin goes over here. I'll need to build up a mound of dirt for good drainage."

He glanced at her, and Emma could have sworn she detected uncertainty in his expression. What was he suddenly so worried about? "This is an acre of soil. Preparing it will take all day. Maybe I should hitch up Dawdi's plow."

Emma shook her head. "No need. Even with a plow, I'll need to break down the clods of dirt. I'll work for a few hours today and come back tomorrow and the next day if I need to."

He grabbed the shovel from the wheelbarrow. "I'll help. This dirt is as hard as a rock."

"Don't trouble yourself. I know you need to prune the peaches." *And I'd really rather not bite my tongue off trying to hold back tears all day.*

He showed that half smile again, as if he really wanted to help but really wanted to avoid her too. She couldn't make heads or tails of it. He gestured to the bag of Pumpkin Pro lying innocently on the ground. "You'll need help with that, and I think the other fertilizer Dawdi bought is even heavier. I'd hate to find you buried under a hundred pounds of bone meal at the end of the day."

Emma ignored her heart, which did all sorts of acrobatic tricks inside her chest. She couldn't very well refuse his help without being rude. And he was right. Without Ben, she might end up being the first person to be assassinated by a bag of fertilizer. "Okay," she said, sounding like she had just agreed to a root canal.

"Okay." He gave her a reassuring smile before plunging the shovel into the dirt and turning it over with a mere flick of his wrist. That dirt didn't stand a chance against Ben's muscles.

Emma sighed quietly so that not even she could hear herself. Then she followed with the hoe, breaking up the large clods of dirt he left behind. Once they'd loosened the soil, they'd go back over the ground with a rake and the fertilizer.

Breathing a little harder now, Ben looked back at her and smiled again. Three times already today. That was a surprise, for as adamantly as he disliked her. "How is your family? Is Mahlon still working at the sawmill?"

"Jah, he is still there, plus he helps Dat on the farm, of course. Percy is helping with the cows. When his turns sixteen this summer, he's going to find work with an *Englischer* in town. He can't work at the sawmill with Mahlon until he turns eighteen."

"Percy is a *gute* worker."

"Jah, he's always searching for ways to earn money."

"How are the little ones?"

"Not so little. This is Rose's last year in school, and Andy and Lisa are in fourth grade and sixth grade."

Ben shook his head. "I can't believe they're that old already."

"Rose is learning how to make quilts. Dat bought her a fancy battery-operated sewing machine."

"I'll bet she can go fast with that."

"Jah. She can."

He didn't look at her as he cut dirt with the shovel, but she could see his brows inching closer together. "Have you tried the new machine?"

"I don't dare. It goes so fast, I'm afraid I might sew all my fingers together."

He nodded as if she'd answered the question correctly, then turned from her as if he'd said something slightly rude and felt embarrassed about it. No doubt he was thinking about Emma's treadle accident.

Emma winced. The week after they had gotten engaged, Emma had started on a quilt for the wedding. In her haste, she had sewed right through her finger with the old treadle machine. She'd never finished the quilt and had gotten a very swollen finger and a tetanus shot for her trouble.

Emma hoed with renewed vigor. Tears threatened, and she wasn't about to invite them by reminiscing about Ben. The day she'd sewn through her finger had been one of the best of her life. Ben had taken her to the emergency room for a shot and a bandage, and after the hospital, they had spent a wonderful afternoon at Shawano Lake, dipping their toes into the water and talking about the day when they could marry and be together forever. Ben had told her that the only present he wanted for his wedding was Emma herself and that after they married, she never had to sew anything ever again.

Ben grunted as he buried his shovel blade into the hard dirt. By the shadow overspreading his features and the hard line of his lips, she could tell his mind was at the lake too. Maybe he remembered the sunset that tinged the clouds pink and orange before fading to a deep crimson and finally giving way to the darkness.

Did he remember how they had sat so close that her sleeve had brushed against his arm and made her tingle all over? Or how he had told her that he wanted to kiss her so bad that it took every bit of strength inside him not to go ahead and do it?

She studied the frown on his face as he labored with the dirt. Maybe he was thinking about how she'd accidentally sprayed mosquito repellant into his mouth while they were at the lake. He had laughed about it then, but maybe it wasn't as fond a memory to him as it was to her. Mosquito repellant tasted pretty nasty. It was probably one of the reasons he'd left her.

She frowned to herself. Doubt and self-condemnation always accompanied thoughts of Ben—always the second-guessing and what-ifs. If she hadn't burned down the chicken coop and sewed through her own finger, would Ben still love her? If she hadn't sprayed repellant into his mouth or burned his birthday cake, would they be married right now? Thoughts of what might have been left her breathless.

Silence prevailed between them for a few minutes. Emma didn't know how the silence could be any better than the conversation. If she stayed silent too long, Ben might start to notice how she hoed the dirt and determine that she was not a good enough gardener to be his wife.

"How is your family?" she blurted out. Talking was better than thinking about the regrets.

He paused, as if considering how to answer her question. "They're gute. I went yesterday for supper." He almost choked on his next words. "Lizzie said to tell you hello."

Emma immediately decided she preferred the silence. It was impossible to talk about anything without dredging up memories too painful to contemplate. She most definitely did not want to talk about Lizzie, her former best friend. Lizzie blamed Emma when Ben ran away, and Emma couldn't bear to face her.

Of course, Lizzie had been right to cut Emma off. How could they hope to be friends when Lizzie had lost her favorite brother because Emma was too flawed to be loved?

"My family is going to the lake when it gets a little warmer." His face suddenly brightened. "I bet they would love it if you came. You and Lizzie could take that old canoe out." Why did he smile like that at another memory that only made her want to weep? "Remember the first time you got into that canoe with Lizzie, and it started rocking something wonderful?"

Emma turned her face away so he wouldn't see it glow bright red. "I remember."

"It tipped over, and you thought you were drowning, but then you stretched your feet out and touched bottom. The water barely went to your waist."

He'd obviously forgotten the best and the worst part of that story. She'd panicked when the canoe tipped and had started flailing her arms and praying for some sort of rescue. Even as her feet found purchase on the bottom of the lake, Ben had jumped into the water without hesitation and scooped her into his arms. They both laughed when they discovered how shallow it was, but he had still insisted on carrying her to shore.

It was the day they had met and the day she knew she loved him. Love at first sight, so to speak, although Mamm would say that notion was a bunch of baloney. Emma had been seventeen years old and had never looked back. Ben would always be the only boy she ever loved.

Her eyes stung with those blasted tears again. She attacked the dirt clod at her feet with renewed determination and pretended Ben wasn't standing five feet away staring at her. The tears retreated.

"In the summer, you and Lizzie towed that canoe behind Dat's buggy and went floating in the lake at least once a week."

"She liked to row around the lake, but she always wanted to be the one to steer."

Ben grinned. "That's Lizzie. Bossy as a wren guarding her nest." He dropped the grin and transformed into a minister giving a sermon. "You are blessed to have each other."

Emma twitched her eyebrows in surprise and turned her face to her task so Ben couldn't see her reaction. Didn't he know that she and Lizzie hadn't spoken since he left for Florida? She risked a glance at his face. His expression looked as if a plow had done its work on his brow.

Jah. He knew. Did he feel guilty that she had lost a friend as well as a fiancé?

Of course he felt guilty. She searched for a way to reassure him that things weren't so bad, that she had plenty of other friends to paddle canoes with. She didn't want him to feel any worse about this than he already felt. Her penchant to burst into tears at the slightest provocation wasn't helping either.

She forced a cheerful—but hopefully not overdone—smile. "Martha Weaver, Amanda Coblenz, and I like to quilt together. And Edna Fern Glick and I go to *singeons* all the time. I have lots of friends. Besides, Mahlon still drags me to go fishing sometimes, although he says I scare away the fish with all my talking."

Ben nodded with a weak smile on his lips. "Mahlon likes to fish."

"I don't. A hook stuck in your thumb hurts worse than a needle sewing through your finger." Oh. She shouldn't have mentioned that. Ben was already fully aware of how accident-prone she was.

His eyebrows rose two inches on his forehead, and his lips formed a silent *O*. "Did you have to go to the hospital?"

Her face got warm, and with her hoe she reduced the nearest clod to dust. "Dat pulled it out with his pliers. He said I didn't need stitches." Emma rejoiced that she wore garden gloves. She did not want Ben to see the scar. It would serve as further confirmation that he'd made the right decision to dump her.

"Titus caught a hook in his earlobe once. He has a little scar. Mamm says he looks like one of those Englischers with piercings all the way up their ears. One day, Titus stuck a tiny rhinestone over the top of his scar and told Mamm he'd gotten his ear pierced. You should have heard her squeal."

Emma loved the sound of Ben's laughter. Next to his singing, it was the best sound in the world. She smiled at him and tried to enjoy his company without thinking about what she had lost.

Unfortunately this was impossible for more than about ten seconds. But it was a gute ten seconds.

Ben proved to be quick with the shovel. They fell into an easy rhythm with each other as he turned up the soil and she broke it down. Emma started to feel comfortable. Her heart resumed a relatively normal pace. Relatively. The hard work diverted her attention from the handsome boy who was definitely working up a sweat and helped her focus on dirt and earthworms. She barely noticed how the muscles of Ben's thick arms bulged with every slice of the shovel.

Once they'd turned up the soil, Ben shoveled dirt to make a little hill for the pumpkin plant. "You're only planting one?"

"Jah, the giant one." Emma didn't want to say any more about giant pumpkins. Growing the giant pumpkin was the last big thing she and Ben had done together.

He didn't mention it either. "Did you sell all those pumpkins you grew last year?"

"I had over two hundred yet."

"Two hundred? That's wonderful gute."

"Mamm thought I was foolish to plant two full

acres, but Dat said he had enough room for feed corn and he wanted to rotate the crops anyway. Mamm put seven big ones in the root cellar, and I made pies for several neighbors." Emma trained her eyes to the ground. That had been after Ben left for Florida. She made pies until they came out her ears. The hard work hadn't made her feel better about Ben in the least. But the pies had made her neighbors happy.

"When Yost Newswenger came to me and asked if he could have a few to sell, I let him have the rest of the crop. He sold most of them."

The line between his brows deepened. "You gave Yost your pumpkins?"

Her heart sank. "Do you think that was foolish of me? Mamm scolded me for doing all the work and then giving away all the money. But Yost needed a bike to make deliveries for his *fater*. With his mamm feeling poorly, they don't have extra money. I wanted him to have a bike." She studied Ben's face. He was probably counting all the reasons she would make a bad wife, like the fact that she gave away her hard-earned money like candy.

His expression revealed a mixture of delight and sadness, which didn't make sense, but that's what she saw. "You are the kindest person I've ever met, Emma."

The way he said her name sent tendrils of electricity traveling up her spine. Maybe he didn't think she was such a dolt after all.

Heat rose to her cheeks. "You haven't met very many people, have you?"

"Thousands," he said, almost breathlessly.

She couldn't endure his penetrating gaze for long. "We're almost ready for the bone meal. And how are you at shoveling manure?"

He buried his shovel in the dirt and lifted a heaping scoop. "You tell me."

She glanced at his straining muscles and cleared her throat. "You'll do fine."

He slit the bag of bone meal with his shovel and carried the powdery fertilizer to wherever she asked him to dump it. Then he did the same with the other fertilizer and finally took the wheelbarrow to fetch an ample batch of manure while Emma worked everything into the soil with the rake and another shovel.

Sometimes, she wished she was hard of hearing. Everything had been going along so well. She hadn't thought of crying for over half an hour when Ben came out of the barn with another load of manure, singing with his powerful bass voice.

"*No tears in heaven, no sorrows given. All will be glory in that land.*" Ben's dawdi Felty was known for his beautiful voice. The sound could carry all the way to the highway on a good day. But Felty had nothing over Ben. Ben's voice could charm wings off hummingbirds and stingers off wasps. When he sang, the breeze stopped playing with the trees so it could listen.

Last summer when they were alone together, Ben used to sing hymns to her. Emma had almost come to believe that God's gift to Ben was only for her and that no other girl in the whole world would be sung to after she died.

Oh sis yuscht.

She had worked so hard to maintain her composure, and she felt it slipping away the moment he started singing.

"*No tears in heaven fair, No tears, no tears up there.*"

How could he know that every note broke her heart a little bit more?

She dropped her hoe and started running. If she was going to disintegrate into a puddle of tears, she would do it in the privacy of Anna's bathroom. And she was determined not to ruin the toilet paper roll this time.

"Emma? Are you okay?" he called after her.

She kept moving. Even with his long legs, he wouldn't be able to waylay her. She had a pretty good head start.

"Emma, what's wrong?"

She couldn't leave him standing there guessing. He would blame himself for yet another outburst from Emma Nelson. "I have something in my eye," she yelled, hoping that he could hear her with her back turned and her hand covering much of her face.

That wasn't a lie. She had a thousand tears in her eyes that would escape as soon as she set foot in that bathroom. Once she left her bathroom sanctuary, she'd have to sneak away. She refused to show the puffy eyes ever again. The garden would have to wait.

By suppertime, Mahlon would be throwing eggs at Ben's house for sure.

Chapter 4

Ben tilted his head to one side and nearly groaned out loud. His neck felt so stiff, he almost couldn't move it. Trying to be as subtle as possible, he pressed his fingers into the tight muscles of his shoulders and worked his way up the right side of his neck. The firm pressure helped the stiffness a little, but he didn't want Mammi to notice, so he didn't really work himself over like he usually did. Hopefully Mammi was too engrossed in her knitting to pay him any heed.

Dawdi sat in the front seat of the car so he could get a good look at every license plate that passed by. Their driver, Roy, pointed out unusual plates, which wasn't much help since there were about twenty different kinds of Wisconsin plates. Dawdi's hopes were dashed more than once with an unfamiliar Wisconsin plate.

Dawdi had played the license plate game every

year since Ben could remember. Last year, he had found his last plate, Nevada, three days after Christmas in a hospital parking lot in Milwaukee.

"Here comes one yet," Roy said.

"I can't see it," Dawdi said. "Change lanes."

"It looks like Rhode Island," Roy said, as the car lurched to the right while he tried to get a better look.

Since Ben had the best eyes of the bunch, he leaned forward stiffly and looked out the windshield. "It is Rhode Island, Dawdi. See the anchor?"

"Well, what do you know about that!" Dawdi said, jotting down his find in his miniature notebook. "I thought having surgery would be a waste of time, but now that I've found Rhode Island, I don't feel so bad about the whole thing."

Roy and Dawdi refused to rest on their laurels. While careening down the highway, they glued their eyes to every car that passed in case they'd be fortunate enough to see New Mexico or Louisiana.

Ben leaned back and held on to the door handle for dear life. Nobody seemed to be paying attention to the driving while the hunt for license plates went on. The trip to Green Bay took less than an hour. They'd get there in one piece, Lord willing.

Mammi, oblivious to all the excitement of finding license plates, sat in the backseat next to Ben concentrating on her knitting or purling or whatever she worked on today. She reached over and patted Ben on the leg. "Don't worry. We're almost there."

Her knitting creation looked as if it would be a very big forest-green blanket. "That's pretty, Mammi," Ben said, trying to keep his mind off the road while keeping his eyes glued to it. If they were going to crash, he'd rather it not come as a complete surprise.

"I'm making a shade covering for my pumpkin," Mammi said. "Emma told me that if I want a really big one, I've got to keep it in the shade."

Ben couldn't nod well with the stiffness, so he smiled as best he could at Mammi and concentrated on the road while pressing a thumb into the long muscle that ran up the length of his neck.

The discomfort in his neck was nothing to the pain in his heart. As long as he stayed on Huckleberry Hill, it would be impossible to keep thoughts of Emma from burying him. He'd seen her three days last week, and his endurance was weakening. Dear Mammi had no idea how she tortured him when she pushed Emma and him together at every opportunity. His emotions were a raging fire that would consume him if he let down his defenses. He had come dangerously close last week when he and Emma prepared the soil for planting. The vivid memories of working side by side with her in the pumpkin patch last summer had nearly overwhelmed him.

He resolved to do a better job of staying away from Emma, no matter what Mammi wanted. Better to risk Mammi's displeasure than to be so tied up in knots over Emma that he couldn't function.

That had already happened once. He wasn't strong enough to pull himself away from Emma's love twice. He had to stay away from her, encourage her to keep her distance as well. His life would be so much easier if she had already given him up, if she had found another boyfriend. It would have been so much easier on everybody—especially him. He craved Emma the way most people craved air.

He shifted on the seat and kneaded the other side of his neck. Today was Dawdi's nasal surgery. Depending on how well Dawdi recovered, Ben could be on a bus to Florida this time next week.

It couldn't come soon enough.

"Look," Dawdi exclaimed from the front seat. "*Ach, du lieva.* That's Hawaii!"

No matter how reluctant Dawdi was to have surgery, he would consider the trip worthwhile.

Examining her handiwork, Emma grimaced and a low growl rumbled in her throat. She'd already unpicked the brim of this prayer *kapp* twice and there were three spots of blood on the crisp white fabric where she had pricked her finger on a sharp pin.

She grabbed her seam ripper for the third time and began picking out the stitches, wondering whom she could hire to sew a prayer kapp for her little sister Rose. Mamm had assigned the covering to Emma because she desperately needed the sewing practice. Emma longed to tell her mamm that kapps looked better without bloodstains, and quilts sold better if all the corners matched up—a skill that Emma had yet to master and probably never would. She didn't have nimble fingers, but she had a green thumb. Why wouldn't Mamm leave the sewing to Rose and let Emma tend produce all day? They'd make a lot more money from her cucumbers than they ever would with her clumsy quilts. As an added benefit, she didn't usually bleed on the vegetables.

Except for that one time.

She felt a twinge of pain where her heart should have been if it hadn't broken eight months ago. Ben used to tell her that he didn't care if she had trouble with the treadle machine or if she burned the chicken every night. He assured her that he would hire a cook if they ever really needed to eat. He loved her and only her.

Correction. He had told her he loved her, but he hadn't really meant it. Either that or her frequent mishaps had prompted a change of heart. Either way, she'd done plenty to drive him away, and she couldn't be good enough or smart enough or graceful enough to get him back.

A tear plopped onto the white fabric, joining the three spots of blood and a gray smudge from her thumb. She might have to throw the whole thing away and start over.

But she was learning to control her emotions better when she had to be around Ben.

Surely she was getting better.

In the five occasions she'd been on Huckleberry Hill, she'd run to the safety of the bathroom only three times. Yesterday, she hadn't needed to blink back one tear while she soaked pea seeds. Of course, Ben had been gone the whole day and she hadn't seen him, but dry eyes under any circumstance was progress.

Mahlon strolled into the kitchen where the sewing machine sat. Studiously working on her covering gave her the perfect excuse not to look up. Mahlon would see the tears and get all riled up about Ben again. If there was one thing she didn't need, it was Mahlon dumping rotten tomatoes on Ben's doorstep.

"You coming to the gathering tonight?"

She silently sniffed back the tears. Lord willing, the moisture on her cheeks would dry before he looked too hard, and he'd be none the wiser. "Probably. But I'll be late. Felty Helmuth is having surgery this morning, and I want to go visit him later today."

Mahlon plucked an apple from the bowl on the table and took a hearty bite. "Will Ben be there?"

Why did her voice crack at the most inconvenient moments? "Don't talk with your mouth full."

Mahlon took an even bigger bite and smacked his lips. "Is that better?"

Keeping her face turned away, Emma giggled. "Jah, much better."

Mahlon pulled a chair from the table, scooted it next to the sewing machine, and sat down. He leaned sideways so he could get a good look at Emma's face.

She dipped her head lower.

Mahlon grunted. "Emma. Look at me. Is Ben going to be there?"

She promptly swiveled in her chair and turned her back on her brother. "Of course. He lives there. I see him all the time."

"So why are you crying about it?"

She twisted around to look at him. His expression loomed as dark as if a tornado were about to come through.

"I pricked my finger."

Mahlon pounded his fist on the sewing machine cabinet, making pins hop and dust motes take flight. "Anna Helmuth does not need help growing pumpkins."

"Mahlon Nelson, you control your temper or you'll get no supper."

The trenches around his mouth deepened. "You mean perfectly cooked bread and crispy brown fried chicken? I don't want it."

"It's getting better, Mahlon. I've only gone to the bathroom three times."

He lifted his eyebrows as if she had stunned him beyond speech, but he still managed to expel the words from his mouth. "In your life?"

She cuffed him on the shoulder and laughed until tears ran down her face. Or rather, her tears of laughter mingled with the other ones and washed them away.

Mahlon merely grunted again and watched her laugh, probably wondering if he should put her in an asylum.

Emma wiped her eyes and sighed. It felt so good to laugh about something.

Mahlon picked up the pins that he had knocked onto the floor and pushed them into the pincushion sitting next to the machine. "You should wash your hands of that whole family, Emma. They've brought you nothing but grief. You don't owe them anything."

"Jesus said to love my neighbor as myself, and it was Pilate who washed his hands."

"That doesn't mean you have to plant pumpkins for them. Why don't you just love them from the safety of your own vegetable garden? I'm sick of seeing you in tears all the time."

Emma sniffed and blinked the moisture from her eyes so she could see well enough to finish picking the seam on the kapp. "I'm doing much better."

Mahlon stood and shoved his fingers through his hair. "I know. I know. You only go to the bathroom when absolutely necessary."

Mahlon turned when someone knocked on the back door. "I don't like seeing you like this, Em."

"I'm doing better."

Emma's heart jumped to attention and pounded in her chest like a bass drum. Ben's younger sister Lizzie, Emma's former best friend, stood on the back stoop clutching a brown paper bag to her chest like a shield. She'd probably need it the way Mahlon scowled at her.

"If it isn't Dizzy Lizzie," Mahlon said. His voice dripped with disdain. The only person who made him madder than Ben was Lizzie Helmuth. She had rejected Emma at the same time Ben had. Mahlon hadn't forgotten.

Lizzie arched an eyebrow and pinned Mahlon with a sharp eye. She and Emma had been best friends for years. That meant Lizzie was more than capable of dealing with Emma's annoying twin brother. She had never let him intimidate her before. "I wish I could say I am glad to see you, Mailman, but I don't like to lie."

He motioned to the bag she still clutched to her chest. "That better be fifty letters of apology, or you can forget about coming in my house."

Despite her distress at seeing Lizzie after all these months, Emma leaped from her chair and shoved Mahlon aside. He didn't resist, but merely threw his hands in the air and turned his back.

Lizzie lost all the swagger she'd used on Mahlon moments before. She turned bright red and stared at Emma as if she wished she could say something but couldn't speak the language.

Emma decided that she must break the ice. Jesus said to love your neighbor. "Hi, Lizzie."

Obviously embarrassed, Lizzie forced a smile and held out the bag to Emma. "The orphans are having a benefit sale."

"The orphans?"

Mahlon made unnecessary amount of noise as he pulled a chair out from under the table. Training his eyes on Lizzie, he sat and made no indication that he would ever move again.

"There is an orphanage in Mexico that needs money. My aunt and uncle went there last year. They need diapers and stuff."

"Oh, that's interesting," said Emma, with no idea how to keep the conversation going. She and Lizzie had never had trouble finding things to talk about before. My, how things had changed. What did Lizzie mean by coming over?

Lizzie forged ahead even as Emma drew back. "I am wondering if you would like to help me make a quilt. We used to quilt together every Thursday night."

"There are a dozen girls better at quilting than me."

Lizzie nibbled on her bottom lip and lowered her eyes. "I thought maybe we could be friends again."

Mahlon glared at her and took a giant bite of another apple from the bowl. "Why would she want to be friends with you, Lizzie-Lizzie-in-a-Tizzy?"

Flames leaped into Lizzie's brown eyes. Mahlon certainly knew how to make things significantly worse.

Emma turned to him. "Mahlon, close your mouth."

Lizzie squared her shoulders, marched past Emma, and slapped the paper bag down on the table next to Mahlon. "I want Emma to help me make a quilt, and if that's too difficult for your tender feelings to bear, then you should go stand in the corner and suck your thumb, you big baby."

Mahlon nearly choked on his apple. Emma's lips twitched upward as she pounded Mahlon on the back while he coughed and sputtered in surprise.

Lizzie always knew how to take Mahlon's pride down about three notches. It was one of the reasons Emma liked her so well.

It didn't take Mahlon too long to recover. "Why don't you go tell your brother to quit bothering us, Busy Lizzie? Better yet, why don't *you* quit bothering us?"

"Stop it, Mahlon," Emma ordered.

Lizzie snatched the apple from his hand and threw it out the open door. "Why don't you go fetch your apple, Mailman?"

Mahlon's scowl could have peeled the paint off the barn—actually, off every barn in the county. He should have known better, but he got up anyway and strode out the door to retrieve his apple. Lizzie followed and slammed the door behind him, then slid the latch into place and clapped her hands together as if she'd dispensed with a household pest.

She and Emma met eyes, and they giggled. They heard Mahlon's body crash against the door as he attempted to reenter the room. They laughed harder.

"Can you believe he actually fell for that?" Lizzie said.

Emma gave her an exaggerated nod. "Jah, I can.

You haven't been around to keep him on his toes. He's gotten lazy."

As expected, they heard the front door open, and Mahlon's quick footsteps echoed across the living room floor. He entered the kitchen with the half-eaten apple in his fist.

"I see you were able to rescue your apple," Lizzie said.

Mahlon held it up so Lizzie and Emma could see the dirt and leaves and bugs embedded in the apple's flesh. "You wasted a perfectly good piece of fruit," he said.

Lizzie took it from him and rinsed it off in the sink. The lines of Mahlon's face might have softened when she carefully dried off the apple with her apron and kissed it. He cocked an eyebrow.

"There," Lizzie said. "All better."

"All better?" he complained as she handed it to him. He shook his head and ambled to the back door. He slid the latch and walked out for the second time. "I'm going to feed this to the horse," he said. He eyed Emma with compassion. "Unless you need me to stay."

"I'll be okay."

He nodded and hopped off the stoop while mumbling under his breath. "Girls" was all Emma heard.

She shut the door and turned to Lizzie. "Sorry. He's still learning how to behave himself."

"He's always been fiercely loyal to you," Lizzie said. "It's his only good quality."

"I'm glad you think he has at least one good quality."

Lizzie laughed easily, but the tension hardened like ice as soon as the laughter faded. "So, do you want to help me make a quilt?"

"Why?"

"For the orphanage, like I said."

"Why do you want my help after months of getting along fine without me?"

Lizzie sighed as if she were exhausted and sat down at the table. "You know why, Emma. Ben asked me to come."

Emma slumped her shoulders. She wanted a real friend, not one who'd been assigned to her. "He feels sorry for me."

Lizzie folded her arms and pressed her lips together before speaking. "I don't know why. Everyone knows you acted as if you never cared about him at all."

"I didn't want him to feel any worse than he already did."

Lizzie rolled her eyes. It wasn't an attractive look. "Sure you didn't."

Emma sat at the table and leaned toward her ex-best friend. "Think about it, Lizzie. Ben would have felt worse knowing how I suffered. I had to pretend so he wouldn't worry and so my brother wouldn't take a bus to Florida to throw mud at Ben's house."

Lizzie blinked twice before looking away. "He lives in a trailer."

The tears stung her eyes. She and Lizzie used to hide in the haymow and talk for hours about cute boys at school and pets they wanted and what color dress they would wear if they could wear any color they desired. Emma studied Lizzie's face. She had missed her so much. And she wanted her back.

She should have made her apology long before now. Taking a deep breath, she said, "I'm sorry that you lost your brother because of me."

Lizzie bit her bottom lip. "Me too."

"I'm sorry that I drove him away. I didn't mean to, but I have too many weaknesses and sins to count. He moved clear across the country to be away from me. I can imagine how he must hate me."

Lizzie reached over and put her hand on Emma's arm. "You know how honest I am. Or blunt. Most people say blunt. But I want to get this all out in the open, even if it hurts your feelings."

"Okay," Emma said, bracing herself for something terrible.

"I only came because Ben asked me to. He acted like it was a matter of life and death, and he's been through so much heartache already, I couldn't say no."

Emma frowned. She'd spent too much time in Anna's bathroom. Ben hadn't been fooled at all.

"I know I need to forgive you," Lizzie said. "I want to forgive you. But I'm still mad for the way you treated him. I've never seen anyone so broken, like he had nothing in the world to live for." She squeezed Emma's arm as sorrow flooded her expression. "I thought I knew you better than that. How could you do that to him? You were engaged. You told him yes. Doesn't that mean anything to you?"

Emma caught her breath. "It means everything to me."

"Then why did you do it?"

Feeling as if she were about to explode, Emma grabbed both of Lizzie's hands and held tight. "You know that Ben broke up with me, right?"

"But . . . I thought . . . No, Emma. You're the one who called it off."

"Nae, I'm not."

Lizzie rocked backward as if she had been shoved. "Emma, that can't be true. He loves you with his whole soul."

Goodness gracious. More tears. "He doesn't. He is so repulsed by me that he had to get far away. Far enough away that he wouldn't have to see me every day and be reminded of how revolting I am."

Lizzie's voice trembled. "Nae, Emma, I don't believe it."

Emma stared at her ex–best friend with all the intensity she felt. "Lizzie. Look at me. I love Ben. I'd marry him tomorrow if he asked me, but it doesn't matter. He doesn't want to marry me."

"He loves you. I know he loves you."

"Nae."

Lizzie must have seen something in Emma's

eyes that finally convinced her. She stood up so quickly that the chair toppled over behind her. "All this time, he let me believe it was your fault." She lifted her hand to her eyes and kneaded her brows with her fingers. "I lost your friendship because I believed that Ben would never, ever break up with you. I blamed you, all this time. Why didn't you say something?"

Emma wiped at the tears traveling down her cheeks. "You told me you'd lost your brother because of me. My faults drove Ben away. Of course you'd be mad about that."

"That's not true," Lizzie said. "You're perfect. Nothing you did could ever stop Ben from loving you."

"Even driving his buggy into the ditch?"

Lizzie put her hands on either side of Emma's face. "Not even that."

Emma swallowed hard. She refused to tell Lizzie the worst of her sins. "For whatever reason, he doesn't want to marry me."

Lizzie pulled a chair right next to her and wrapped an arm around Emma's shoulders. "To think I've wasted all these months because I was too angry to get your side of the story." She wrapped her other arm around Emma's neck and pulled her close. "Why did I hold on to my stubborn pride? Can you ever forgive me?"

The feel of Lizzie's tears on her shoulder reduced Emma to a blubbering mess. She wept and let Lizzie pull her closer. "Of course I forgive you. I was so lonely for a close friend. I didn't have anybody to talk to except for Mahlon."

Lizzie giggled, and while she cried, the laughter came out more like a grunt. "Some confidant he'd make. How many times did you have to lock him out of the house?"

They pulled apart and shared a smile. "Truth be told, Mahlon proved a true friend yet. He offered to throw eggs at your house more than once."

Lizzie smirked. "Yep, I can believe it."

"Don't be mad at Mahlon. He's a little annoyed that his sister got her heart broken."

"A little annoyed?" Lizzie pursed her lips and raised an eyebrow.

Emma surrendered a grin. "Okay. He's been madder than a wet cat."

"He smells like one too."

Emma took Lizzie's hand. "Please don't be mad at Mahlon. He is only watching out for his little sister."

"Little by five minutes," Lizzie protested. She shook her head and sighed. "I'm not mad at Mahlon. We used to tease each other all the time. He put spiders in my lunch, and I threw spitballs at him during arithmetic. I'm only mad at myself for being so pigheaded. It's my fault and only mine." She twisted her mouth thoughtfully. "And Ben's. Now that I think about it, this is almost entirely Ben's fault. I'm going to give him a large piece of my mind, and he's going to feel pretty foolish."

"Ben is hurting enough already. Don't make it worse for him."

Lizzie propped her elbow on the arm around her waist and drummed her fingers on her cheek. "He *is* hurting. That's what I can't understand."

"He's sad that he made me feel bad. That's all."

Lizzie sprang from her chair and clapped her hands so unexpectedly that Emma nearly jumped out of her skin. "You've got to get him back. I don't know what his problem is, but you've got to get him back."

Emma's heart and hopes sank to her toes. "Nae. I can't."

Lizzie reached out and pulled Emma to her feet. "He loves you, Emma. He's so unselfish that he probably thought it was wrong to marry you and keep all your loveliness to himself."

"Ha-ha."

"It must be true. It's the only reason I can think of for his leaving you and his family. The only reason. You've got to win him back, Emma. I'm his sister. I can help you. What better way to learn where his defenses are the weakest than by having a spy under the same roof?"

Emma managed to keep tears from pooling in her eyes. "Nae, Lizzie. I won't break my heart all over again."

Lizzie let go of her hands but didn't reply.

"I can't make somebody love me who doesn't love me."

"But that's what I don't understand. I truly

thought he loved you. How could he leave you like that?"

Emma deflated and sat down next to her mangled prayer kapp. "I can think of a thousand reasons. The water accident, the burned auction cookies, the broken buggy axle. And let's not forget the chicken coop. What kind of girl sets fire to a chicken coop? I mean, how hard is that to do?" She picked up her kapp and pretended to take a stitch. She hadn't told Lizzie the worst, but since they'd just become friends again, she figured it was too early. Besides, it didn't really matter. She'd never get Ben back, no matter how hard she contemplated her faults.

"He loved those things about you, Emma. It made him feel protective."

"Because I'm like a toddler, the way I get myself into one pickle after another."

Lizzie nudged her playfully. "Because everything you do is for other people. He wanted to be the one to do nice things for you."

Emma almost burst into tears again. That was exactly what Ben had told her the night he proposed.

"I want to take care of you, Emmy. You watch out for everyone else, and I'll watch out for you."

Lizzie nodded encouragingly. "Ben is back. I think we should try to get you two back together."

"I'm trying to endure being around him again without making a fool of myself."

Lizzie went to the drawer next to the fridge and pulled out a pencil and a notebook. "Let's make a plan to lure Ben back to you." She wrote *Ben and*

Emma at the top and drew a line under it. "What shall we do first?"

Emma shook her head. "Nope. I'm not going to do it, Lizzie. Any glimmer of hope would drive me over the edge of a cliff. My heart is too fragile to survive that twice. I'm done, and I won't put Ben through the ordeal of having to let me down gently again."

Lizzie bit her bottom lip and thought about it. "I don't want Ben to be hurt."

"Then we should leave him alone. Both of us."

"Okay," Lizzie said, not looking terribly convinced of her own words. She tore her very short list out of the notebook and crumpled it in her hands. "If that's what you think is best."

"I do."

"But it won't hurt to get an explanation from Ben. Just to hear his side of the story."

"Nae, Lizzie," Emma insisted. "You'll make him uncomfortable. If he had wanted to explain himself, he would have done so by now."

"What explanation did he give for calling off the engagement?"

It took all the discipline Emma possessed not to let the memory reduce her to tears. She curled and uncurled her toes inside her shoes as a distraction. "He said he didn't want to marry me and then raced to his buggy, probably so he didn't have to watch me bawl like a baby."

Lizzie put an arm around her. "Or so Mahlon wouldn't throw rotten pumpkins at him."

Emma cracked a smile. "That's probably true."

"I'm still going to demand an explanation from him."

"Don't ask him. He'll think I put you up to it." She already knew why her fiancé had left. She'd rather not be reminded of it yet again.

Lizzie didn't consent to anything. Emma hadn't expected to gain her cooperation. Lizzie had a mind of her own. She'd do precisely what she wanted to do. Emma just hoped that Ben wouldn't be hurt and she wouldn't be further humiliated. Ben already pitied her enough.

Lizzie shrugged and grabbed both of Emma's hands. "So, can you forgive me? Are we friends again, no matter what an idiot Ben has been?"

Emma gave Lizzie a warm hug and savored the feeling of having a best friend again, in spite of her misgivings. Being friends with Lizzie would put her in Ben's path more often than ever, at least while he stayed in Bonduel. She comforted herself with the knowledge that Felty was as spry as any seventy-year-old. He'd recover quickly from surgery. Ben could be gone by the end of May. Maybe sooner. She and Lizzie could go on like before, as if Ben had never come into her life. She could be almost happy again. Tonight she would pray for Felty's speedy recovery. Then her heart could begin to heal.

Her new best friend pointed to the bag on the table. "So, do you want to help with a quilt?"

"Of course, if you don't mind that the corners don't match up."

"That's part of the charm."

Mahlon opened the back door and scowled when he saw who still lurked in his kitchen. "You haven't left yet?"

Lizzie picked up her bag. "Emma and I are friends again, and I admit I was in the wrong. Does that make you feel better?"

Mahlon's scowl relaxed, although it didn't disappear, and he folded his arms across his chest. "A little, but it still doesn't make up for all those nights Emma cried herself to sleep."

"I did not," Emma said.

He glanced at her. "You can't hide stuff from me, Em."

Regret flitted across Lizzie's face before she pinned Mahlon with a steely gaze. "Don't bother trying to get under my skin, Mailman. You'll lose every time."

Mahlon raised his arms as if stopping traffic. "I'm just pointing out your shortcomings. If you can't handle the truth, don't come over."

Lizzie narrowed her eyes. "Don't worry. I'm coming over. I'm coming over to torment Emma's irritating twin brother."

Mahlon matched her glare and added a frown. "Just to make sure you're sincere and won't hurt Emma's feelings again, bring me an apple pie, and I'll think about letting you back in the house."

Emma pressed her lips together in an attempt to keep a straight face. Lizzie and Mahlon had always picked at each other like a pair of cackling hens.

"I'd like to see you try and stop me," Lizzie replied.

Mahlon puffed out his chest like a rooster protecting his territory. "I'm looking forward to it."

"So am I," Lizzie said with her nose in the air, which inspired a look of indignation from Mahlon.

She picked up her bag, smiled brightly, and gave Emma a swift hug. "I'll come by tomorrow."

"With an apple pie," Mahlon added as Lizzie swept out the door like a leaf caught in the wind.

She turned around and winked. "Don't you wish," she said, before whirling around and marching across the lawn and into the field that was the shortest way to her house.

Mahlon stood with his hand holding the door and watched her go.

Emma lifted her eyes to the ceiling and sighed. "You're almost twenty-one years old, Mahlon. You've got to start being nicer to girls or you'll never get married."

"I'm only nice to the ones who don't have a brother who broke your heart."

"You and Lizzie have always butted heads, even before me and Ben."

"She likes it when I needle her a little."

She shook her finger at him. "You'll be nice to

Lizzie or you'll find bread crumbs in your bed tonight."

"That's nothing new. I eat in bed all the time."

"You do not."

Mahlon stared out the door at the very spot where Lizzie had disappeared from sight. "Do you think she'll bring pie? I really like Lizzie's pie."

Chapter 5

Dawdi reclined in his chair, trying to read without going cross-eyed. A puffy bandage sat beneath his nose like a miniature sling to catch any blood that might still be flowing from his surgery.

Mammi stood at the kitchen sink fiddling with a bottle of painkillers, trying to open the lid and read the instructions at the same time. "Ben, dear, will you come and open this for me? The pharmacist must have been very strong. I can't seem to budge it."

Ben left his post next to Dawdi and went to see what he could do about Mammi's bottle.

"I don't need any of that, Banannie," Dawdi said, forming the words as if each of his lips was four inches thick. "I'm not in hardly any pain, and in any case, I want to keep my wits about me."

"Now, Felty, you're taking some painkiller," Mammi insisted.

Ben wasn't sure if he should open the bottle for

Mammi or throw it in the trash for Dawdi. He chose Mammi. She looked the most determined.

Dawdi, with his strange bandage strapped to his face, turned his head to look at Mammi out of the corner of his eye. "I'm feeling pretty gute. The doctor said I would. When Jonas Hoover had nasal surgery, they shoved about six feet of gauze up his nose."

The thought that Dawdi might be feeling fine seemed to agitate Mammi. "Now, Felty. You're not doing gute at all. You'll be off your feet for at least a week, probably two."

"I've done my part, Annie. I'll not lie around any longer than I need to."

Mammi propped her hands on her hips. "We need at least two more weeks."

"I've got to tend to the animals," Felty said.

Mammi smiled at Ben as if she were embarrassed that he was listening in on their peculiar conversation. "That's why Ben is here, dear. He is taking care of everything."

Even with his hands tingling, Ben opened the bottle with ease and handed it to Mammi. "That's right, Dawdi. I don't want you to worry about a thing. Just concentrate on getting better."

Dawdi curled his lips until the corners disappeared beneath his nose bandage. "I don't even have to concentrate on that. The surgery wasn't so bad."

"Now, Felty," Mammi said, the scold rising in her voice, "there will be no talk of getting better."

Ben raised his eyebrows. Mammi certainly had a peculiar way of nursing her husband back to health. But Ben couldn't argue with it. Mammi and Dawdi had been together for over sixty years. Mammi knew better how to care for Dawdi than anyone. If Dawdi needed words of discouragement, who was Ben to question her methods?

Mammi tried to read the tiny directions on the pill bottle label. "Stuff and nonsense. Where are my glasses?" She handed the bottle back to him. "What does it say, dear?"

"Take one every six to eight hours as needed for pain."

Ben handed Mammi one pill, feeling guilty for conspiring against Dawdi. Mammi filled a glass with water and took it to Dawdi.

Ben tried to smooth things over with Dawdi. "The doctor said you'll heal faster if you take something for the pain. It helps reduce the inflammation."

Mammi snapped her head around to look at Ben and stopped in her tracks. "He did say that, didn't he?" She reversed direction, away from Dawdi's chair. "Never mind, then."

Felty held out his hand with a smug look on his half-covered face. "Come here, Annie Banannie. I'll have my pill now."

Ben pressed his lips tightly together to keep from chuckling. Had Mammi tricked Dawdi into taking a pill, or had she really changed her mind? Maybe she was way more clever than Ben could ever hope to be.

Sixty years of marriage was no small thing.

The door opened, and Ben's sister Lizzie charged like a bull into the great room. She had a basket slung over one arm and a smile pasted on her face, but one look at her expression told Ben that she was irritated about something. She glanced at him and her eyes flashed.

Jah, she was irritated at him.

"Mammi, how are you yet?" Lizzie said, depositing her basket on the table, striding to Mammi's side, and giving her a firm hug.

"Lizzie, it's wonderful to see you."

Lizzie quickly moved to Dawdi and sat on the sofa. "How are you, Dawdi?"

Dawdi lifted his head from the recliner. "A lot better than your mammi thinks I am. Hardly any pain at all."

"How did the surgery go?"

"The doctor told us it went well," Mammi said. "But you never know. There could be unexpected complications. He'll have to be very careful for the next three or four weeks."

Dawdi shifted in his recliner. "Not at all. I feel so gute, I could get up and milk the cows tomorrow."

Lizzie took Dawdi's hand. "You must take it easy. We wouldn't want you back in the hospital if you overdo it."

Mammi tapped Ben on the arm. "Ben will take excellent care of us. He's got all summer."

All summer? Ben wasn't planning on even being here through May. Unless Dawdi needed him, of course. He'd suffer through months of being close to Emma for Dawdi's sake.

Lizzie studied Dawdi's bandage. "You look like you're wearing a bright white and red mustache."

"Did you bring us some goodies?" Mammi asked.

Lizzie stood and went to the table. She pulled a golden-brown pie from the basket. "I made apple pies today. One for you, one for our family, and one to take to Emma's tomorrow, maybe," she said, lowering her eyes.

Ben's heart turned over in its grave. Lizzie was going to visit Emma.

Lizzie gave Ben a pointed look. Jah, she was irritated about something. He had a feeling he'd find out soon enough what it was.

Mammi clapped her hands. "I love apple pie."

"It's not really the season for them," Lizzie said. "But Lark Country Store had some." She turned back to Dawdi. "What can I do for you?"

Dawdi patted her hand. "I don't need any help, Liz. I'm feeling much better."

Lizzie leaned closer to Dawdi's chair. "I want to help wherever I can, even if Ben has things so well in hand." She shot him an accusatory look again, as if everything in the world were his fault.

"Alrighty then," Dawdi said. "You can read the paper to me."

Lizzie picked up *The Budget* sitting on Dawdi's small table and started reading. Ben helped Mammi tidy the kitchen while Lizzie read out loud. Dawdi loved *The Budget*, but Ben's eyes tended to glaze over after about half a page.

Once they'd cleaned the kitchen, Mammi sliced the apple pie and scooped generous pieces onto four small plates. Ben sprayed whipped topping from a can onto each piece. They handed plates to Lizzie and Dawdi and sat together to eat. Lizzie stopped reading, even though she was at an incredibly exciting part about who had come to services in Wautoma last month.

"This is the best pie I've ever tasted," Dawdi said. "Fit for a king."

For some unknown reason, Lizzie blushed. "I hope everybody likes it."

"Very gute," Ben said, studying Lizzie's face.

Her embarrassment didn't last long. She cleared her throat and remembered to glare at Ben. "I saw Emma Nelson today," she said, as if Emma were a regular topic of conversation.

Ben felt the heat travel up his neck as he clenched his jaw. Lizzie obviously had a bee in her bonnet about something, but he'd rather not discuss Emma in front of Mammi and Dawdi. It was tricky enough when Emma came to Huckleberry Hill and Mammi insisted Ben spend hours with her in the garden.

He didn't know how strong he could be. And he certainly didn't want Mammi and Dawdi to get their hopes up about Emma.

Jah. He wouldn't want to upset Mammi and Dawdi for anything.

He shot to his feet and nearly lost his piece of

pie in the process. "Thanks for coming, Lizzie. The pie tasted wonderful gute."

Lizzie stood as if she'd been expecting some sort of reaction from him. "Why don't you come outside and see me off, big brother?"

She retrieved her sweater from the hook and handed him the coat hanging next to it. It happened to be Dawdi's coat, which was about four sizes too small. He looped it back on the hook, gave her a smirk, and opened the door. They walked out together. The late-afternoon sun felt comfortably warm at his back. No need for a sweater.

"Okay," he said, deciding not to mince any words. Lizzie never did. "I'm really sorry for whatever it is I did." Then a depressing thought came to him. "Have you changed your mind about being Emma's friend?" The way she frowned at him made his heart sink. "I take it the reunion didn't go well."

Lizzie's face turned a pale shade of purple. "Go well? Emma thinks everything is her fault. She welcomed me back with open arms. We're best friends again."

Ben almost breathed out a sigh of relief, but her expression stopped him short. Maybe he shouldn't be happy just yet. Lizzie still acted as if he were waving a red bandanna in front of her face and taunting her. "Okay?" he prompted.

She shoved her hands onto her hips and stared him down even though he towered over her by seven or eight inches. "All this time. All these months. How could you?"

"How could I what?"

She narrowed her eyes to barely visible slits. "Don't interrupt me."

He shut his mouth and pretended he didn't have one.

"It must have been very hard when Emma broke up with you."

The memory almost bulldozed him. Why would she bring up such a painful event? He flexed his tingling fingers.

She looked at him as if he'd stolen an Englischer's car. He crushed his lips tighter together. "Well, what do you have to say for yourself?"

"You told me not to interrupt."

She stomped her foot and turned a deeper shade of purple. "It's true, isn't it? You're the one who called off the engagement."

A puff of air could have knocked Ben to the ground. He couldn't keep his voice from shaking. "You didn't know?"

"All I know is that you told me you had to get away from Emma, that you weren't going to get married." The anger seemed to melt from her expression and she looked truly hurt. "You loved her so much, Ben. I assumed she called it off because you never would have."

Ben's throat went dry. He loved Emma with every beat of his miserable heart. But sometimes love had to be unselfish. He briefly closed his eyes and told himself for the millionth time that it was better this way. Emma would recover in time, and in the end, she would be glad she hadn't married him.

"I feel so *deerich*, foolish," Lizzie said.

"It doesn't matter. Now you know."

"All these months I've been blaming Emma for driving you away. I told her that I'd lost my brother because of her."

Lizzie's words felt like a slap in the face. Emma must have been devastated—more devastated than she already had been.

And her pain was his fault. Again.

Lizzie's face clouded over, and she hooked her elbow around his arm. "*Cum.* You need to sit down before you fall."

He did as he was told. He suddenly didn't feel so strong.

Lizzie softened her voice and spoke as if she were delivering very bad news. "Everybody thought Emma had broken it off. You moved to Florida, Ben."

"But didn't she explain everything to you?"

She huffed out a breath. "I accused her of driving you away, remember? She wouldn't have wanted to explain anything to such a rotten friend. She just pasted on that fake smile and tried to work herself to death. I thought she acted that way because she was happy to be rid of you."

A black pit threatened to swallow Ben whole.

Poor Emma. He had found some measure of peace in Florida because he thought Emma had somehow moved on, that she wasn't mourning for him. Now all that disappeared. She must have suffered more terribly than he had anticipated.

Lizzie scooted closer to him and draped her arm over his shoulder. She kept her voice low and soothing even though Ben could tell she was rumbling like a volcano beneath the surface. "I don't understand. Why did you call things off with her? You two were everybody's ideal couple. We were all a little jealous at how good-looking you both are. Although it was no mystery you found each other. Good-looking people seem to find other good-looking people to live happily ever after with."

"We found each other because you invited her to the lake four years ago. It's all your doing."

"So?" She studied his face. "Why did you break up with your perfect match?"

He held his breath for what seemed like ten minutes and thought of all the things he *could* say to Lizzie but wouldn't. "I don't deserve her."

Lizzie raised both eyebrows and blinked exactly twice. "That is the stupidest thing I have ever heard in my life."

He lifted his hat and ran his fingers through his hair. Stupid or not, that was all he could give her. If he told her everything, she'd argue with him, and he didn't want to argue. He'd debated with himself so many times that he had a permanent headache.

But still, he thought that maybe he could make Lizzie see reason without really giving her all the information. "Emma would have been miserable being married to me. I know you think that's dumb, but it's truly the way I feel. I love—loved—her too much to let her chain herself to me for life. I won't do it."

Lizzie batted her eyes as if a stiff wind had blown chimney ash into her face. She patted his hand as if she were explaining things to a five-year-old. "I believe you're suffering from a severe case of low self-esteem."

He pulled his hand away. "It's not right for Emma and me. Can you trust me when I tell you it's just not right?"

Lizzie seemed unmoved by his plea. "If I don't know why you broke up, how can I help you get back together?"

Ben's heart leaped at the possibility even as he recognized what a disaster it would be to Emma's tender feelings. "Nae. We won't get back together."

Mischief twinkled in her eyes. "You can't stop me from trying to make it happen."

He turned to stone. Couldn't Lizzie see how hazardous such an attempt would be? "If you push me, I'll go back to Florida in a second and ask cousin Aden to care for Dawdi."

All the light seemed to drain out of her. "You'd leave us again?"

He sighed in resignation and put a comforting

arm around her. "I'm not going to be here much longer anyway. You know that."

"Then it won't matter what I do. Offended or not, you'll be going away again."

"I'm sorry, Lizzie. That's how it has to be."

She nestled closer under his arm. "Then I should enjoy the time we have left together."

"Jah, instead of wasting your time trying to match me with girls I don't want to be with."

He flinched as Emma came around the bend in the lane. Had she heard any of their conversation?

Her mouth quivered as if she were trying to smile but found it impossible to actually do it.

An empty space yawned in the pit of his stomach. She'd heard enough. Hurting her had become a regular habit, even though he would as soon move to Africa as injure his dear Emma. He didn't know how his heart could take much more of being near her and watching both of them suffer.

"Emma," Lizzie said, a little too loudly as if to warn Ben of Emma's approach. "I was just giving Ben a piece of my mind."

Could he say anything to wipe that forlorn look off her face? "My dawdi's surgery went well."

The surgery went well? Was that the best he could do? He ran a hand down the side of his face. Why had Emma ever fallen in love with him?

Emma nodded gravely, marched up the porch steps, and bolted into the house. "I have to go to the bathroom," she said over her shoulder as she disappeared down Mammi's hall.

Lizzie frowned and cuffed him on the shoulder. "I'm so mad at you right now."

Ben spread his arms in surrender. "I don't know what to do. What do you want me to do?"

"Stay in Bonduel and marry Emma."

"I can't, Lizzie. Don't ask. Don't ever ask again."

Chapter 6

Ben's legs felt as stiff as boards as he shuffled into the barn through the side door. Enough sunlight streamed through the high windows to let him see by, and if he propped the door open, he'd have no need for a lantern.

It had been two weeks since Dawdi's surgery, and Emma had avoided him as if he had a foul smell hanging about him. It was better this way. As long as she stayed away from him, he wouldn't have to gaze into those lake-blue eyes and dream about what a paradise it would have been to have Emma as his wife.

He also didn't like to be reminded of how badly he'd hurt her last August and how deeply she still felt it. Even though she forced a painful smile when he was near, he knew his presence tortured her. Why else would she retreat to the safety of Mammi and Dawdi's bathroom every time he looked at her the wrong way?

The sooner he could get out of Bonduel, the better. Emma must be allowed to heal.

He gathered the tools he would need from Dawdi's bench and walked to the hooks on the wall where Dawdi hung his harnesses and other tack. He fingered the harness that needed repair yesterday and decided he might need that lantern after all. He could have sworn one of the straps was nearly worn through. Today it looked as good as new. Better than new. Someone had already replaced it.

He rubbed the back of his neck as he took a closer look at the buggy. The leather had been oiled and the buggy's exterior buffed. Even the velvet seats had been brushed and the floor cleaned. Had Mammi done this? Or Emma?

Well then, one fewer item on his long list of things that would need to be done today. He limped to the bench and stowed Dawdi's tools where they belonged.

The door on the other side of the barn opened and flooded the space with light. Emma walked into the barn and began searching for something on the shelves along the far wall. Ben turned into a statue. He was partially hidden behind a stout pillar and the buggy, so if he didn't make a sound, Emma would never know he was there.

Why did his chest ache and his heart hammer against his ribs every time he laid eyes on her? He'd done his very best to let her go and move on. His body hadn't gotten the message. He indulged in a little self-pity. She was so beautiful. Why had God required this sacrifice of him? Didn't God want him to be happy, to have Emma beside him for a long life dedicated to God's service? He squeezed his eyes shut and banished those thoughts from his head.

God is good. His ways are not my ways.

Emma stood on her tiptoes rearranging pots and seed boxes, still looking for something, but she wasn't tall enough to see the highest shelves. Ben resisted the almost overpowering urge to go to her aid. He was tall enough to reach anything Emma might need.

She stretched her arm all the way up and her fingertips brushed against a ball of twine on the top shelf. She wouldn't be able to get it down by herself. Too late he decided he should help her. Before he had a chance to step out of the shadows, her sleeve brushed against a teetering watering can on the shelf below, and it toppled off its perch and clocked Emma on the forehead.

Ben gasped, forsook his hiding place, and went quickly to her side. She groaned as her hand flew to her right eye. Blood had seeped between her fingers by the time Ben reached her.

"Emma, are you okay?"

While she pressed her hand over the right half of her face, he led her to the milking stool and helped her sit. Then he found another milking stool and sank next to her.

Emma pulled her hand from her face, caught sight of the blood on her fingers, and immediately slapped her hand back over the wound. "Oh, bother," she mumbled.

Ben had to concentrate on keeping his breathing steady. He usually didn't mind the sight of blood, but this was Emma's blood. Why had he not set aside his own selfishness and helped her in the first place?

"Can I have a look?" he said, as calmly as if he were asking for a glance at the latest news in *The Budget.*

She faithfully clutched her face. "Head wounds always look more serious than they are. I'll go in and get a little bandage from Anna." She tried to stand.

Ben nudged her back down. "It wouldn't be very gute if you fainted on your way to the house and flattened Mammi's newly planted petunias."

Frowning in concentration, she studied him with her good eye. "I need the twine for measuring to the center of the pumpkin mound. I want to move Anna's plant from the pot this morning. I'm a little clumsy today, I guess."

"That watering can was bound to come over on you. It was teetering before you even walked in the barn. Someone didn't scoot it back far enough on the shelf."

"I'm the one who put it away," she said.

"Oh."

Her mouth drooped. "I'm all thumbs, in case you haven't noticed."

"I've never noticed that about you. Some people are naturally accident-prone."

"Same thing."

"Can I see your very impressive cut?"

"How do you know it's impressive?" she asked.

"Because there's enough blood running down your arm to donate to a hospital."

She gave him a sheepish twitch of her lips and pulled her hand from her face. A deep cut gaped half an inch above her eyebrow. She'd definitely have a scar.

"You'll probably need a tetanus shot when we take you to get stitches."

She held out her left finger for his examination. "Already got one, remember? When I sewed through my finger?"

"Well, that's good news. No need for a tetanus shot." He leaned close and touched her forehead just above the nasty-looking cut.

She stiffened as soon as his skin brushed against hers. "I don't need stitches. I'll be right as rain with a gauze pad and some antibiotic ointment."

"Nope. I know what a tough girl you are, but trust me. You need stitches."

"It's that bad?"

"I wouldn't look in the mirror if I were you. You might freak out."

"Thanks for the words of comfort," she groaned.

"Just trying to be helpful."

"You've seen me in enough scrapes to know when I need medical attention, I guess." She grimaced and lowered her eyes as if she were suddenly seized by a gripping headache.

Ben stood up, ignoring the tightening in his chest. "Stay here, and I'll get something for your head."

"Don't trouble yourself. I can go."

"We're trying to avoid fainting, remember? I'll be right back."

He jogged to the house where Dawdi sat in his usual place reading the paper and Mammi busily prepared dinner. Ben didn't even want to guess what kind of smell wafted from her bubbling pot.

"Ben," Mammi said, without looking up, "will you make sure Emma knows she is invited for dinner? I've decided that I need to learn how to cook pumpkin if we're going to have a giant pumpkin come autumn time. I'm trying out my first recipe today."

"What is it, Mammi? It smells delicious." He knew it was a sin to lie, but Mammi always got so enthusiastic about her cooking. He couldn't hurt her feelings.

"I call it Chunky Pumpkin Soup. It was supposed to be just pumpkin soup, but I can't make the lumps disappear, so I've renamed it."

"Sounds gute." He marked off another lie on his sin chart.

"Also," Mammi continued in her bossy voice, "I want you to help Emma tie up the tomato plants. It's too big a job for one little girl to do all by herself."

"I'll see they get done today," Ben said, rifling through Mammi's cupboards for a first aid kit.

"What are you looking for, dear? The twine for

the tomatoes is on the top shelf above the potting soil in the barn."

"Emma already found it. A watering can fell and clunked her on the forehead."

Mammi put her hand to her mouth. "Is she all right?"

Dawdi's recliner groaned as he lowered the footrest. "She can take my place on the recliner. I don't want to sit in it ever again."

"Now, Felty," Mammi said with a wink at Ben. "We know how brave you want to be, but you are nowhere near well enough to rise from your bed and walk around."

Dawdi stood and harrumphed dismissively. "Nonsense. I'm fit as a fiddle." He wildly swung his arms back and forth and marched smartly around the great room. Then he got down on the floor and did two push-ups. He couldn't manage a third, but for a man of almost eighty-five, Ben found it quite impressive.

"Now, Felty," Mammi scolded. "See what happens when you overdo it? You end up flat on the floor, worse off than you would have been if you had stayed put in your chair."

Dawdi stifled a grunt and got slowly to his feet. "Banannie, how much longer do you think I can sit in that chair without going crazy?"

Mammi and Dawdi continued discussing Dawdi's health while Ben found the supplies he needed to tend to Emma's cut. Even with his doctoring, she would need a trip to the hospital. As soon as he saw to Emma, he would go to the nearest phone shack and find a driver.

Mammi was trying to get Dawdi back into his chair. "The doctor said you shouldn't blow your nose for three months. The minute you go outside, you'll catch a late-spring cold and your nose will swell up like a one of Emma's pumpkins."

He really couldn't help it. Ben curled one corner of his mouth and bit his tongue. Neither Mammi nor Dawdi would take it well if he burst into laughter while they were discussing very important matters— like if Dawdi should be admitted to a hospital.

He ran back outside, and to his relief, Emma sat right where he had left her, with her head cradled gently in her hands. He rejoiced she hadn't tried to stand and ended up facedown with a mouthful of dirt or something even more disgusting from the floor of Dawdi's barn.

"How's your head?"

"Throbbing."

He placed his supplies on the milk stool and knelt on one knee in front of her. "Let me clean it off, and we'll see how bad it is."

"Or how good it is."

"I'm glad you're thinking positive thoughts."

Being grateful he'd brought an extra rag, he handed her one of the wet ones, and she cleaned the blood from her hands. While she concentrated on her hands, he carefully wiped the blood from around the cut, working his way from the outside to the center. She hissed when he got too close to the actual wound. "Just a little more?" he asked. "I want to make sure it's clean."

"Of course. I'd rather not come down with an eyebrow infection."

"I hear those are terrible." He fell silent as he tried hard to concentrate on the ugly cut on Emma's forehead instead of her perfectly shaped lips, which were almost irresistible. Unfortunately, his imagination hijacked his discipline, and he pictured himself brushing his lips softly against hers. Longing overpowered him as fire seemed to travel through his veins.

He jerked his hand away from her forehead, jumped to his feet, and put three strides between them. As soon as he got his wits about him, he turned his back on her and pretended to look for something on Dawdi's work table so Emma wouldn't wonder if he'd completely lost his mind—which he had. But she certainly didn't need to know that.

"Are you looking for something?" she said, gazing at him doubtfully, as if his sudden retreat had somehow been her fault.

He motioned with the rag. "I think I'll go squeeze a little soap on this."

He ran back to the house, faster this time, concern for Emma warring with anger at himself. He had to be stronger than this. He had to give up this ridiculous fascination with Emma's mouth.

"How about Lasik?" Mammi was saying as Ben entered and made a beeline for the kitchen sink.

She sat at the sofa reading a stack of colorful

pamphlets, though Ben didn't take the time to see what they were about.

Dawdi stretched out on the floor near his recliner doing sit-ups. Sparky barked her encouragement every time Dawdi came up. "I can do dozens of these," he said, grinning at Ben.

Ben furrowed his brow. Lord willing, Dawdi would not break his back.

No time to find out. Ben was already in the process of treating one injured person in the barn. Dawdi's future injuries would have to wait.

With a clean rag and a dab of soap, Ben went back to the barn determined to ignore his rapid pulse and Emma Nelson's rose-petal lips.

Emma sat patiently on her stool with a cloudy expression on her face, dabbing the blood off her hands. He didn't dwell on what he suspected she was probably thinking. Instead, he knelt down and sponged the cut with his soapy washrag. She flinched. "Sorry," he said.

She managed a half smile. "It's not bad. The soap stings a little. I've had worse."

He returned her smile with a weak one of his own. "Jah, I know you have." He dabbed his rag once more at her cut before taking her hand and pointing to her scarred thumb. The skin there was jagged and white.

She blushed and slowly pulled her hand away. "For as clumsy as I am, it's a wonder I don't have more scars to show for it."

"That wasn't your fault. The knife was dangerously sharp. They use it to gut fish."

She wouldn't meet his eye. "I thought it might work well on carrots."

"I'm glad they were able to save your thumb." He nudged her chin up with his finger. Her brilliant eyes almost took his breath away. "Although I felt bad I never got a chance to call you by the nickname I made up."

A grin played at her reluctant lips. "What was that?"

"I wanted to call you 'Stumpy.'"

She giggled cautiously. It was the most delightful sound he'd heard for several days. "I only sliced the tip of my thumb. Not the whole thing."

"Then I would have called you 'Half-a-Stumpy.'"

"It takes too long to yell, 'Hey, Half-a-Stumpy, watch out for that ditch!' I would already have fallen in by the time you finished saying my name."

Ben fingered the stubble on his chin. "True. It's very good those doctors were able to sew you back together."

"It's funny when you really think about it. I'm all thumbs, yet I almost lost one of them."

Chuckling, he took her hand in both of his and ran his finger lightly across the back of her thumb. He held on for longer than he meant to. Her skin was just so soft.

Emma coughed as if she had a large boulder stuck in her throat, and Ben feared that she might bolt for the house and the safety of the bathroom at any moment.

Instead, she cleared her throat and stood her ground. "Lizzie and I are making a quilt together," she said.

Relieved at the change of subject, Ben found a gauze pad in Mammi's first aid kit and began to dab the blood from Emma's cleaned forehead. It didn't want to stop bleeding yet. "For the orphans' fund."

"Jah. We are almost done piecing the top together. It is very pretty."

Ben furrowed his brow, hoping that Lizzie's quilt project hadn't been perilous for Emma's fingers. She didn't always do so well with pins. "She says she's been to your house every day this week."

"I told her we could go to her house, but she says she doesn't mind coming over to mine. Maybe she likes getting on Mahlon's nerves."

"I haven't seen Mahlon since . . . I haven't seen him for a long time."

She wouldn't look him in the eye. "He always seems to have a chip on his shoulder about one thing or another."

"Did he get baptized yet?"

"No, he's still in rumschpringe, though I don't know why. I've been baptized, but most of his friends haven't yet. They like Davy Burkholder's cell phone."

"But he'll stay in the community, won't he?" Ben said.

"I don't wonder that he will. Maybe he thinks

he'll have to stop being grouchy once he's in the church. Or maybe he's waiting to find the right girl before he decides to be baptized. Lizzie lectures him frequently about the evils of waiting too long to join the church. When she talks like that, he just grins and winks at her. That's usually enough to get her good and riled up."

Ben nodded. It wasn't hard to get Lizzie riled up. He sobered when he thought of Mahlon. At least Mahlon talked to Lizzie. He would probably never speak to Ben again. He couldn't forgive Ben for leaving his twin sister.

If Ben had been in Mahlon's shoes, he might have felt the same way.

He reached out and tucked an errant lock of hair behind Emma's ear. She never could quite manage to keep her unruly hair underneath her kapp. He'd tucked her hair behind her ears dozens of times when they were engaged.

She lost her smile and clasped her fingers together in her lap. He withdrew his hand and pretended that he hadn't just done something incredibly stupid—something that dredged up all sorts of pleasant and painful memories.

He squeezed a dollop of ointment onto her cut, spread it around, and covered it with a gauze pad.

He wasn't surprised to see tears pooling in her eyes. "I'm sorry," he stuttered. "My hands aren't very gentle. It can't be comfortable to have me poking you like that."

She valiantly blinked back the tears and nodded.

"You've been very kind. It's starting to hurt a little bit, now that the shock has worn off."

He cleared his throat. "Let me look at your eyes."

She turned her trusting gaze to him, and he tried not to melt like a snowman in July. "It doesn't look like you have a concussion. That's good news."

She smiled weakly. "Jah. That last concussion was painful. I don't remember much about driving your dat's buggy into the ditch, but I remember how kind you were to me when it happened. You carried me for more than a mile until you could flag down a car to help us."

Ben folded his arms across his chest to keep the emotions safely bound and gagged. He remembered that day vividly—his anguish at seeing Emma in pain, the comfort of holding her safely in his arms, and the overwhelming need to protect and care for her. That memory haunted him every night.

He reached out and, with his thumb, caressed the side of her forehead not covered by the gauze pad. Emma was a special, wonderful girl who tried so hard to do everything right that sometimes she went overboard in her eagerness. He loved her for that.

The longing to shelter her clobbered him upside the head and left him breathless.

He jumped to his feet and turned his back on her once again so she wouldn't see the despair that must surely be written all over his face. "I will ride to the Millers' and use the phone they have in their shop. We should get you to a doctor."

He didn't wait to hear what she had to say. With long, purposeful strides, he walked back to the house. He had to get out of Bonduel. If he had his way, he'd already be on a bus.

Dawdi reclined in his chair, looking like he'd worked up quite a sweat while Ben was out. Mammi sat next to him on the sofa knitting furiously. A faint whiff of what was in the pot hung in the air, but Mammi didn't seem to be in any hurry to remove it from the stove. Perhaps it would boil itself down to mush.

Ben wiped any hint of distress off his face and sat on the sofa next to Mammi. "Dawdi," he began, "you know I would do anything to help you on the farm."

Mammi took her hand from her knitting long enough to pat Ben's knee. "I know you would, dear."

"But now that you've recovered from surgery, it's time for me to go back to Florida. I'm helping Marvin Shrock mind his store. He needs me back there as soon as I can."

And I must get away from Emma and the memories.

Mammi went so far as to drop her knitting needles in her lap and stare at Ben in shock.

Dawdi rocked his recliner and let it catapult him to his feet. "Two weeks is long enough to sit in one place. I'll go feed the chickens."

Mammi could have set fire to the sofa with the glare she sent in Dawdi's direction. "Now, Felty. Don't you care about what happens to your grandson?"

Dawdi was halfway out the door. "We'll miss you, Ben. Send us a postcard so we know you got home okay."

"Felty, stop right there. You know Ben can't leave." She looked at Ben and the wrinkles bunched around her lips. "Felty is trying to put on a brave face, as he always does, but he hasn't told you about the other surgery he must have."

Ben's gut clenched. "Other surgery?"

"Other surgery?" Dawdi said.

Mammi glanced at Ben like they were in cahoots with each other. Then she turned to Dawdi with a patient expression on her face, as if he had misplaced his own head and she was eager to help him find it. "Felty can't hardly walk with those plantar warts on his feet. The doctor's been urging him for months to get them removed. Two weeks from now is the day."

Dawdi stepped back into the house and shut the door. He didn't exactly slam it, but he didn't go gentle on it either. He stroked his beard as his gaze darted between Ben and Mammi.

"Pumpkins take a long time to grow," he said.

The sit-ups must have been taking their toll on his faculties.

Mammi picked up her knitting needles and took up as if she'd never stopped. "Yes, they do. We can't rush these things."

Dawdi slumped his shoulders and groaned in surrender. "These plantar warts have been bothering me for months."

"That's what I want to hear," Mammi said. She nudged Ben with her elbow, a movement she could execute without dropping a stitch in her knitting. "Are you sure you can't stay? Felty won't be able to walk."

Shrugging off the distinct feeling he'd been hoodwinked, Ben nodded. "I will stay. I'll do everything I can to help Dawdi." He stretched his spine and rubbed the back of his neck. But he'd stay away from Emma. No good could come of it. For either of them.

As he rode to the Millers' so he could use their phone to call a driver to take Emma to the hospital, an idea struck him. It wondered him if he might not be going about this in the wrong way.

Why couldn't he help Emma at the same time he helped Dawdi?

But what did Emma need besides a few stitches and a first aid kit strapped to her wrist?

Chapter 7

Ben climbed out of his buggy and took a deep breath. He hadn't been to a gathering for months. Would everybody stare at him, like a leper?

He shook off that immature teenage anxiety. He wasn't looking to be accepted into a group of friends or even trying to check out the cute girls. He had come for one purpose. Once he did what he came here to do, he'd retreat to Huckleberry Hill and never have to dodge giggling girls again.

Lizzie jumped out of the buggy and grinned at him. "Feeling a little awkward?"

"I'm too old for this."

"You'll be fine. Try not to break a hip during volleyball."

"Whatever you say."

She sidled next to him as if she had a wonderful secret to tell. "Emma will be here."

"I'm not here to see Emma."

"Maybe not," Lizzie said, "but you'll see her. And she'll see you. Maybe sparks will ignite."

He clenched his jaw. He'd rather not have Lizzie working against him. "The only sparks I might see are if you and Mahlon Nelson stray too near each other. Just don't get into a fistfight."

Lizzie rolled her eyes. "Mahlon won't dare start an argument with all these people around. I always win. He doesn't want to be humiliated in front of his friends."

The Yutzys had set up a volleyball net in their backyard and a game was in full swing. Ben's gaze traveled around *die youngie* milling near the snack table. John Shirk lugged a five-gallon jug across the lawn toward the table. Might as well start with him.

He turned to Lizzie. "Bye. I've got people I need to see."

Lizzie raised her brows. "Ooh. People. It sounds so mysterious."

He gifted her with an unamused smile and walked away.

Meeting John halfway across the yard, he said, "Can I help?"

John nodded, set down the jug, and let Ben grab one of the handles. They lifted together and hefted the jug onto the table next to the paper cups.

For a split second, Ben reconsidered his choice. John Shirk was a fine young man, stocky and solid, who had a gute job at the sawmill and wasn't afraid of hard work. Emma would never go hungry if she were married to John. He'd take good care of her.

But John wasn't all that quick on his feet. Would he be able to rush in and save Emma from a speeding train or a runaway horse? And how could he hope to tend to Emma's cuts and scrapes with those thick fingers of his?

He studied John out of the corner of his eye while he filled a few cups with lemonade. John wasn't nearly good enough for Emma, but what choice did Ben have? He had to find someone, and John was one of Ben's top three prospects. He'd have to make do.

He handed John a cup of lemonade. "How have you been, John?"

John took a gulp of lemonade. "I thought you weren't coming back. At least that's what Mahlon said."

"I'm here just long enough to help my dawdi while he has surgery."

"It's gute to see you for whatever reason," John said.

"So, what have you been up to? Do you have a girlfriend yet?"

"Nae. I thought Elizabeth Zimmerman and I might get along all right, but she wasn't interested."

Ben shook his head. "Her loss."

"But I did buy that hunting rifle I've had my eye on."

How would John be able to keep Emma safe when he went hunting? Maybe he could take her hunting with him. Ben ground his teeth together and tried not to imagine what could happen if

Emma and a gun ever came within several hundred feet of each other.

"Have you been out to shoot it yet?"

"I used it all winter. Tagged myself a big buck."

"Congratulations." He rested a hand on John's shoulder and hesitated only for a moment. Did he really want to see Emma with someone else? He took a breath and let the pain wash over and through him. More than anything, he wanted to see Emma happy. "Talking about girlfriends—"

"Were we talking about girlfriends?"

"Have you ever considered taking Emma Nelson home from a gathering?"

John swallowed down the wrong throat and began coughing violently. Ben pounded him on the back. "Emma Nelson?" John said.

"Jah. She's pretty. I bet she'd be delighted."

John furrowed his brow. "I could never take Emma out, Ben. Her candle is still burning for you. I'd rather not waste my time on another man's farm."

"It's been almost nine months, John. She's ready to move on. Ready to find someone who can make her truly happy."

"Are you sure?" John asked.

"I moved to Florida. We both know it's over."

John lifted his eyebrows. "She's real pretty. After you left she acted like she was okay with it, but I didn't really believe it. She'd lost that light in her eyes, you know, like she was still hoping for you to come back. I would have tried before now, but she doesn't seem interested in anybody."

"It's over between us. Everybody knows that."

John regarded Ben with a suspicious eye. "Why are you so eager to match me up with Emma?"

"I want her to be happy." He pushed the words out of his mouth. "And you're a gute man."

John tilted his head and drained his lemonade cup. "I'll think on it. Emma is a wonderful-gute girl, even though she attracts accidents like honey attracts bees. I'll have to secure my buggy," he said, laughing at his own cleverness.

Maybe John wasn't such a gute idea. Ben didn't like it when people made fun of Emma. But it was too late now. The seed had been planted. He'd just have to wait and see if it germinated.

He shook hands with John and stalked off to seek his next target. Adam Wengerd played volleyball with a gaggle of young females who spent more time looking at him than they did at the ball.

Adam was sufficiently tall, with dark brown hair and tawny eyes that the girls found dreamy—at least according to Lizzie. Adam taught school, so he would be out of a job if he married Emma. That was one strike against him. Emma's husband had to have a steady job or a good farm to support his family. Ben would not have Emma living in a hovel. But Adam was quite charming with the girls. He'd keep Emma mesmerized with his light brown eyes and straight, white teeth. Ben didn't like him already.

He was perfect.

Ben charged right into the volleyball game, hit a

ball that came his way, and stood next to Adam in the front row. The little girl to his left who looked as if she'd turned sixteen yesterday glared at him for taking her place beside the man of her dreams. "Adam," Ben said, ignoring the girl shooting darts at him with her eyes, "I need your help with something. Can we talk?"

Adam jumped high in the air and blocked a volley coming from the other side. "Sure. Anything for you, Ben."

He winked at the little girl next to him, which catapulted her into a fit of giggles. "Edna, you'll have to cover the front line for me. Do your best, and I'll be right back."

Adam led Ben to the shade of a large oak standing watch over the backyard. "Is something wrong? How can I help?"

"This is going to sound out of the blue, but have you ever thought about dating Emma Nelson?"

"Thought about it? I've almost asked her to ride home with me twice. But I don't think she'd say yes. How can any boy compete with the memory of Ben Helmuth?"

Ben looked at the ground and shook his head. "I want you to take her on a date or something."

"Why?"

"I'm going back to Florida. She needs to find somebody else."

Adam rubbed his jaw, considering Ben's proposal. "I don't like being any girl's second choice."

"I was the *wrong* choice. Emma sees that now. Don't you think she's worth a try?"

Adam's face brightened. "She's definitely worth a try. If you want me to ask her out, I'll ask her out. My dawdi wouldn't have that new roof over his head if it weren't for you."

"Forget about that. I'm glad I could help."

Adam glanced behind him. "I've got to get back to the game, but I'll be sure to do something about Emma. It would be really fun."

Ben thumbed his suspenders and surveyed the crowd once again. So far, his plan was working out better than expected. Now he just had to have a visit with Freeman Kiem.

He furrowed his brow and hoped that assigning three boys at the same time wasn't a mistake, but he wanted to give Emma plenty to choose from. They couldn't all court her simultaneously, but maybe three at once would give her a chance to quickly cull out the choices and find the one she wanted to marry come autumn.

Pain twisted in his gut, like it did every time he thought of giving Emma up to some other boy. The fact that it had to be done didn't make it any less painful, and it certainly didn't make him feel any better. In fact, he felt more miserable than he had for months.

He had to get out of Bonduel.

As soon as Dawdi got his plantar warts frozen off, he would go home.

Lizzie and Emma stood by the lemonade. Emma

sported an oversized gauze pad on her forehead that covered half of her eyebrow. Ben supposed people were probably used to seeing her like that, with some sort of bandage or cast at gatherings.

Although it had been difficult, he had insisted on taking Emma for stitches himself. He could have sent Mammi or Dawdi, but he wanted to make sure that she was properly cared for. It had always been that way. He felt so protective of her that no treatment or care seemed good enough unless he saw to it personally.

The doctor had given her three stitches, which didn't seem like near enough, but he insisted that Emma would be good as new, except for a new scar that would give her a good story to tell.

The accident with the watering can happened almost a week ago. She would be able to take off the bandage soon. The corner of Ben's mouth curled involuntarily. It was so cute the way the gauze pad draped over her eyebrow like a pirate's eye patch.

Lizzie acted as if she were planning some secret spy operation, whispering instruction in Emma's ear and keeping her eyes darting from one person to another. In between sips of lemonade, Emma shook her head and seemed to be resisting whatever Lizzie was planning. She glanced Ben's way once but quickly averted her gaze. He quickly averted his.

He saw Freeman Kiem huddled in a cluster of other boys, acting as if he were trying to work up the courage to talk to one of the many girls who also seemed to congregate in packs at these gatherings.

Ben marched across the lawn once again. He'd talk Freeman into dating his ex-fiancée, then get out of here. Lizzie could find some nice young man to drive her home.

"Freeman," Ben said. He stopped short as Freeman turned, and he caught sight of Mahlon Nelson standing in the midst of Freeman's pack.

Too late to retreat. Mahlon had already seen him. Mahlon's expression didn't change, but Ben could see the muscles of his jaw tighten ever so slightly. "Hello, Mahlon. Hello, Joshua." His mouth felt as if it were filled with sawdust. "Have you tried the lemonade? It's wonderful gute."

He hoped that wasn't a bald-faced lie. He hadn't actually tried the lemonade, but lemonade was a safe and nonthreatening topic of conversation. What would Mahlon think if he knew that Ben was collecting boys for Emma to date? He'd probably be glad. He certainly wanted Emma to find someone worthy of her as much as Ben did. At this point, Mahlon felt so mad at Ben, he wouldn't approve of Ben and Emma getting back together even if they wanted to.

"How long are you going to be in town, Ben?" Joshua asked. "We heard your dawdi is feeling poorly."

"He's getting surgery on his feet next week. Once he's recovered, I'll be going back. Maybe three or four weeks."

Freeman put a hand on his shoulder. "We've

missed you. No one can wield a hammer like Ben Helmuth."

"Jah," said Davy Burkholder. "I never thought anyone could rebuild a chicken coop so fast."

Everyone in their little circle laughed except for Mahlon and Ben. The whole community knew of Emma's penchant for accidentally destroying small structures. They always talked of her mishaps with affection instead of scorn. But the chicken coop was another painful memory of what Ben had lost. If he judged the look on Mahlon's face correctly, Mahlon's thoughts turned in the same direction.

Joshua slid his hands into his pockets. "Emma tells me she's gonna grow a giant pumpkin for Anna Helmuth. That was quite a sight last year."

Never one to hold his tongue, especially in defense of his sister, Mahlon snapped, "Your mammi can grow her own pumpkins."

Joshua, Freeman, and the other boys stared at him in dismay, probably wondering why he cared about pumpkins and if he would throw a fit about them.

"She's really grateful for the help," Ben said, in his soft voice that usually placated even the most hostile of foes.

"Did you put your mammi up to it? Are you regretting breaking up with Emma, or don't you care about her feelings at all?"

Ben would be trapped no matter how he answered that question. He smiled weakly and made his posture as humble as possible. "She's doing a gute job. The plant has spread out on the mound almost four feet. She's got a real talent for it."

"*You* broke it off with Emma?" Joshua asked. "I thought she broke up with you."

"That's what he wanted everybody to think," Mahlon said. "So he wouldn't look like the bad one."

Ben wanted to crawl into a little hole. He'd really made a mess of things. Leave it to Mahlon to point out one of his many flaws. "I thought everybody knew that I broke it off."

"I did," Davy said. "It was pretty obvious the way Emma acted."

"I never wanted to hurt anybody, especially not her," Ben said. But he hadn't gotten what he wanted. He'd hurt Emma and, no doubt, her entire family. Not to mention his own family.

"So now you won't even say Emma's name out loud."

The boys standing in Mahlon's little circle slowly began to find other places to be. They tiptoed away from the simmering confrontation and toward the volleyball game or the lemonade table.

Mahlon and Ben were left standing alone. "Mahlon, I know how angry you are."

"Do you?"

"Can you forgive me for how this has hurt your sister?"

Mahlon tilted his head back. "I can see you are so concerned about my sister. That's why you led her on for months, got engaged to her, and then dumped her. She trusted you. How hard do you think it will be for her to trust anyone ever again?"

"I hope she can get past it—"

Mahlon threw up his hands. "Well, me too. At least there's one thing we can agree on. But you're sure making it hard for her, aren't you? Does your dawdi really have plantar warts, or is that a rumor started by your family? It wonders me why you want Emma growing pumpkins on Huckleberry Hill. So you can gloat about breaking up with her?"

"No, of course not. I just want Emma to be happy." If only Mahlon knew how many nights he had spent pleading with God for Emma's happiness, maybe he wouldn't be so quick to judge.

A whirlwind flew past Ben and pushed Mahlon back about three feet. It took Ben a split second to realize the whirlwind was Lizzie. She shoved her index finger into Mahlon's chest and propped her other hand on her hip. "What do you think you are doing, Mailman?"

To Ben's surprise, Mahlon shrugged and grinned weakly at Lizzie. "I'm picking on your brother," he said.

Lizzie poked him again. "Well, stop it. You're making a pest of yourself."

Mahlon folded his arms across his chest. "You're the pest, Lizzie Tizzy. I don't go around poking people."

Lizzie only poked him harder. "I don't go around attacking people."

Ben wasn't quite sure what to make of this exchange. Did Lizzie and Mahlon like irritating each other?

Emma came from behind him and joined Lizzie, and they stood between Mahlon and Ben as if they thought Ben needed protection—the pirate girl and the kid sister. Ben found the sight of two girls staring down big, arms-like-trees Mahlon Nelson quite amusing. Lizzie had no trouble beating anyone into submission with her glare, but Emma had always been so timid. It was nice to see her stand up for herself. Or rather, see her stand up for him.

He swallowed hard at the lump forming in his throat.

Lizzie pulled her finger from Mahlon's chest. "Don't you remember we have a strategy, Mahlon? This is not it."

"We do not have a strategy," Emma said.

Ben had no idea what they were talking about. He took Lizzie's hand and pulled her backward. "We were just talking."

"Sure," said Lizzie. "I could hear Mahlon 'just talking' from a hundred feet away. In fact, everyone at the gathering could hear Mahlon just talking. He's making a fool of himself."

Ben glanced at Mahlon and then settled his gaze on Emma while trying to ignore her bright eyes. "It's okay. Mahlon hasn't said anything to me that I don't deserve."

Mahlon narrowed his eyes and studied Ben's face as if to ascertain whether he was sincere. He nodded and nudged Emma with his elbow. "See? Don't get huffy."

Emma lowered her eyes while a sad smile played at her lips. "Of course Ben would say that. He's so kind, he would gladly take the blame for all your sins."

Mahlon grunted his disapproval. "Why are you accusing me? I haven't done anything wrong."

"You're being a bully," Lizzie chimed in.

Mahlon glanced at Ben with grudging respect. "A bully? He's taller than I am and stronger."

"But he won't fight back," Lizzie said. "If you want to pick on somebody, pick on me. I always fight back."

"Jah," Mahlon said, in mock indignation. "I've noticed."

"And I always win." Lizzie flashed a sparkly smile that seemed to leave Mahlon speechless. She turned her back and strolled away from all of them.

Mahlon recovered himself enough to think of a reply. "You *wish* you always won," he insisted loudly as he seemed to forget about his sister and Ben and chased after Lizzie.

Emma fingered the bandage at her forehead. "I'm sorry about Mahlon. He doesn't mean to offend you."

"No offense taken."

"He's a very protective brother."

Emma inspired that protective instinct in more than one person.

Ben swiped his hand across his eyes. With Emma, he had to learn to suppress those urges. He would never be able to look after her the way she needed to be looked after.

"Anna says Felty's getting his warts out next week."

Ben nodded.

"That will be about the time to pollinate and seal the pumpkin buds."

His hand caressed her cheek before he could stop it. "Are you making sure to apply the ointment to the doctor gave you and checking for infection?" So much for suppressing his protective instincts. "I don't want to them to have to amputate."

Her lips curled in spite of the uncertainty in her eyes. "I've never heard of an eyebrow amputation."

"There's a first time for everything," Ben said.

"Especially with me. I'm probably the first girl ever to burn down a chicken coop and lose her shoes in Cobbler Pond on the same day."

"The chicken coop needed to come down. It listed badly to one side."

"I never liked those shoes," she said.

"And if you hadn't lost them in the pond, they might have been destroyed in the fire."

She motioned toward the massive oak where Mahlon and Lizzie were engaged in a heated conversation. "Maybe I should go pull those two apart before they start throwing rocks at each other."

"They seem to be enjoying themselves."

Emma's eyes flashed, and she cocked her head to the side. "I never thought of that before."

He grinned. "Me either."

He shouldn't have been standing there staring at her, but he couldn't make himself walk away. Besides, if a stray volleyball came hurtling through the air, he'd be able to stop it before it hit her in the head and split her stitches open.

Freeman, who had disappeared with the rest of his gang when Mahlon had started fussing, marched resolutely across the lawn to Ben and Emma. He must have thought the danger was over.

"We're going to do some singing in a minute," he said, "if you want to join us."

Emma glanced at Ben. "Sure. I will come over."

Ben just needed to get Freeman alone for a minute, and he'd be all set. He was about to ask Freeman if he could speak with him privately when Freeman blurted out, "And Emma, it wonders me if I could drive you home tonight."

Perfect. He hadn't even had to ask. Freeman was already interested in his fiancée. Ex-fiancée. This was very good news.

Then why did the blood in his veins feel as thick as peanut butter?

Maybe Freeman wasn't such a suitable boy for Emma after all. He was young. How would he ever watch over her properly? He had all those wood-working tools in his shop. Emma might cut off an arm or something if she were ever to set foot in there. Freeman would never do.

But what could he say without being extremely rude? He could volunteer to give Emma a ride home himself, but that would defeat the purpose of showing everyone that they were over each other.

Freeman must have felt like he needed to convince her. "I just installed a new heater in my buggy, although I won't need to use it until wintertime. And brand-new headlights to make it extra safe."

Ben almost protested. Brand-new headlights weren't all that safe if the person steering the buggy drove carelessly on the roads.

Freeman turned to Ben. "You don't mind, do you?"

His hands were tied. Unless he wanted everyone to believe that he still loved Emma, he'd have to let her go with Freeman, who had headlights but probably didn't have proper reflectors on the back. Maybe Ben should follow them home to make sure they didn't have any mishaps along the way.

Instead, he bowed gallantly, which considering how stiff he felt was quite a feat. "It's not my place to mind. Emma and I mean nothing to each other."

Emma's smile stretched across her face as if it had been pulled tight and stapled there. Her face drained of color. Only then did Ben realize what he had said. He wanted to smack himself upside the head.

He didn't really mean the "nothing" part. Emma meant everything to him and always would. He meant that he wanted to be nothing to her but a memory. Likely, all Emma had heard was "You mean nothing to me," and she looked as if she might melt into a puddle of tears any second.

The words he wanted to say stuck in his throat in an attempt to get them all out at once. "I mean . . . we used to be . . . Emma's so good at gardening, and she's helping my mammi. We're good friends." He couldn't have sounded more ridiculous if he had planned it. It was plain that every word sliced Emma to the core.

With that smile firmly in place, she nodded at Freeman. "I'd like for you to drive me home tonight. I made cookies." She walked away with Freeman, seeming to hang on his every word, and didn't give Ben a second look.

He felt as low as a snake in the cellar. He'd hurt Emma's feelings once again and let her go off with someone who had absolutely no idea how to take care of her.

He couldn't do anything to repair Emma's feelings now. Growling, he marched to the front yard to see if he could locate Freeman's buggy with the brand-new headlights.

If Freeman didn't carry a first aid kit in his buggy at all times, he couldn't be trusted to take Emma home.

Chapter 8

Emma plopped herself into the overstuffed chair in her living room. "See? I can't match a corner to save my life."

"You're not patient enough," Mamm called from the kitchen.

Ever since Emma and Lizzie had renewed their friendship, Mamm hovered within earshot of every conversation, clearly trying to make sure not a word about Ben was spoken between them. Her strategy worked. Lizzie and Emma never mentioned Ben's name between them unless they were in Emma's bedroom with the door closed and towels stuffed into the crack under the door.

Mamm had practically popped a blood vessel in her neck when she found out Ben had returned from Florida, until Mahlon had persuaded her that Emma would get over Ben faster if she saw him more often. Convincing Mamm had been quite an accomplishment, especially since Mahlon didn't believe it himself, but he knew how determined Emma was to keep her promise to Anna and how hard it was to bear Mamm's scolding.

Lizzie fingered the seams of Emma's latest quilt square, squinting in concentration. "This really isn't that bad. I'm just going to unpick it right here and tuck the fabric in a bit on this side, and no one will ever be able to tell the difference." She pulled her seam ripper from the sewing basket. "Log Cabin squares are hard."

"Give me the Bear Claw next time."

"Even harder."

Emma sighed. "Maybe I could sit on this chair and watch while you make the quilt."

Lizzie carefully separated the seam that needed to be fixed. "You're fine, Emma. You can do the Nine Patch."

"Too many corners."

They heard the back door close as Mahlon and Andy strolled into the room with indecently large bowls of ice cream.

Emma tilted her head to peek into the kitchen. "Did Mamm send you in to spy on us?"

Mahlon grinned. "She had to get the laundry off the line and wanted us to make sure that you two didn't talk about any forbidden subjects."

Emma smirked. "She bribed you with ice cream?"

"Did you save any for the rest of us?" Lizzie asked.

Mahlon licked his spoon. "None for you, Tizzy."

"Mamm bought a whole tub of ice cream," Andy said between bites. "And butterscotch topping."

Emma smoothed her hand over one of Lizzie's perfectly shaped quilt squares. "Well, Andy, show some manners and fetch Lizzie a bowl of ice cream."

"No, thanks. I don't want to get the fabric dirty. Besides, I'm not going to be here much longer. Emma has a date," Lizzie said, her voice ripe with resentment.

Mahlon looked as if he'd choked on three scoops of ice cream. "You have a date?"

Emma felt her face get hot with both embarrassment and guilt. She should never have accepted the invitation, even if Mamm encouraged it. It wasn't fair to Freeman. "We're going to Shawano Lake overlook. Just for a ride."

Mahlon raised his eyebrows. "It's about time boys took notice. You two are the prettiest girls in Bonduel." His mouth twitched as if he hadn't meant to share that piece of information. "I mean, Lizzie would be pretty if she weren't so contrary."

Lizzie probably blushed all the way to her toes. "I am not contrary."

"Jah, you are."

"I'm only contrary with you, Mahlon Nelson. You shoot off your mouth when you shouldn't, and you're wrong about everything. Somebody needs to save you from making a fool of yourself. I've taken on that heavy responsibility."

"Nobody asked you to," Mahlon said, trying not to smile.

"I know. That's what makes me such a charitable person."

Andy stirred his melting ice cream. "Who's your date with?"

Mahlon snapped his head around to stare at Emma. "That was a gute trick to get Lizzie to distract me."

"I did no such thing."

Mahlon gave Lizzie a fleeting glance before turning his full attention to Emma. "Why didn't you tell me about this new boyfriend?"

"He's not her boyfriend," Lizzie insisted.

Mahlon frowned. "Maybe he is. The old boyfriend isn't hanging around much anymore."

Emma hadn't expected the hurt that flashed in Lizzie's eyes. Of course she still held out hope for Ben, but Emma hadn't recognized how fervent that hope was until now. They hadn't talked about it much.

Mahlon studied Lizzie's face, and his frown deepened. "Freeman is a gute boy. He'll own his dat's harness shop one day. And he has a nice family," he said, with much less swagger than he normally showed around Lizzie.

"He's too tall," Lizzie murmured.

"He's shorter than Ben."

"He's too short," Lizzie replied.

Mahlon's eyes strayed to Lizzie once again before he said, "This is good news, Emma. It's about time you moved on with your life."

Lizzie stood up and slammed the quilt square and seam ripper on the end table. "No, it isn't, Mahlon. You don't know anything. Anything."

The fight leaped into Mahlon's eyes. "I know that Emma has been miserable for months because of your brother." He put his bowl down and threw his hands up. "Admit it, Lizzie. This is all Ben's fault."

She matched his fire with a blaze of her own. "You don't know my brother like I do. Something is wrong, and I'm going to find out what it is."

That sinking feeling in the pit of Emma's stomach kept sinking. Did she have to catalog her faults for Lizzie? Why did Lizzie find the truth so hard to accept?

Lizzie folded her arms and stared down Mahlon, all six feet of him. "You and I are going to get Ben and Emma back together."

Mahlon's voice rose about seven pitches. "Me? You want me to push them back together so he can break her heart all over again? I won't do it. Let your brother go back to Florida and leave well enough alone."

Emma tried to disappear into the folds of the extremely comfortable overstuffed chair. They talked about her as if she weren't even in the room, as if she were a broken wheelbarrow that could be fixed if only they thought hard enough. Didn't they see she couldn't be fixed? She wanted to be with Ben so badly that she had to pinch herself to keep from crying out.

She relinquished her comfy chair as her distress

helped her find her voice. "I'm standing right here. If you want to discuss my life, argue with me instead of each other. Freeman asked if I'd go to the lake with him. I told him yes. That's all. I'm sorry to disappoint you, Mahlon, but he is not my boyfriend, and I plan on telling him I don't want to go out again. I'm not . . . He's not . . ."

"He's not Ben," Lizzie said softly, as if speaking louder would cause Mahlon to erupt.

Instead of jumping down Lizzie's throat, Mahlon deflated. He put his arms around Emma and actually spoke to Lizzie without scowling. "Do you see why I'm so firm about this? You're not doing her any favors by fanning hopes that are better left to die. You're making things worse. Much worse." He glanced toward the kitchen. "Besides, Mamm would never let you near Emma again if she heard such talk."

Squaring her shoulders, Emma pushed Mahlon away with an overdramatic shove and a halfhearted grin. "You're still talking about me like I'm not here." She lightly shoved Mahlon again for good measure. "I'm stronger than you know"—she motioned toward Lizzie—"and smarter than you think. Too smart to believe for one minute that Ben wants me. He doesn't. And I'm going to get over it. But not now. Not while Ben is in Bonduel, being so kind and looking so handsome." She took a deep breath. "There. I said it. I still love him."

The embers in Mahlon's eyes flared to life.

With her frown, she warned him to be still. "I'm going to be okay."

Lizzie bit her lip, no doubt to keep from arguing with either of them.

Emma glanced at Andy, who sat eating his ice cream, seemingly oblivious to the tension hanging in the air. Either that or he was a better spy than Emma could have guessed. "Andy, it looks like you're out of topping. Why don't you go get some more?"

Andy stuffed another bite into his mouth. "Okay," he said. He headed toward the kitchen. "I liked Ben a lot. He played baseball with me and Lisa. I hope you get him back."

Emma threw up her hands and shot a helpless look at Lizzie. Lizzie giggled. "Sorry. I hope we haven't started the rumor mill."

Mahlon shook his head. "As long as Andy has ice cream and baseball, he's pretty content to let other stuff go right over his head."

Emma reached out for her annoyingly loyal twin brother and her irritatingly persistent best friend. "Come here," she said, pulling them into a three-way hug. Lizzie hesitated briefly, and Mahlon stiffened as if he were having a heart attack. But they both relented and let her wrap her arms around them. "Denki for loving me enough to fight about me."

Freeman knocked on the door so loudly that both Lizzie and Mahlon jumped. He was four minutes early.

Emma pasted on her friendliest smile, the smile that she hoped said *I'm so happy to be going to the lake with you, but I'm not interested.* Freeman probably wouldn't get that subtle hint. No doubt she'd need to make herself clear at the end of the evening.

Freeman stood on her porch grinning as if he were looking forward to being with her. "Hullo, Emma. You ready to go?"

Emma grabbed the black sweater that Anna had knitted for her. The first week in June would be cool at the lake.

"Hullo, Lizzie. Hi, Mahlon," Freeman said.

"Have a gute time," Mahlon mumbled, watching Lizzie out of the corner of his eye—probably trying to tell if his good wishes irritated her.

Why were her hands trembling? Emma fumbled with her sweater, pushing her hand through the sleeve but managing to turn the other sleeve inside out. Freeman leaned in to help her untangle her twisted sweater as she shoved her balled hand through the sleeve. Unfortunately, she shoved hard and caught Freeman on the chin with her fist. His head snapped back, but he didn't fall over. Surprise popped onto his face, but he soon recovered himself, rubbed his chin, and kept on smiling. Good thing. It was never good to have to revive the boy on the doorstep before the date even started. She'd already done that once.

"I'm so sorry."

"That's all right," he said, "It's always good to

know if a girl has a good left hook to fight bears with."

Emma laughed sheepishly. "I don't usually attract bears."

Freeman chuckled. "Well, you can take on the dangerous squirrels, then."

They finally made it out the door and into Freeman's courting buggy. Emma sighed as she examined the red mark already forming on his chin. After their date, she wouldn't even have to be careful to let him down gently. With her penchant for accidental mishaps, Freeman would be running for the hills within the hour.

Ben's eyes flew open. Light streamed between the slats of his blinds. How could he have overslept? He groaned as he tried to jump out of bed. His legs felt as if they weighed three tons each. He didn't see how he would even be able to get dressed this morning, let alone help Emma with the pumpkins or milk the cow for Dawdi. He'd overdone it at the doctor's office yesterday, helping Dawdi in and out of a wheelchair and up and down the stairs. Dawdi's surgeries seemed to be harder on Ben than they were on Dawdi.

Ben rolled onto his stomach and raised himself with his arms. They didn't feel too bad today. A little weak, but he'd rather have that than the pain. He shifted his legs off the bed and set his feet on the floor. He gasped as he flexed his leg muscles and did what he could to get the blood flowing. Once he felt stable enough to stand, he shuffled around his room until he was certain he wouldn't topple over in Mammi and Dawdi's presence. They had enough to worry about with Dawdi's procedure yesterday.

He walked with long strides into the great room so he could show everyone how hale and hearty he felt. Mammi stood at the stove making what Ben assumed was breakfast, although it smelled like fish. Maybe he'd slept in longer than he thought.

Dawdi sat in his recliner, reading the paper as usual. One of his feet sported a work boot while the other foot was wrapped thick with gauzy bandages. It looked like a snowy white pillow. Things hadn't been as serious as Mammi had led Ben to believe. The doctor froze Dawdi's warts off and told him they would blister, hurt for a week or so, and then he'd be good as new. Ben could be back in Florida before the end of June.

Dawdi eyed him curiously as he came into the room. Ben stood taller and didn't even wince at the tightness in his spine. Dawdi would not discover his secret, even if he searched as hard as he could. "*Gute maiya*, Dawdi. I can't believe I slept in."

Dawdi waggled his finger at Ben. "No need to apologize. It was a hard day for all of us. I'm glad we didn't have to go to the hospital to get my warts off. I don't like the smell."

"How are you feeling?"

"Right as rain. Thanks to you, I found three new license plates."

Washington, Maryland, and Ohio had almost made the surgery worth it for Dawdi. "It wasn't all thanks to me. Roy saw Ohio."

Dawdi patted the small notebook that he always kept in his shirt pocket. "If I get another surgery or two, I'll have all my license plates by September."

"You won't have to have any more surgeries," Ben said, patting him reassuringly on the hand. "You're going to get better in no time, Dawdi."

"I'm sure of that. My foot don't even hurt one bit."

"Now, Felty," Anna said with her head still bent over the stove. "You'll be on crutches for weeks. How are you ever going to harvest beans on crutches?"

"I'll take care of everything," Ben said, even as his legs screamed for him to sit down. He resisted the urge. If he sat, he might not be able to stand back up.

"Oh, Ben," Mammi gushed, "always so helpful. I know we can count on you."

"It smells delicious," Ben lied, going to the stove and planting a kiss on his mammi's cheek.

"I'm making another pumpkin recipe. Pumpkin-stuffed trout. Your cousin Moses was kind enough to give us his catch."

Ben stifled a shudder. Sometimes it was quite taxing eating at Mammi's table. "Sounds wonderful gute. When will it be ready? Do I have time to milk the cow first?"

"Emma's already milking."

"Emma?"

Mammi nudged the trout and mushy pumpkin around the pan with a spatula. "She wanted to get an early start on the vegetables, but when I told her you hadn't got up yet, she offered to milk for me. That girl is a treasure—always so good to both of us."

Ben swallowed the bile that rose in his throat. This was why he would never marry Emma. It shamed him that she needed to do his chores because he had accidentally slept in.

"She might need your help," Mammi said. "I don't know that she can manage a full bucket with crutches."

"She's on crutches?"

"Jah, but her foot didn't look that bad to me. Not all wrapped up like Felty's."

Ben was out the front door before Mammi finished her sentence. There was Emma. She shuffled from the barn trying to drag the milk bucket behind her while negotiating the dirt with a pair of crutches. She'd spill it, as sure as you're born.

Instead of a kapp, she'd tied her hair up in a scarf, the way a lot of girls wore it when they did chores so they wouldn't soil their head coverings. Ben thought it was an especially attractive look on Emma.

"Can I help?" he said, ignoring his stiff legs and bounding down the stairs.

Something like regret traveled across her features before she twisted her mouth sheepishly and released the bucket, almost tipping it over in an effort to set it down. Its contents sloshed over the side, but most of it stayed in the bucket.

He picked up the bucket and pointed to her ankle, wrapped in an Ace bandage and glowing a light purple color. He didn't like it when Emma got injured. At least the huge gauze pad didn't dangle over her eye anymore. The scar would be almost invisible in a few months. "You milked my mammi's cow?"

She shrugged. "Anna said you haven't been feeling well. I want to help."

An ache formed right between his eyes. Mammi had noticed he hadn't been feeling well? He obviously hadn't been good at keeping a stiff upper lip. He'd have to work harder. "I overslept. I never meant for you to do my chores."

She smiled the way she always did when she got praise she didn't think she deserved. "I'm not a very gute milker, if that makes you feel better."

"What happened to your foot?"

She fiddled with the handles of her crutches. "Nothing serious. I twisted my ankle."

"What happened?"

"You know. I was just being clumsy, like I always am."

"That's not an answer."

"Well," she said, "John Shirk invited me over to his house to play Scrabble with his family."

Ben should have been thrilled. John Shirk had asked Emma on a date. But all he felt was emptiness, as if life were marching on without him.

"Scrabble seems safe enough."

Emma blushed. "We played Race Scrabble, where the tiles are scattered on the patio and you have to run for them. You have to go fast or other people will make their words before you do."

"I see." Running was never one of Emma's best activities. John should have known that. Ben narrowed his eyes. He had always suspected there was something a little irresponsible about John Shirk. "Does it hurt?"

"It did. The doctor said I should be able to put weight on it in another few days."

Ben fell in step with Emma, and they strolled to the house. "Careful of that divot in the grass."

"It looks like your dawdi's surgery went well."

"His recovery shouldn't take long. And then I can get back to Florida."

He didn't mean to say it so eagerly, as if he were looking forward to leaving Emma again, but he really did need to be away from her in order to hold on to the shreds of his sanity.

Her expression didn't change. He'd probably already wounded her as deeply as it was possible to hurt her. She held her crutches in one hand and hopped up the steps. She paused before going into the house, looking as if she were thinking very deep thoughts.

He waited for her to excuse herself to go to the bathroom.

Instead, she sprouted a smile. "Anna invited me for breakfast."

He could certainly be cheerful if she could. "I

have to warn you. Her pumpkin-stuffed trout looks pretty rough."

"Don't worry. I can eat just about anything, especially to spare Anna's feelings. Remember when we ate those little octopus things at the food festival?"

Ben groaned at the memory. "You ate three, and I threw up."

"Don't throw up in front of your mammi. You'll hurt her feelings."

"I've eaten enough of Mammi's cooking to know what to expect. It hasn't killed me yet. I try not to show her my weaknesses."

She gazed at him with what looked like affection. He wished he hadn't noticed it. "I've never seen any weaknesses."

"I have plenty." But she would never, ever see them. He'd be long gone before Emma or Mammi or anybody else had a chance to find out how weak he really was.

"Not you, Ben. You are so capable. I always depended on your strength when we were . . ." Emma pressed her lips together and didn't say another word.

Ben followed her as she marched into the house. She seemed determined to get somewhere quickly but didn't race to the bathroom like he expected she would. With only a little hesitation on both sides, they sat next to each other at the table and watched Mammi pour the trout-swimming-in-pumpkin into bowls because it was too runny to serve on plates. "Come on, Felty. Let's eat."

Mammi's concoction didn't turn out so bad. It tasted more like pumpkin clam chowder than anything else—not that Ben had ever tasted pumpkin clam chowder, but he suspected that this is what it would have tasted like, except with slimy, undercooked trout and stringy, overcooked pumpkin. Emma had two bowlfuls. Ben could only stomach one.

Once the dishes were attended to, Ben made sure Dawdi was comfortable in his chair and went outside to help Emma in the garden. He left without knowing whether Dawdi would take his pain pill. Dawdi and Mammi were still discussing it as he walked out the door.

With her crutches beside her, Emma sat next to her giant pumpkin plant, which seemed to spread a couple of feet every day. Yellow flowers already appeared from each stalk. She didn't look at him, probably still trying to recover from that little dish of pain he'd handed her right before breakfast. Or maybe trying to recover from breakfast itself.

"Do you want me to tear fabric?" he asked, as the memories overtook him. Last year, they had hand-pollinated dozens of pumpkin flowers and then tied the petals closed with narrow strips of fabric. Those times were some of Ben's fondest memories. Emma hadn't hurt herself while tying flowers, and their hands had touched more than once while passing fabric back and forth.

"Okay," she said with a serene but unreadable expression on her face.

"Maybe I should go weed tomatoes," he suggested. If she would rather not have him around, tomatoes would be a perfect excuse to get rid of him.

She forced a smile. "Nae. Stay. It helps to have somebody measure and cut, especially when I'm not very mobile."

If she could be strong, then he could too. He knelt beside her and measured lengths of fabric while she stretched and pulled out what tertiary vines she could reach sitting on the ground. Then she picked up her crutches.

"Can I help?" he said.

"Not unless you can tell a female flower from a male flower."

She didn't seem too steady on those crutches.

"You could teach me."

"It's okay. I think I can manage all right. It's like walking on three legs instead of two. That should make me more stable than ever."

She hobbled amongst the pumpkin vines while Ben kept a sharp watch out of the corner of his eye. If she took a tumble, at least it wouldn't be a long way down.

"Mammi will be so happy about her giant pumpkin," he said.

"Lord willing, it will grow. There is so much that can go wrong. Here's one," she said as she bent and plucked a flower from one of the vines. She tore all the petals off and then stuck it into a female flower still on the vine. "With just one plant, pollinating won't take long."

Ben shook his head in awe. "How did you get to be so smart?"

She pretended not to be pleased with his compliment as she balanced on her crutches and tied the female flower closed with a piece of fabric. "I'm not smart. Everybody knows how to pollinate pumpkin plants."

"I don't."

"I think you're the very last person in the world who doesn't know how to pollinate pumpkins," Emma said.

"Are you saying I'm not very bright?"

"I think you know what I'm saying." Her eyes sparkled when she grinned. It was the first genuine smile he'd seen from her since he came back to Huckleberry Hill.

"Hey, I'll have you know I could calculate the area of a triangle better than anyone in the eighth grade."

She reached out her hand for another strip of fabric. "I can figure out the volume of a cylinder with my eyes closed."

"I can add fractions with both hands tied behind my back."

Emma certainly had nice white teeth. "Are you sure? You might need your fingers to count the high numbers."

"You wouldn't think that was funny if you only had nine fingers to count on, Stumpy."

She laughed. The sound was so spontaneous and delightful that he joined her. He'd forgotten how much he loved to hear her so happy.

"I still have all my fingers, thank you very much," she said. "You are not allowed to use that nickname until I actually do lose one of them."

"It's kind of growing on me. I might have to call you that anyway, but only in private, of course. We'd bore everybody with the story of how you almost had nine fingers and then didn't."

"The part with the fishing knife is pretty exciting."

"What about Thumbkin?" he said.

"Huh?"

"Instead of Stumpy, I could call you Thumbkin. Thumbkin, the girl who grows pumpkins."

Laughter tripped from her mouth. "Very clever."

Emma continued to look for male and female flowers while Ben sang "Where Is Thumbkin" until Emma begged him to choose another tune. After that, he made up songs about the trees and the bees and the flowers every hour and the butterflies and mosquitoes, because he couldn't think of a rhyme for "butterflies."

He was enjoying himself so much, he didn't hear Adam Wengerd until he came up right behind him. "Ben," Adam called, three feet from his ear. "I'm here."

Emma looked up from the flower she tied. "Hi, Adam."

Adam motioned to her crutches. "What happened?"

"I sprained my ankle. Another couple of days and I'll be fine."

Ben loved that Emma wasn't a complainer.

"Did you come to help with the pollinating?" she asked Adam.

"I wouldn't even know where to begin. What exactly are you doing?"

"We're pollinating pumpkins for Anna," Emma said. "She wants a great big one."

"Like the one you grew last year," Adam said.

Emma bent over and plucked another flower from one of the vines. "Jah. Did you come to help?"

Adam flashed his blinding, charm-the-girls'-socks-off smile and gave Ben a small nod. "I'm delivering feed for my dat, but I really wanted to talk to you."

Ben's heart raced with dread. Adam wasn't going to ask Emma on a date while he stood there, was he?

Don't do it, Adam. At least let me excuse myself to go get a drink of water. Or go to the bathroom. That works for Emma.

"I need to go check on Dawdi," Ben stuttered.

"Don't go," Adam said, still beaming, still carrying that overconfident air about him. What did Ben expect? Adam's good face was one of the reasons he'd chosen Adam in the first place. He thought Emma might be more inclined to agree to a date if the boy was good-looking. "I want to talk to both of you."

Emma eyed Ben and Adam suspiciously, as if she expected them to gang up on her. Stuffing the extra fabric strips into her pocket, she maneuvered her crutches around the abundant pumpkin vines and came to the edge of the pumpkin mound. "What can I do for you?" she asked, a pleasantly curious curl on her lips.

Ben clenched his fists. This was not how he wanted Adam to go about courting Emma.

"I am wondering if you would like to help me at the benefit haystack supper two weeks from to-morrow."

Ben almost passed out with relief. Nothing threat-ening about a benefit haystack supper.

Emma raised her eyebrows, as if she had been expecting something else. "Of course. For the Kauf-manns' hospital bills?"

"We expect maybe a hundred people," Adam said. "Mamm wanted me to round up some help."

"I'll help," Ben said, so glad he could have given Adam a crushing bear hug.

"Gute," Adam said. "Because after the dinner, I want Emma to be my date for a bonfire at the lake, and Ben, I want you to come with us and bring a girl too."

The air around Ben grew stale. Why hadn't he fled for the bathroom when he still had a chance?

Emma's eyes darted between Adam and Ben as she pressed a wide smile onto her face. She spoke with forced enthusiasm. "Denki, Adam. I would enjoy going to a bonfire with you."

"Will you be okay to walk by then?"

"Of course. Do you want me to bring marshmallows?"

What was Adam thinking? Emma and fire did not mix well together. Why had Ben ever imagined that Adam would make a gute husband for his Emma?

Adam shook his head. "You don't need to bring anything. I've got it all taken care of. It'll just be a few of us. We'll do some singing. Ben can make up lyrics to his heart's content."

Emma tightened her grip on the crutch handles. "I am pleased that you would invite me."

Adam jabbed his thumb in Ben's direction. "Don't thank me. Ben's the one who suggested I should ask you on an outing. He told me that you're not interested in each other anymore and wanted me to give you a chance."

Emma didn't change her expression, but the dancing lights of her eyes immediately went out. She inclined her head stiffly. "Then I'm very grateful to Ben."

Adam wasn't finished yet. Why, oh why wouldn't he shut up and go away? "Truth be told, I've wanted to drive you home from a gathering for a long while. Ben gave me the push I needed."

Neither Emma nor Ben said anything in reply.

After standing in awkward and painful silence for what seemed like three days, Adam cleared his throat and slid his hat onto his head. "I guess I should finish my deliveries. My mamm will contact your mamm about the haystack supper. I appreciate your help."

Adam marched away with all the confidence of a runner who had just won a big race.

Ben didn't move a muscle until Adam disappeared from sight. Then he glanced at Emma. She stood with her face toward the lane and her hands firmly gripping her crutches. Her eyes held no expression whatsoever. How could Adam have been so stupid? How could Ben have been so stupid?

"Emma, I didn't mean for it . . . That isn't the way it was supposed to happen."

She pressed her lips into a rigid line.

"I'm sorry if that embarrassed you." He tried to smile. "It definitely embarrassed me."

Balancing on one crutch, she pulled a fistful of fabric from her pocket. Her hand trembled so badly, she looked as if she were shivering with cold. In June. "No need to apologize, Ben. I got the message."

"What message? There wasn't any message."

"I must be making a horrible pest of myself if you have to persuade young men to ask me out."

Ben's mouth went dry. "That's not true. I thought you might enjoy—"

"You talked to John and Freeman too, didn't you?"

With every miserable breath he took, he wanted

to pretend she hadn't asked that question. "Okay, I did, but only to—"

She couldn't move far, but she swiveled a quarter-turn away from him. "And Lamar Zook and Wallace Sensenig?"

Those names struck him momentarily mute. Lamar and Wallace had asked her on dates too?

"Emma, look at me."

She completely ignored his request. Turning even farther away from him, she said, "You don't need to help me with the pumpkins."

"Emma."

"I don't want your help with the pumpkins anymore. You've got plenty to do on the farm without coddling poor, helpless Emma Nelson."

"I didn't mean it that way."

"Leave the fabric on the ground next to my trowel. I'm going to the bathroom."

Ben had never seen anyone move so quickly on crutches, as if her life depended on her speed. Ben didn't stop her. He'd made a horrible mess of things already. No use chasing her if it meant that she would trip over her own foot in an effort to escape.

The hoe lay near the pumpkin mound with its head buried in the dirt. He yanked it out and then pounded it furiously against the ground over and over again.

Why, God? Why? You made the heavens and the earth.

Why can't you make me strong and able? All I want is to serve you and love Emma. Is that too much to ask?

He persistently drove the hoe into the ground until the dirt looked like cottage cheese and his arms were so stiff he couldn't move them.

The Bible said that Jacob wrestled with God, and God gave him a blessing. To Ben, every day felt like a wrestle with God and a wrestle with his own deteriorating body, but no blessings were forthcoming. He ached to be faithful instead of full of doubt and dark thoughts, but sometimes he felt he was losing the battle within himself.

And if this was his cross to bear, why did Emma have to suffer too?

He sank to the dirt and buried his face in his hands. "Please, Heavenly Father," he whispered. "Please give me strength for this fight. Help me to be still and know that you are God."

It was the only prayer he uttered anymore.

Whenever he asked for more, God always told him "no."

Chapter 9

Emma liked the chicken coop. Except for the smell. And the chicken droppings. And the inconvenient chickens that tried to peck at her toes and fingers.

At least it was secluded. And no one, not even Mahlon, would think to look for her here. The perfect place for someone who wanted to be left alone.

Someone knocked on the door of the coop. *Bother!* Last week Mahlon had found her in the hayloft and the week before that in the small hut Andy had built in the lower branches of their cherry tree. She was quickly running out of quality hiding places. Wasn't there someplace a girl could go to cry in peace?

"Emma?" It was Lizzie. At least her brother's scowl wouldn't be the first thing she saw when she emerged from seclusion. "Can I come in?"

"Just a minute," Emma squeaked. She quickly wiped her eyes and hobbled across the dirt floor on her crutches, being careful not to step in any surprises on her way out. Opening the door, she twitched her mouth into a smile and then wondered why she even bothered. Lizzie already knew she was upset. No need to pretend in front of her best friend, even if she was Ben's sister.

"You don't have to come out on my account," Lizzie said. "I just came to see if you're okay."

Emma sniffed and swiped her sleeve across her cheeks for good measure. "I'll come out. It really stinks in here."

Lizzie sighed, pulled Emma into her arms, crutches and all, and gave her a tight hug. "I'm sorry, Em."

Emma let a sob break free before she got control of herself. It was ridiculous to cry over this.

Lizzie released her. "You really do stink."

They laughed through the tears. "I think I will reconsider using the chicken coop as my personal space," Emma said. "I don't want to scare my friends away."

"Or your mamm. She'll make you sleep outside." Lizzie put her arm around Emma, in spite of her odor, and led her across the lawn to the house. "How is the ankle?"

"Better. Although I might have tweaked it running away from Ben today."

Lizzie gave her a wan smile. "Let's get you cleaned up before the neighbors start complaining."

"How did you know I was out here?"

"Ben came over to our house today. He told me he made you cry. He feels horrible about it."

Emma wanted to contradict Lizzie, but she couldn't. Ben always felt bad about hurting other people's feelings. That was surely one of the reasons he'd asked about a dozen boys to take her off his hands. He wanted someone to distract her so that his presence wouldn't upset her anymore. It wouldn't work, but Emma couldn't blame him for trying.

The tears pooled in her eyes. "It's my fault he's so miserable. If he didn't have to tiptoe around my feelings so often, he'd be much happier."

"That's not true. He loves you."

"I'm going to tell Anna I can't help with her pumpkins anymore. Or her beans. And the tomatoes were coming along so nicely."

"You'll do no such thing," Lizzie said as she walked up the stairs while Emma hopped. "Mahlon and I have a plan."

"No plans, no schemes, and no getting me and Ben back together."

Mamm stood in the kitchen with her hands in a bowl of hamburger. "Emma, where have you been? I need you to wash potatoes." She wrinkled her nose. "You smell like something the cat dragged in."

"Chicken," Lizzie corrected, "Like something the chicken dragged in."

"Why on earth would I allow a chicken in my

house?" Mamm said. She turned and took a good look at Emma. "You've been crying again, haven't you?"

Emma sniffed twice. "Yes, Mamm."

When Mamm got cross, her eyes narrowed to slits. "I tell you, Emmy, if you waste one more day crying over spilt milk, you can go live with your aunt Ginny in Missouri. I'll not have any more of this, do you hear?"

"I'm sorry, Mamm."

"And where have you been doing your crying? In the pen with the hogs?"

Emma curled her lips sheepishly. "Chicken coop."

"Well, go wash up. I'll have Rose do the potatoes."

Lizzie followed Emma down the hall. "Me and Mahlon have been talking."

"Talking or fighting?" Emma teased.

Lizzie stepped in front of her and blocked the way to the bathroom. "Come out to the barn."

"Mamm said to wash up."

"It will only take a few minutes, and you won't want to take a shower and *then* go to the barn. You'll end up stinky again."

Emma glanced behind her. "What are you up to?"

"Mahlon wants to discuss things while he milks cows."

"I said, no schemes."

Lizzie tugged on one of Emma's kapp strings. "Come on, Emma. Just for a minute."

Against her better judgment, Emma continued down the hall, through the washroom, and out the back door. Earlier today, she'd found that she could go quite rapidly on her crutches. She hobbled to the barn double-time. Whatever Mahlon and Lizzie had to say, Emma wanted to get it over with right quick. They weren't going to convince her of anything.

Lizzie tagged behind her but caught up at the entrance to the barn. Mahlon sat on the milking stool next to Lavender, and Emma could hear the bright ping-ping of thin streams of milk hitting the pail. Her brother turned his head when Emma and Lizzie entered. "Where were you, Emma?"

Lizzie folded her arms. "I found her crying in the chicken coop."

"The chicken coop? You should stick to the tree house. The chicken coop is a little punishing to the nose."

"I wanted to be alone." She glanced at Lizzie and turned up one corner of her mouth. "And I didn't want anyone to know I was crying."

"Not like we couldn't have guessed," Mahlon said. "Pull up a bucket or something."

Lizzie found a stool for Emma and a bale of hay for herself. Mahlon finished milking Lavender, untied her tether rope, and led her outside to pasture.

Emma leaned her chin on her elbow. "Not that I don't love watching Mahlon milk cows, but I really should take a shower before the flies start buzzing around my head."

Lizzie smiled. "Just wait."

Mahlon reappeared and pulled his milking stool

next to Emma's. "Now, Emma. I want you to know this is all Lizzie's idea. If it were up to me, I'd cut Ben loose and let him wander back to Florida, but Lizzie kind of likes her brother around."

"If you're thinking of using me to get him to stay in Bonduel, you're going to be very disappointed," Emma said.

Lizzie leaned forward and pinned Emma with an exasperated glare. "Listen, Emma. Ben told me that he doesn't deserve you. I think that's why he broke up. He believes you're too good for him."

Emma glanced at Mahlon. He shrugged. She wouldn't get any help from him. "That's the silliest thing to ever come out of your mouth," she said. "I don't believe it for one minute. And neither does Mahlon."

She nudged him when he didn't immediately agree with her.

He shrugged again. "Don't look at me. I don't really care what your ex-boyfriend is thinking."

It was Lizzie's turn to nudge him. Only her nudge came out more like a smack on the shoulder. "You agreed with me not an hour ago."

"That's because you batted your eyes at me. I got confused."

Lizzie's frown disappeared. "Ben sees himself as a big, strong man."

Emma felt worse. "He *is* a big, strong man."

"But he's always the one to fix things for people. He likes to take care of the less fortunate and downtrodden. He thinks he has to be everybody's hero."

Mahlon folded his arms. "Lizzie thinks Ben felt bad that he didn't watch out for you the way he should have. Maybe he feels guilty about all those accidents and thinks he doesn't deserve you."

"Didn't watch out for me? He always watched out for me. He helped me and a dozen other people put out that chicken coop fire."

"But he wasn't there to stop you from setting the fire in the first place," Lizzie said.

"He pulled me out of the lake."

"Maybe he wishes he never would have taken you there," Mahlon said.

"He carried me a whole mile after that buggy accident."

Lizzie nodded as if this proved her point. "He shouldn't have let you drive our buggy."

A seed of doubt grew in Emma's mind. "So you think he blames himself for all my accidents?"

"And he thinks someone else will protect you better," Lizzie said.

"Nae," Emma said. "That's not why he called off the wedding."

Lizzie twirled a piece of hay in her fingers and stared intently at Emma. "It's the only possible explanation. Ben is crazy in love with you."

Emma held up her hand. "Don't tell me that, Lizzie. I can't let myself believe it." Her hope couldn't survive another crushing blow. She refused to give it wings.

Mahlon cleared his throat and studied Lizzie and then Emma, as if trying to decide which one of them to side with. "Lizzie thinks Ben should save you from an angry bull or a speeding train."

Lizzie nodded enthusiastically. "If he does something heroic, then he'll be convinced that he really is capable of taking care of you, and he'll want you back."

"You want me to step in front of a speeding train?"

"Nae," Lizzie groaned, even though she looked like she might be open to the possibility. "We'd have to manufacture something that looks like an accident but really isn't. We could lower you into that cave near Zooks' farm and let Ben pull you out."

"Too many spiders," Emma said lightly, because they surely must have been joking.

Lizzie inclined her head in agreement. "You could get stuck in the tree house."

"What if she sprawls out by the side of the road with some fake blood on her head and lets Ben find her?" Mahlon said. "Then she wouldn't have to actually do something dangerous, and Ben would be none the wiser."

Emma gaped at them. Mahlon's expression held pure concentration. Lizzie couldn't have looked more earnest. They weren't teasing.

She grabbed her crutches and stood up. "I would never deceive Ben like that."

"We're brainstorming," Lizzie protested. "We're not set on one particular accident."

"I won't agree to tricking Ben like that," Emma said. "Besides, have either of you considered what could go wrong while faking an accident? I have a talent for getting into my own accidents without any help from anybody else."

Mahlon nodded thoughtfully. "You probably won't be lucky enough to have an accident in Ben's presence."

Emma growled in irritation. "Mahlon, do you hear yourself?"

"But, Emma," Lizzie said. "This is the best plan we have."

"There is no need for a plan," Emma said, wishing she could stomp her foot, but she only had one good foot with which to stomp. "Ben was quite close when that watering can fell on my head. He cleaned off the cut and took me to the emergency room for stitches, and after all that, he didn't ask to get back together. It's not going to happen."

"You're right," said Mahlon. "It's silly to plan an accident."

Lizzie propped her hands on her hips. "Mahlon Nelson, don't you dare back out on me now."

Mahlon threw up his hands. "There are too many things that could go wrong."

"And it wouldn't make any difference," Emma said through clenched teeth. Did her brother grasp what she was trying to hammer into that thick skull of his? She turned to Lizzie. "And shame on you for scheming to deceive your brother."

Lizzie didn't look the least bit apologetic. "We wouldn't be deceiving him. We'd be helping him to the best wife he could ever hope for."

"We could cause an accident without Emma knowing, then she wouldn't feel deceitful about it."

Emma swatted the hat off Mahlon's head. "Don't even joke about that. You'd end up killing me."

Lizzie sighed. "She's right, of course."

Mahlon rubbed the stubble on his chin. "I know. I'd never put Emma in danger. I'm just throwing ideas out there."

"Well, quit throwing out bad ideas," Lizzie said.

"Well, maybe we should forget the whole thing, Lizzie Tizzy."

Lizzie scolded Mahlon with her glare. "You said you'd help come up with a gute plan."

Emma was ready to go back to the house and leave Mahlon and Lizzie to their argument. She wouldn't take part in any plans, no matter how good they sounded.

Lizzie picked up Mahlon's hat and handed it to him. That was probably the closest thing to a peace offering Mahlon would get. "What kind of girl catches your attention, Mahlon?" she asked. "Does something in particular turn your head?"

Mahlon tapped his hat back onto his head. "Does Ben know about all the boys who have taken an interest in Emma? Maybe we could make him jealous."

Emma sank back to her stool and burst into tears. It would be impossible to make Ben jealous, and she wouldn't even consider such an underhanded trick.

"Oh, dear," Lizzie said as she slid off her hay bale,

knelt on the ground, and sidled next to Emma. "Was it something Mahlon said?"

"Don't blame this on me. I've already seen Emma cry enough to last two lifetimes."

Emma cried until she started hiccupping. Lizzie pulled three tissues out of her pocket and handed them to her. They were soaked in seconds with her copious tears. "Adam Wengerd came to visit me this morning on Huckleberry Hill."

"Did Ben see?" Lizzie said.

Emma nodded. "Adam told me that Ben had asked him to take me on a date."

A few inches lower and Lizzie's jaw could have scraped the ground. "Ben?"

"All those boys who've asked me out," Emma said, "Ben told them to."

Lizzie gasped as if she'd been slapped.

Mahlon furrowed his brow. "Not Wallace Sensenig. I'm the one who asked him."

Stunned, Lizzie and Emma stared at him as if he had pumpkins growing out of his ears.

Emma felt as if she would disintegrate into a million pieces. The only boys who asked her on dates were the ones who felt obligated to Ben or Mahlon. That fact made her feel about as desirable as a bag of potatoes.

Lizzie found her voice first. "How could you, Mahlon? You know how much I want Emma and Ben to get back together."

Mahlon pressed his lips together and looked as

if he wouldn't utter another word for the rest of his life.

"So you see, you can't make Ben jealous," Emma said. "He wants to get rid of me."

"I don't believe it," Lizzie said. "He isn't thinking straight." She looked at Mahlon. "Would Wallace be willing to help us make Ben jealous?"

Mahlon shrugged. "Maybe Emma's right. Maybe we should—"

"Would he help us?" Lizzie said, scowling with her whole face.

"Probably."

"Stop this," Emma said. "You're supposed to be offering me comfort, not plotting against your own brother."

Lizzie tapped her chin with her index finger. "How are we going to make Ben jealous when he seems to want other boys to date Emma? It doesn't make sense."

Emma snatched her crutches from the ground and stood up. "I'm finished with the both of you." She shoved her finger in Mahlon's direction. "If you ask any more boys to take me out, I'll crack an egg on your head in your sleep. And, Lizzie, I don't want to hear another word about deceiving Ben. He doesn't deserve it." She had to show them she was perfectly capable of moving on without Ben. Now, while he was still in town. Even if she didn't believe it herself. "I've changed my mind about not returning to Huckleberry Hill. Even if we're together every day, you'll see that Ben won't ever want me back, even if I burn down every chicken coop from here to Florida."

"But Emma . . ."

"And I'm going to go to that bonfire with Adam Wengerd and have a wonderful-gute time." She lifted her chin and practically dared them to contradict her. Neither said a word. They were too busy being surprised at her boldness.

Gute. Maybe they would think long and hard about trying to kill her.

She hobbled out of the barn and made a beeline for the house, still able to hear Mahlon and Lizzie discussing boys and weddings. But she refused to listen to another word. Now that she'd gotten used to them, she could be pretty speedy on those crutches.

Ben shuffled out of the barn with a galvanized metal bucket. His hands were tingling as if they had fallen asleep and his knees felt as if someone had jabbed a screwdriver into each of them, but he had to get those peas off the vine. Emma proved to be too good a gardener. The trellises overflowed with peas, and by tomorrow, the ripe pods would grow too big to be sweet.

Even with the debilitating tightness, he wasn't about to wait for Emma to do his picking. No one would take up the slack for him while he had any strength left. In Florida he'd trained himself to work around the stiffness. It was a part of him, but he refused to let it defeat him. He flexed his leg muscles. Some days it definitely felt like he was losing the battle.

He stopped short at the trellis of pea plants as he came upon a bucket brimming with pea pods. Somebody had already picked this morning. He gazed around the garden. Had Emma come early? Or maybe Mammi had picked them before he awoke. She would have had to get up before the rooster. And Dawdi? He hadn't budged from that chair in a week even though the doctor told him the pain would only last a few days.

He heard Dawdi's clear voice ringing through the air. So much for relaxing in his recliner. "*In my childhood days, when I was strong, I could climb to the hilltops all day long, I am not in my prime like I used to be, Time has made a change in me.*"

His grandparents came around the side of the barn holding hands. Dawdi wore both of his work boots, and he didn't even limp. He stopped his song when he spied Ben. "Look who's up."

"Ben, did you see my pumpkin?" Mammi said. "It's just a little nub of a thing."

Ben stood up straighter. His grandparents needed to see how vital and healthy he should have felt. "Emma says when it gets going, it can grow twenty-five pounds a day."

Mammi's eyes twinkled. "She's coming to tend the garden today."

Ben nodded.

"It would be a gute time to ask her to Adam

Wengerd's bonfire. They're having a bonfire after the haystack supper."

Ben took a deep breath. "She already has an invitation. Adam is taking her."

Mammi's jaw dropped in indignation. "Adam Wengerd? Ben, you were supposed to ask her. Bonfires with *die youngie* are always so lovely. The perfect place to rekindle old romances." She nudged Felty. "Remember when we took Tyler and Beth to a bonfire?"

Felty's mouth twitched in amusement. "She got so mad at him, she stormed off and he had to chase after her and apologize. And when we got there, we found out he had a date with a different girl."

"Now, Felty. It all worked out in the end, didn't it?" Mammi looked pointedly at Ben. "Your cousin Beth and Tyler Yoder are very happy together. All because of that bonfire."

"Then I suppose Adam and Emma will be very happy together after this bonfire." He shouldn't have said it. Mammi's expression drooped like a snowman in April.

Emma hadn't said a word, not one word to him since last Thursday when Adam had asked her to the bonfire. He'd really done it this time, and there would be no recovering from such a mistake. If she hadn't before, she surely hated him now. It was better for her if she did hate him. Then at least the anger could replace the hurt and hopefully eventually give way to indifference.

Even though a knife twisted in his chest at the

thought, he truly wanted Emma to be indifferent. Then she would stop hurting so badly.

"Well, then. I hope Adam and Emma have a nice time." Mammi pursed her lips together and paused as if she were measuring her words carefully. "I think being around two old people for so long, you've become too serious. You need to get out and have some fun. Won't you go to the bonfire anyway? Just to be sociable?"

Although it would be pure torture to see Emma enjoying herself with another young man, Ben would go to the bonfire, partly because he'd been invited and mostly to watch out for Emma. Adam had no idea the destructive force he would be unleashing when he put Emma near an open flame. Someone needed to be there to protect Emma from herself.

Ben attempted a pleasant, dutiful expression. "I'll go to the bonfire, Mammi."

Mammi burst into a smile and patted his cheek. "You'll have a wonderful-gute time."

Her reaction pulled a genuine smile from Ben. Mammi truly loved to see her grandchildren happy. If only she knew that Ben could never be happy again.

Her eyes got big. "No one asked me to bring any food. I suppose they think I'm too busy with Felty laid up."

That wasn't the reason Mammi hadn't been

asked to bring any food, but Ben wasn't about to enlighten her as to the real reason.

"I think I'll take a dessert, all the same," Mammi said. "Something with pumpkin in it, like pumpkin rhubarb pie. Doesn't that sound delicious?"

"Delicious, Banannie," Dawdi said. Ben marveled at how sincere Dawdi always seemed to be in his compliments about Mammi's cooking.

As easy as you please, Dawdi strolled to the peach trees and plucked a small green fruit from the nearest tree. "These are coming along real gute, Ben. You did a crackerjack job thinning them. They'll be nice and big."

Ben put his arm around his mammi. "I've had a wonderful-gute time helping you this spring."

"Sunday is officially the first day of summer. June twenty-first," Dawdi said.

"I'm glad you're feeling better, Dawdi, and I'm glad I could help you on the farm. But now it's time for me to get back to Florida. I can leave on the bus Friday morning."

"We'll miss you something terrible," Dawdi said. "You're the kind of boy we want around all the time."

Mammi glanced at Dawdi and pasted a smile on her face. "But you can't go yet. The worst surgery of all is coming up."

"Worst of all?" Ben said.

"Worst of all?" Dawdi said.

Mammi nodded. "Do you remember when Dawdi had to get that tooth pulled three years ago?"

"Nae."

"The dentist wants to put in a new tooth so Felty can chew his food even when he gets old."

"A new tooth?" Dawdi said, as if this was news to him.

"The dentist has to put a screw into the bone and then attach a false tooth to the screw. It will stay securely in place that way."

"Annie, I—"

"Now, Felty," Mammi scolded, "I know that tooth has been bothering you for a long time. I won't have you being unselfish about this. You need this surgery, and we will scrape together enough money to do it, even if we have to skip one meal every day. Your health is more important than anything in the world."

Ben nodded. "She's right, Dawdi. We want you to be around for a very long time."

"It is a little known fact that dental health can prolong your life," Mammi said, sounding like some sort of expert herself. She put her hand on Ben's arm. "I know this is a lot to ask of you, but if you could stay for a few more weeks . . ."

He should have said no. He really did need to get back to Florida, where he always saw the sun and he never saw Emma Nelson. Mammi and Dawdi had plenty of grandchildren who could help them take care of the farm. Moses lived not fifteen minutes away and Ben's own brother Titus wasn't much farther, plus at least ten others who surely wouldn't mind helping.

Ben massaged the back of his neck. The other cousins had jobs and farms and lives of their own. Ben didn't have anything. He'd been gone for months, unable to help his grandparents from so far away. He should at least do his duty to his family while he still could. Besides, a few more weeks in Bonduel would mean a few more weeks of watching out for Emma, even if she despised him, and making sure she didn't do any permanent damage to herself or anybody else. Summer was always the worst time of year for accidents.

Of course, no matter how much she needed him, he couldn't be here forever. Why prolong the inevitable? Why not let other boys, like Adam, step up and learn to care for her?

Because they couldn't. Not yet anyway. Ben would stay a little longer. What could it hurt besides his fragile heart? And in his short time here, he might be able to do a lot of good for Emma. If he prevented even one accident, the time would be well spent.

"I will stay as long as you need me," Ben finally said.

Dawdi groaned and shook his finger at his wife. "Annie, you're lucky you're so pretty, or I'd have put my foot down sixty years ago."

Mammi laid a kiss on Dawdi's cheek. "Stuff and nonsense. You put your foot down plenty."

Dawdi chuckled. "And I usually step in a pile of horse pucky."

Mammi snapped a pod off one of the pea plants.

"Ben, I see you've already picked the peas. I'll shell them right now, and we can have pea and pumpkin potpies for dinner. I've been working on a new recipe."

Ben picked up the full bucket and followed Mammi and Dawdi into the house.

If he went back to Florida, he'd never get to taste exotic foods like pea and pumpkin potpie. He'd better stay a while.

Chapter 10

The fire crackled to life as Adam set a match to the kindling at the bottom of the pile of wood. It was a beautiful night for a bonfire at the lake. What a thoughtful young man Adam was.

There were a dozen or so of *die youngie* who had come to the lake after the benefit supper. The haystack supper had been a huge success. Over a hundred people attended, and they'd raised some $2,000. Not enough to pay all the hospital bills, but enough to put a dent in them.

Emma had helped on the food line, as far away from Ben as possible. She already saw him three days a week on Huckleberry Hill. She didn't need any more time with Ben Helmuth.

Why had he come? There was plenty of help with tables and other heavy stuff, and he certainly didn't act as if he wanted to be there. She couldn't figure him out, and she wearied of trying to guess what he was thinking. He already owned the throbbing ache in her heart. She refused to give him any more of herself than she had.

Adam fed more wood to the flames as Emma stared into the fire in the gathering darkness. Ben sat next to John Shirk and Eli Lambright with a bucket and without a date. It didn't surprise her. Ever since his return, Ben had kept himself isolated on Huckleberry Hill. Did he ever feel lonely?

Mahlon and Lizzie relaxed in the sand whispering to each other. Probably discussing possible accidents they could get Emma to fall for. She had no illusions that they had abandoned their plan to get her and Ben back together. Emma only hoped they wouldn't kill her with their good intentions. She kept a wary eye on both of them in case they decided to throw her into the lake.

Dinah Hoover came close and gave Emma a hug. "My mamm says thanks for the soup. She's feeling much better today."

"I burned it on the bottom a little. I hope it tasted okay."

"Jah. The burning gave it a smoky flavor. Like you'd added bacon or something. It was kind of you to think of us."

"I'm sorry your mamm's been sick."

"How are your pumpkins coming?" Dinah said.

"Wonderful gute. I planted three acres. I'll have lots to sell come September."

"I hear you are growing a giant pumpkin for Anna Helmuth."

"I went yesterday. The pumpkin is the size of a

baseball. Lord willing, by the end of the summer it will be over five hundred pounds. Anna will be so happy."

Since the day they pollinated pumpkins, Emma's time on Huckleberry Hill had been bearable. She steered clear of Ben, and he had made no attempt to converse with her. Once the pumpkin grew big enough, Emma would never need to set foot on Huckleberry Hill again. She was counting the days, or rather, measuring the pumpkin until she could be done. The sooner she put Ben Helmuth out of her life, the better.

She sighed. What could possibly be better about having Ben Helmuth out of her life?

The fire soon engulfed Adam's pile of wood. They sang songs while waiting for it to cool to a useful pile of coals. Emma sang loudly so that she wouldn't be able to hear Ben. Even over the roar of the fire, his voice caressed her with too many memories, and she willed herself to keep her composure in his presence. She was on a date with Adam Wengerd, for crying out loud. She should be giving him her full attention. Ben's beautiful singing voice should have been the furthest thing from her mind.

She turned her attention to Adam. He smiled at her while trying to keep up with the singing. His voice didn't sound all that bad, and he mostly didn't go flat, but she didn't expect him to be as good a singer as Ben. Everybody had their own talents. Singing was only one talent and not even the most important one to possess.

Adam leaned close to her ear and whispered, "Why don't you take your shoes off?"

Emma looked around. Almost everybody had their shoes off except for her. "Should I?"

"The sand is nice and warm."

She almost always wore her shoes outdoors. While others seemed to be able to take off their shoes without consequence, she would inevitably be the one to step on a rusty nail or stub her toe on the porch step. She glanced at Ben. His shoes were still on. He had told her once that he always wanted to be ready to run to her aid, and a dead run proved easier with shoes.

"Okay," she said. "I'll go put them by your cooler."

Sensing Ben's gaze on her, she walked away from the fire and up an incline to the place where most of the shoes rested in a pile. She sat in the sand, unlaced her shoes, and pulled off her stockings. After stuffing her stockings into her shoes, she stacked them on the pile and sifted her toes through the rough sand. It felt good to be so reckless.

Plunging her feet into the sand, she shuffled back to the fire as if she were ice-skating. She lifted her gaze to see if Adam saw her enjoying the sand. Dividing her attention turned out to be a bad idea. By now, she should have known how dangerous it was to take her eyes off the path directly ahead.

Her toe caught on a jagged rock buried beneath the sand, and she lost her always-precarious balance. The ground rushed to meet her. Before she made contact with a nasty piece of driftwood, a pair of strong arms caught her from behind and set her back on her feet.

How had he made it from the fire so fast? Probably because he was wearing his shoes.

She gasped. "Oh. I'm sorry." Sorry for what? Making a fool of herself? She glanced in Lizzie's direction, half suspecting her of planting that rock right where Emma would find it. Lizzie and Mahlon innocently sat in the sand chattering as if they didn't even know Emma had come to the bonfire party.

Ben still had his arms securely around her, which was good because her knees had turned to jelly. "You okay?"

Unsure of what she would see, she didn't dare look into his face. She'd received enough pity to last a lifetime. "Jah, denki. I can't believe I fell." That wasn't precisely true. Of course she could believe she had fallen. It was what she did best.

"Did you hurt your foot?"

Leaning on his arm, she lifted her foot out of the sand. Even in the dim light, she could see the shiny, dark blood dripping from her big toe. *Ouch*. She'd hurt it worse than she thought.

"I've got a first aid kit in my buggy," Ben said.

"Nae, don't go to the trouble."

"It's no trouble."

Emma pulled away from him and hopped back up the incline. "I'll put my shoes and stockings back on and tend to it when I get home. I don't want your first aid kit to get sandy." She sat down, brushed the grit off her feet as best she could, and started to pull her stockings on.

"Are you sure?" Ben said.

She braved a look at him. It surprised her not to see pity on his face.

She shoved her shoes onto her feet and stood up, hiding a wince as she put her weight on her throbbing toe. She refused to burden Ben by being needy. "Denki for your help," she said, leaving him behind as she tromped back to the fire, keeping her gaze squarely on her path. The embarrassment would be unbearable if she tripped twice.

As quickly as she could, she returned to Adam's side and joined him in singing. Her toe felt as if it were the size of a golf ball, and she could sense a miniature heartbeat inside her shoe, not to mention the sticky blood that made her foot feel squishy. It was going to be a long night.

Adam looked down at her feet. "You decided not to take off your shoes."

"It's better this way," she said.

Once the fire had cooled, Adam pulled a bag of marshmallows from his cooler. "Who wants s'mores?"

He passed out marshmallow roasting sticks from a long cloth bag. "These are dangerous. Do not point them at people's eyes. Especially you, Emma." Some of his friends chuckled. Emma felt the heat travel up her neck, but she didn't take offense. Adam knew enough to be cautious.

Emma passed out marshmallows and didn't even think of bawling when she gave one to Ben. He told her "denki" and met her gaze, as if he didn't injure her with his very presence. As if those icy green eyes didn't send her reeling every time she looked into them. As if he hadn't just saved her from falling on her face and ending up with sand between her teeth.

She looked away as soon as she could pull her wits about her. Her friends shouldn't go without marshmallows simply because Ben's eyes made her incapable of rational thought.

Turning her back, she skewered her marshmallow even as she felt his gaze bore into the back of her head. She would ignore him completely. After all, that was what he wanted. He'd have liked nothing better than to be rid of her. Ben found her annoying, and he saw her as an object of pity and disgust, nothing more.

She knelt next to the fire to get close to the glowing orange coals at the base of the flames. Even if it killed her, her marshmallow would be golden brown and perfectly roasted this time. She usually didn't have gute fortune roasting marshmallows. Last summer, Ben had ended up roasting them for her. Tonight, she had found the perfect spot near the coals, and her marshmallow would turn out just the way she liked it.

She heard a hiss right before her marshmallow started smoking. Before she could pull it away from the heat, it burst into flames.

Ach!

The last time she had tried to blow out a flaming

marshmallow, the ash had splatted onto her face and burned her lips. This time she waved her roasting stick over her head like a flag, hoping to put out the fire with the rush of air.

She must have whipped it around too forcefully. Her blazing marshmallow flew off her stick and sailed into some dry grass near the shore. "Oh!" she cried as a tuft of grass in the marshmallow's path caught fire. Out of nowhere Ben ran to the tiny blaze and dumped a bucketful of sand on it, effectively extinguishing it before it could spread up the hill. Where had he found a bucket of sand so quickly?

He glanced at her, and a frown tugged at his lips. Her throat dried up like a piece of chalk. Ben must have been overjoyed that he wasn't engaged to this walking accident anymore. It didn't matter how hard she concentrated, she would never be graceful enough to make Ben love her.

Adam stepped around the fire. "Are you okay?"

"What?"

"I heard you shout."

He hadn't seen the flying marshmallow of destruction. "Jah, I am fine. Something startled me, that's all."

He looked at her stick. "Do you want a marshmallow?"

"Um, jah. I would like a marshmallow."

"I'll get you one."

Adam jogged to his cooler and retrieved a marshmallow for Emma. She should have brought her own bag. She had a feeling she'd need several test marshmallows before she managed to achieve golden-brown perfection.

What did it matter? A perfect marshmallow wouldn't bring anybody any happiness. Not tonight.

When Adam handed her another marshmallow, she stuck it right into the flames and let it catch on fire. Then she pulled her stick from the fire and made no attempt to extinguish the marshmallow. She held it away from any flammable objects like her dress or Dinah's hair and let it burn to a black stump at the end of her stick. Then, after being careful to let it cool a sufficient amount of time, she closed her lips around her mouthful of ash and pretended to enjoy it. Ben wouldn't get the satisfaction of seeing her struggle with marshmallow after marshmallow, giving him one more reason to be glad he'd broken off the engagement.

"Do you like them burned like that?" Adam asked.

She hadn't realized he'd been watching. She *must* quit fixating on Ben. "Delicious" was all she said.

"I like mine toasty warm and gooey," Adam said. "They taste better in a s'more that way."

Emma could only nod. Melted chocolate and a golden-brown marshmallow between two graham crackers sounded like about the most wonderful thing in the world. Her mouth tasted like she'd stuck her tongue in the ash can.

Ben, without his bucket, nudged her with his elbow. Her heart carried on like a bass drum tumbling down the stairs. She hadn't seen him coming.

"I like roasting them but I don't like eating them," he said as he slipped a s'more into her hand.

The marshmallow inside was golden brown and melty, and the soft, warm chocolate puddled between the two crackers. Nothing ever looked so good. She studied him in surprise.

Why would he even . . . ?

Before she could thank him, he practically sprinted to the other side of the fire and started a very important-looking conversation with Eli.

Why did he pull something like that when she was trying so hard to steel herself against him?

Emma choked back the tears, found a spot to sit, and ate every bite of that perfect s'more. Adam roasted two marshmallows and made a double-decker s'more. After stuffing his roasting stick into the bag, he trudged across the sand to sit by her. "Did you get a s'more?" he asked, holding his out so she could see it.

"Jah, I did," she said, wishing Ben hadn't made one for her. She'd never be able to eat a marshmallow again without thinking of him.

"The haystack supper went good. My mamm said it's one of the best we've ever had. There are lots of people at the lake this time of year. We got about fifty tourists."

"The tourists love to see the Amish."

Adam scooted closer. "Denki for coming with me tonight," he said, taking a big bite. "I think I've wanted to date you ever since I was in the second grade."

"You used to throw snowballs at me."

"How else was I supposed to get your attention?"

"Oh, I don't know. By saying hi or carrying my lunch cooler home from school."

"I'm glad Ben suggested I ask you out. At first I didn't believe him when he said you were over him. I mean, it's obvious to everyone that he's moved on, but I wasn't so sure about you."

Emma felt like a cold, empty house. Adam should just stop talking.

"But he urged me to ask you out, as if it meant a lot to him. I guess he thinks it's his fault that no one dares to date you."

"Does he?"

Adam took another bite of his s'more and scattered crumbs all over his green shirt. "You know how nice Ben is. I'm sure he felt bad about breaking up with you like that. I don't wonder that he won't be able to marry or even date until he's sure you've moved on. Maybe not until you're married."

Emma thought she might turn to stone. Why hadn't she realized this before? When Ben had left, she had tried to put on a good face, not only for Dat and Mahlon, but for Ben as well. Even though he didn't love her, he had a tender heart. She knew he'd never be able to live with himself if he found out how profoundly hurt she felt. She loved him, heaven help her, and she would rather have done anything than let Ben be hurt by her misery.

But it never even crossed her mind that Ben might not be able to move on with his life unless he saw that she had moved on with hers. That might even have been why he had come back to Bonduel. Maybe there was a girl in Florida he was interested in, but he had to secure a husband for Emma before he could even think about dating someone else.

The thought of Ben loving someone else immersed her in an ocean of pain. She hadn't thought her sorrow could go any deeper. She was drowning.

The lights flickering from the dying fire started to blur as tears clouded her vision. She pressed her fists to her eyes and shoved the tears back. Ben had told her that he wanted to see her happy. She hadn't realized what that meant. He couldn't be truly happy, truly free, unless Emma married and went on to live a life of bliss with another man.

Mahlon and Lizzie had been wrong. Her dating another boy would not make Ben jealous. It would make him happy.

And Ben's happiness was all she wanted.

Chapter 11

Ben stared into the small orange bottle. Three pills left. He'd only been taking two a week. How could he almost be out? Whenever he took one, he felt as if he were swallowing pure gold nuggets. Each pill cost ten dollars.

The doctor said he needed them if he wanted to slow the progression of the disease, but money was running out. What would he do when he couldn't afford to take those expensive little pebbles anymore? Probably crawl to a hospital, where they would put him in a bed and leave him to die.

He clamped his eyes shut, shook his head, and tried to banish such thoughts from his mind. God would not want him to despair. God would not want him to crave death. God would want him to keep hoping, to seek for all the beauty and happiness he could.

Or at least that's what Ben told himself God would want. What God was truly thinking continued to be a guessing game. God refused to heal him, so he would have to fumble around in the dark and make the best of things. But how could he see any beauty in the world when he couldn't have beautiful Emma? How could he be happy when he'd lost everything he held dear?

Ben shook his head again. Harder this time. He'd let his doubts overtake his faith this morning. He shouldn't second-guess God.

My ways are not thy ways.

In truth, he should have been happy. Emma had turned some sort of a corner in the last week since Adam Werngerd's bonfire. The pumpkin in Mammi's garden was the size of a small volleyball. The tomatoes and beans were coming on so plentifully that Mammi would be canning until Christmas. Emma's social life had been active as well. From what he heard from Lizzie, Emma and Adam had spent a lot of time together since the bonfire. They played board games almost every night, and they were going to the fireworks tonight at the airport.

Lizzie broke the news yesterday that Adam had taken Emma to the lake twice and on a bike ride once. The lake and a bike ride! Did Adam have a brain in that thick skull of his? Emma was unpredictable when she got around water, and Ben had never seen her ride a bike without falling over. That explained why Emma had shown up this morning with a skinned hand. Why hadn't she told Adam no when he proposed something as dangerous as a bike ride? And why did she have that brace around her ankle last week?

Ben knew he was being foolish. He couldn't protect Emma indefinitely, even though he still worried. Emma would need to learn to take care of herself because it was obvious Adam couldn't be trusted to do it.

He should have been happy that Emma and Adam were getting along so well, but all he could feel was regret that he had ever suggested Adam take Emma out. Adam was all wrong for Emma. He never paid attention to ways that Emma could get herself into trouble. He'd been chatting like an old hen when Emma had tried to set the entire east shore on fire, and he hadn't even noticed when Emma almost fell face first into the dirt. Adam wouldn't have been so cavalier if Emma had broken her nose. Ben would find somebody else.

He slumped his shoulders. There wasn't anybody else. The only person who loved Emma enough to look out for her was Ben.

In truth, he couldn't stand the thought of Emma being with anybody else. Of course Adam didn't measure up. Ben didn't want Emma to be anybody's wife but his.

Emma hadn't cried in Ben's presence once since she had started dating Adam. It appeared that she had found love again, and that made Ben very happy.

Very, very happy.

He tipped the pill bottle over and one of his

precious pills slid into his hand. He'd figure out a way to earn some extra money once he got back to Florida. For now, he'd make do with the two remaining pills.

Ben walked into the great room where Dawdi rested in his recliner. He didn't look much worse for wear. The swelling in his mouth had gone down considerably since his surgery yesterday. The oral surgeon had screwed a special screw right into his bone. With the screw anchored like that, Dawdi would be able to attach a false tooth that would probably be more immovable than a real tooth.

Amazing what they could do nowadays.

"Where's Mammi?" Ben asked. "Oh, never mind, Dawdi. Don't try to talk."

"I can talk fine," Dawdi said, enunciating around the wad of cotton in his mouth.

"How are you feeling?"

"Like a fifty-year-old."

"Keep this up, Dawdi, and all your body parts will eventually be brand new. You'll probably feel like a youngster again."

Dawdi held up his hand to stop Ben from saying any more. "Whatever you do, don't encourage your mammi."

"Can I get you a drink or anything?"

"Could you find me a gute book? I've already read the paper twice."

Ben searched through the stack of books next to Dawdi's recliner. "How about *The Stargazer's Guide to the Night Sky?*"

Dawdi leaned back and closed his eyes. "I don't have a telescope."

"*The Horse that Worked for God?*"

"Already read it. Three times."

"*History of Mennonites in Virginia?*"

"Nope."

A little book at the bottom of the stack caught Ben's attention. "*Diagnosis and Management of Central Nervous System Diseases.* Planning to go to medical school, Dawdi?"

Dawdi shifted in his recliner and studied Ben's face. "Just doing a little research. That's all. But don't tell your mammi. She'll suspect something is wrong and have me on about five different medications."

Ben grinned. "My lips are sealed."

The front door flew open and banged against the wall behind it. Lizzie stood on the threshold with flushed cheeks and wild eyes. "Ben," she gasped. "Emma is missing."

Emma sat on a boulder and reread the note.

Emma, I must talk to you in private. Meet me at our old secret spot at three o'clock today. Lizzie

She had no idea what was so urgent and so secret that Lizzie couldn't simply come to her house. Even if she wanted to talk about Mahlon, he worked all day. It wouldn't be difficult to avoid her brother altogether if Lizzie wanted to.

Emma suspected that Mahlon was exactly what Lizzie wanted to talk about. She and Mahlon had been so busy scheming to get Ben and Emma back together, they had been almost oblivious to the relationship blossoming between them. But Emma had noticed, and it made her happy. There were very few things that brought her joy these days.

Emma studied the tiny watch she had brought with her. Almost 3:30. Where was her best friend who so urgently needed to talk to her?

Even though she hadn't been to the secret spot for almost a year, she was certainly in the right place. She remembered to turn right at the ancient tree with a knot that looked like a pig's snout and had passed the particular stone rounded in the center and jagged at the edges. She'd forded the trickling brooklet and passed beneath the twin aspen trees. She wasn't lost, was she?

Maybe so. Lizzie wasn't usually this late.

Being scatterbrained was such a bother.

She'd been lost in the woods before. Twice. Well, three times if she counted that one time in Walmart, which she didn't. One time she found her way out on her own before Mamm even missed her. The other time the whole family had to abandon their picnic to look for her. She made it a point never to wander in the woods by herself. She had a terrible sense of direction.

She sighed loudly so that any bears or wild rodents

would hear the noise and stay away from her. She'd rather not figure out how to escape from a bear today.

If she were still with Ben, this never would have happened. Ben had an excellent sense of direction plus an uncanny ability to sense when she was in trouble.

Don't, don't, don't think of Ben.

Whenever Ben's face popped into her head, she tried to drive it away with thoughts of Adam and chocolate. Thinking of Adam didn't usually chase Ben from her mind, but thinking of her mamm's chocolate truffle brownies did the trick about half the time.

This whole trying-to-be-happy thing wasn't working out all that well. Adam was a nice boy, but he wasn't Ben. Like a lot of Mahlon's friends, Adam lived to have fun. He didn't have a serious bone in his body. He joked so much that Emma often couldn't tell when he was being scornful and when he was being serious. She didn't like the sarcasm so much.

Every time she saw Ben on Huckleberry Hill, she told herself to give it more time with Adam. They'd only really been seeing each other for two weeks. So far she'd seen little to recommend Adam as a husband, but Ben seemed more comfortable around her, as if happy to see her safely in the affections of somebody else.

If Ben was happy, she was happy. It wouldn't hurt

to give Adam a few more weeks. She could always break up with him after Ben left for Florida.

Emma studied her surroundings. Should she wait longer or hike back to the road before it got dark? Would Adam come looking for her when she didn't show up for fireworks? He'd probably be having so much fun that he'd forget he invited her to go with him.

Lizzie and Mahlon would come looking and probably Mamm and Dat too, if she went missing overnight. She leaned back on the generously sized boulder and let her face soak up the sun. The woods were beautiful, lush and green this time of year, and in this secluded spot, she wouldn't have to put on an act for anybody. She could be as miserable as she wanted, and no one would ever know.

She heard Ben calling her name again and again as if he were lost and didn't know how to find her. She tried to answer him, but her lips wouldn't move. Her whole body felt as heavy as lead.

His voice sounded louder now. "Emma," he called, as if his heart would break. "Emma!"

She awoke and sat up with a start. She still reclined on the rock, which hadn't made for a very good bed, judging by the grapefruit-sized knot in her back. How long had she been asleep? Kneading her shoulders, she studied the sky. It couldn't have been later than four. She pulled out her watch. Three fifty-six.

Lizzie obviously wasn't coming. Whatever had been so urgent this morning must have been forgotten by this afternoon. She'd give that girl a piece of her mind when she got home.

"Emma," someone called through the trees and almost made her jump out of her skin. Okay, she hadn't dreamed the voice or even the desperation that lay behind it.

"Over here," she called back.

She might as well have been dreaming. Ben jogged into the clearing looking like some hero from biblical verse—like David must have looked before he slew Goliath—handsome, fierce, and resolute. Except instead of a sling and a stone, Ben carried a shoe.

She held her breath as he came nearer.

"Are you okay?" he panted, as if he'd been running through the woods for hours. As if he actually cared about what happened to her.

She narrowed her eyes. "Ben?"

"When I found your shoe back there, I feared you'd sprained an ankle or something and weren't able to walk." He looked down and furrowed his brow. Both shoes were still firmly attached to her feet. He handed her the shoe. "Isn't this your shoe? It still has the paint splatters on it from last year when we painted the shed."

She turned it over in her hands. It *was* one of her shoes, just not the pair she currently wore. How had it traveled this deep into the woods without being attached to her feet? "I don't know," she said, still befuddled from her nap and bewildered that Ben had awakened her.

He took her face in his hands. She could feel him trembling. "I'm just glad you're safe."

She tried to ignore the sparks that passed from his fingertips to her skin. "Jah. I am safe." Even as she said it, she wasn't so sure.

"Can you walk?"

Did she look crippled? Although she longed to savor his closeness, she put her hands over his and pulled his fingers from her face. "What are you doing here?" she asked.

"I'm relieved I found you before it got dark."

"Was I lost?"

As if he couldn't resist, he raised his hand to her face and stroked her cheek with his thumb. "Did you hit your head?"

"You thought I was lost?"

"Lizzie found your abandoned buggy by the side of a dirt road. She got worried because there isn't a house within three miles of here and the woods are mighty thick. She thought maybe your horse threw a shoe and you got the notion to take a shortcut through the woods."

Emma furrowed her brow. Had she misread Lizzie's note?

Ben's piercing gaze cut through her skull before his lips relaxed into a reserved smile. "I've never seen Lizzie so frantic. She'll probably faint with relief when she sees you."

"But did she . . . ?"

"Did she what?"

Emma pursed her lips and tried not to scowl.

Did she ever intend to meet me at our secret meeting place?

Of course she didn't.

Lizzie had wanted Ben to be here instead. So he'd believe he had saved her. So he'd want to marry her again.

Indignation nearly choked her. Trying to get her to stub her toe was one thing, manipulating Ben's emotions was entirely another. Lizzie and Mahlon were going to catch it good this time.

Ben flexed his hand as if his arm ached. "Are you strong enough to stand or do you need me to carry you back?"

Emma hopped off the rock as if it were blazing hot. "Oh, no," she declared. "I'm plenty strong." Without looking back to make sure Ben followed her, she marched in the direction of the dirt road and her buggy.

Even with his long legs, Ben had to jog to keep up with her. "I'm glad you didn't wander far off the road. Once I found your shoe, it was easy to find you."

Had he found her shoe hanging at eye level in a tree? Or maybe Lizzie had erected a tower of rocks and set the shoe on it so it would be visible from every direction. Emma growled at her own stupidity. She knew she hadn't convinced Lizzie and Mahlon to leave well enough alone. How had she not suspected her best friend and her brother in this cockamamie scheme?

Secret meeting place, indeed.

It only took her ten minutes of vigorous hiking to reach the road where her buggy, Lizzie's buggy, and Felty's horse waited patiently for her appearance. Lizzie and Mahlon stood by her buggy as if expecting her and Ben to emerge from the woods at any moment. Emma rolled her eyes.

Lizzie ran to Emma and practically bowled her over with an embrace. "Emma! I thought I'd never see you again."

"I'll bet you did," Emma said under her breath.

"We're so glad you're safe," Mahlon added, looking more than a little uncomfortable. At least he knew enough to be ashamed.

Lizzie lifted both eyebrows and widened her eyes as a signal for Emma to play along. "Ben, you saved her. What would we do without you?"

Ben looked truly fatigued as he rubbed the hard muscles of his upper arm and trudged to Lizzie's side. "You'll have to get along, I suppose."

They heard another vehicle make its way up the dirt road. Adam appeared from around the bend in his open-air buggy. He showed all his teeth when he caught sight of Emma.

Ben stepped back and let Adam drive his buggy between Ben and the others. "I came to help find you, Emma," Adam said, "but I can see you've already been found, which is gute, because I don't want to be late for fireworks tonight."

Lizzie wrapped a firm arm around Emma's shoulder. "Safe and sound."

Adam brushed a leaf off his buggy seat. "Mamm thinks I should buy a bell to hang around your neck, Emma. That way we'll always know exactly where you are and what kind of trouble you're in."

Mahlon frowned like a bullfrog. "A cowbell?"

Adam chuckled. "Sure, why not?"

Ben's dark expression grew dark. "Maybe if you spent less time polishing that fancy buggy and more time watching out for Emma, she wouldn't get into so many fixes."

The weight of the world pressed down on Emma's chest. To Ben, she was nothing but an incredible burden. And Lizzie and Mahlon had made it worse.

"I'm not Emma's keeper," Adam said, not the least bit offended by Ben's censure.

"Somebody needs to be," Ben said. He wiped the scowl off his face and wasted no time mounting his horse. "I'm glad you're safe, Emma," he said. He turned his horse in the direction of Huckleberry Hill and rode away in a cloud of dust.

Adam dropped the buggy reins and jumped from his seat. "I'm glad you're safe too, Emma, but it's becoming such a common occurrence, I don't get lathered up anymore. Every day at lunch I entertain the guys at the sawmill with your adventures. We get to laughing mighty hard."

Emma lowered her eyes. What girl wouldn't love to be the butt of a lunch-hour joke?

"You shouldn't have a laugh at Emma's expense," Mahlon said.

Thank you, big brother.

Adam's grin widened. "It's all in good fun. Emma doesn't mind." He reached out his hand to her. "Let's get over to Shawano. I want a gute seat for the fireworks."

Emma nodded. "I need a few minutes with Mahlon and Lizzie. Do you mind?"

"Make it quick. All the gute seats get taken by six o'clock."

Emma motioned for Lizzie and Mahlon to follow her several steps into the thicket, far enough away that Adam wouldn't overhear their conversation even if she raised her voice, which she planned on doing. Never mind that she never raised her voice. Lizzie would hear her displeasure now.

Mahlon folded his arms and stiffened as if expecting to be chastised. That was a good guess on his part.

Lizzie, on the other hand, looked as if Christmas had come to Bonduel six months early. She clasped her hands together. "That turned out perfect, Emma, just perfect. Did you see the look on Ben's face when Adam pulled up in his buggy? If looks could curdle milk, he would have made butter for sure."

Emma huffed out an indignant breath. "How could you, Lizzie? I've never seen you stoop so low."

Lizzie's mouth dropped open. "But didn't you see how upset he acted with Adam? He's the one who came to your rescue. Now that we've planted the seed, it's bound to grow."

"Nae. Ben's not jealous. He wants me to date Adam."

Lizzie caught her breath and lunged at Emma so quickly, Emma jumped out of her skin. Lizzie grabbed her wrist. "Somebody needs to break your heart."

"Somebody already has," Emma said, the frustration rising with every breath as she pulled her arm out of Lizzie's grasp.

Lizzie leaned forward and lowered her voice just in case Adam had sneaked into the bushes and listened in on their conversation. "Don't you see? It's perfect. You and Adam date for a few more weeks and then Adam can break up with you in a very public way."

"No."

"He could break your heart at a gathering somewhere Ben is sure to see it. He'll feel so bad for you that he'll want to get back together."

Mahlon's brows inched together. "You want him to take her back out of pity?"

"Whatever works," Lizzie said.

"Listen to yourself," Emma said, planting her fists firmly on her hips. "This is your brother. You purposefully upset him when he didn't need to be upset."

Mahlon nudged Lizzie with his elbow. "I told you we shouldn't do it."

Lizzie turned on Mahlon like a river of water interrupted in its course. "You agreed to this. You said it was a good way to make sure Emma wouldn't get injured and that Ben would still have a chance to rescue her."

Mahlon glared at her. "How can you expect me to think straight when you flash those blue eyes at me? Emma's right. It was a bad idea."

Those blue eyes that so captivated Mahlon flashed with anger. "Don't you dare turn on me, Mahlon Nelson. You've got eyes of your own, you know."

"What's that supposed to mean? This was your idea."

"But you smiled at me and led me to believe you thought it was a good idea," Lizzie protested.

Mahlon softened and burst into a grin. "My smile convinced you of that? What do you like about my smile? My dimple?"

"I like your straight white teeth. They dazzle me."

"And your cute little button nose," Mahlon cooed.

Emma growled louder this time. "I don't care which one of you got hoodwinked into doing this. We're talking about Ben, remember?"

"But, Emma, he loves you."

"You're wrong, Lizzie. He wants me to marry and settle down with somebody else. That is what will truly make him happy. If you care about Ben at all, you'll leave him alone to live his life the way he wants to live it."

Lizzie slumped her shoulders. "I hate to see him so miserable."

"He might be miserable because he has a girl in Florida waiting for him, but he doesn't want to go back to her until his ex-fiancée is married to someone else."

She had stunned Lizzie into silence. But only momentarily. She looked as if she'd swallowed a bitter walnut. "He has a girlfriend in Florida?"

Emma ignored the stabbing ache in her gut. "I don't know."

Lizzie frowned and shook her head. "I don't think so. He'd tell me something as important as that."

"But you said yourself that he is hiding something."

"Not that. It couldn't be that."

Emma took a deep breath and let the pain and frustration flow out of her body. If only Ben had never come back. "I want both of you to promise me that you won't interfere with Ben's life or mine ever again."

"Fine," Mahlon said.

Lizzie pressed her lips together and glanced at Mahlon. "Okay. I promise, but I'm not happy about it. I feel like I'm giving him permission to ruin his life."

"Keep your promise. That's all I ask."

They both nodded. "We'll stay out of it," Mahlon

said. "A plan this elaborate takes a lot of time, and it's too risky when we're talking about Emma."

Emma twitched her lips sarcastically. "Thanks a lot."

Mahlon draped his arm around Lizzie and led her out of the thicket. "I told you we shouldn't have meddled."

Lizzie snapped her head up to glower at him. "No, you didn't. Don't even think about feeding me that line."

"Your brother would make it easier if he went back to Florida and left us alone."

Lizzie cuffed him on the shoulder. "Mahlon, how can you say such a thing?"

When they returned to the road, Adam sat in his buggy fingering the rim of his hat. He plopped it back on his head when Emma appeared. "You ready to go? We've got to get gute seats."

Emma handed her lonely shoe to Lizzie. "See that this gets back to my house, will you?"

Lizzie's face drooped. "I thought I was clever how I made it so easy to find. It led him right to you," she whispered.

"Leave it be, Liz." Emma let Adam pull her up onto the buggy seat.

Adam jiggled the reins to get his horse moving. "Don't worry, Mahlon. I'll see that I keep all matches, sparklers, and sharp objects out of Emma's reach." He laughed at his own joke, poked Emma with his elbow, and prodded his horse into a trot.

Emma turned back to see a black look growing on Mahlon's face like a thundercloud.

Would Adam bring a high chair for her to sit in and give her a rattle to play with?

She was so looking forward to the fireworks.

Chapter 12

It was difficult to make cookies with nine fingers. Well, the cookies didn't have fingers. Emma only had nine gute fingers at the moment. Stirring thick dough was hard when she couldn't grip the spoon tightly. Nearly two weeks since the fireworks and her index finger still had a scab on it where the blister used to be. She had no idea sparklers could get so hot. She hadn't told anybody, not even Mahlon, about the burn. Adam would have laughed at her, and Ben would have tried to take her to the hospital. She hadn't required a tetanus shot, nor had she fainted. All in all, a minor injury.

"Anna, where are the chocolate chips?"

Anna pointed to an impossibly high cupboard above the window. "You'll need a stool."

Emma did her best to remain calm when she heard Ben's voice behind her. She didn't even look up from her stirring.

"Can I help?" Ben stood practically tall enough to

reach the weather vane on top of the barn. He slipped past Emma and took the chocolate chips from the tall cupboard. He didn't even need to stand on his tiptoes.

Grinning, he handed the chocolate chips to Emma. "Show-off," she said.

Things with Ben had been much better lately, maybe because she felt like she had finally given him up. Or perhaps he felt better about leaving her now that she and Adam were dating.

Anna straightened her glasses and gazed at Ben as if he were her guardian angel. "We're so glad to have you around."

"That's about all I'm good for," Ben said. "Reaching high things from high cupboards. It wonders me how you got them all the way up there, Mammi. You're a tiny little thing."

Anna's eyes sparkled. "Stop your teasing. I'm tall enough for kissing my sweetheart. That's all I care about."

"Mammi!" Ben teased. "I am shocked you would talk about such things in the presence of young, innocent ears."

Mammi waved her hand dismissively. "You young folks know a lot more about kissing than you pretend."

Ben took the liberty of opening the package of chocolate chips and popping a handful into his mouth. "What are you making?"

Anna poured the chocolate chips into the batter

while Emma concentrated on stirring. She tucked her finger around the handle so Ben wouldn't see it.

"Remember how I told you I want to try out some pumpkin recipes since I'll have all this pumpkin to cook with?" Mammi said. "Emma is showing me her recipe for pumpkin chocolate chip cookies. And so far, she's doing a very gute job."

Ben smiled weakly as a memory flashed in his eyes. "I love Emma's pumpkin chocolate chip cookies."

Emma concentrated hard on her bowl of batter and stirred as if everything depended on mixing these cookies into submission. The first night Ben had driven her home from a singeon, they had made pumpkin chocolate chip cookies together at Emma's house. He'd stayed until midnight, eating cookies and singing songs. She had known she loved him that night.

Felty came in from outside toting a small basket of brown eggs and humming one of his many tunes. "It's wonderful gute to get outside and work in the yard. I feel as if I've been cooped up for years."

Anna pinned him with a stern eye. "Well, don't get used to it. You're getting your new tooth on Friday."

"No need to worry, Annie Banannie. I'll be off my feet in no time." He placed the eggs on the table and gazed out the window. "Looks like it's going to make down hard."

Emma hadn't even noticed how dark the sky had grown. "I hope the tomatoes don't get waterlogged."

"Will my pumpkin be okay?" Anna said.

"We've planted it on a mound, so the water should give it a good soak, but not puddle." Emma scooped batter by the spoonful onto the cookie sheets while Anna and Felty stood at the window, waiting excitedly for the storm to strike.

Ben grabbed a spoon from the drawer and scooped batter with her. He always saw the need.

A faint rumble of thunder announced the rain. It fell hard and heavy, as if it were giving the whole world a shower. Emma frowned. The sound of pelting rain on the roof gave way to the hard, rat-a-tat roar of hailstones.

Emma came around the counter and peered out the window. Hailstones the size of peas bombarded the ground. The lawn looked like a sea of popping popcorn as hailstones fell, bounced, and finally came to rest.

Raindrops were relatively harmless to a pumpkin plant. Hail was an entirely different matter on those giant fanlike leaves.

Emma gasped. "The pumpkin will be shredded to bits."

Anna brought her hand to her mouth. "Oh, dear. I haven't finished knitting my pumpkin cover."

"We've got to protect that pumpkin." Emma snatched her bonnet from the hook and raced out the door.

"Emma, wait," Ben called after her.

Not pausing for anyone, she ran to the barn, shielding her face from the shower of rock-hard ice. Once inside, she located a large plastic tarp. If she suspended it over the pumpkin plant, she could protect it from the worst damage and salvage her hopes for a giant pumpkin.

Leaving the safety of the barn, she sloshed to the pumpkin mound and unfolded the tarp over the pumpkin, now the size of a small tire. She wouldn't be able to spread the tarp wide enough with her two short arms. This was a two-person job.

Okay, she should have waited for Ben.

Praise the Lord, Ben had long legs and a determined stride. Carrying an umbrella, he jogged to the vegetable patch. When he got close, he raised the umbrella and held it over her head. "Put it down," she yelled over the din of the hail. "We'll need both hands to hold the tarp."

"You're going to get hurt," he yelled back.

"I don't care. We've got to save Anna's pumpkin."

He frowned, collapsed the umbrella, and tossed it onto the ground. Holding out his hands, he grabbed two corners of the tarp. "Stand under the tarp while we hold it over the pumpkin."

"Okay." She wouldn't argue with that. The hail fell harder, and she felt as if a hundred idiotic boys snapped rubber band after rubber band at her head.

Being as careful as they could not to flatten leaves or vines, they spread the tarp above the pumpkin and ducked underneath it. It provided meager shelter, but at least their heads would be protected. Most of the pumpkin vines stretched past the protection of the tarp. The hail pelted the leaves until many of them looked as holey as Swiss cheese. Some of the leaves were stripped clear off the vines. That couldn't be helped. At least the pumpkin and surrounding foliage would be safe. Hopefully they hadn't already sustained too much damage.

Ben's heavy breathing matched hers, and being on the underside of the tarp seemed to magnify it, even as a dump truck of hailstones rained down on them. Ben quirked up the corners of his lips. "Your face glows blue under this tarp."

She shook her head and smiled. "Denki for following me out here. I couldn't have done it by myself."

"I couldn't let you come out here alone."

The hail slid off the tarp and rolled down Emma's back, completely soaking her dress.

"Oh, no," Ben said. He knelt down in the mud so that Emma's side of the tarp sat higher than his. The hail and water found a new path down his back.

She gasped. "No, you don't. You're going to be a mess." She bent her knees so that the tarp paralleled the ground, but that was no good either. The hail piled in the middle of the tarp and made it sag.

"Ben, stand up."

"You stand up. I'm already muddy, and I don't want you to get sick."

She squatted to make her side lower than Ben's. The hail that had collected on the tarp tumbled in an avalanche down her back. She caught her breath as several hailstones sneaked down the back of her dress.

Ben bent so low that his cheek nearly touched

the ground. The hail seesawed back to his side and dribbled down his back. He chuckled and cocked an eyebrow. "I can always go lower."

Seeing she wasn't going to win, Emma growled and stood all the way up. Ben returned to his knees. "This is my project. You shouldn't have to suffer for it."

"I want to save Mammi's pumpkin as much as you do."

After five long minutes and a song about raindrops and tarps courtesy of Ben, the hail gave way to a gentle rain. Ben stuck his head out from under the tarp. "It looks safe to come out."

Emma held out her hand to catch some rain and then lowered the tarp. Light rain like this would be good for the plants. She tugged at the tarp, and Ben let go. "We should let this dry flat in the barn and fold it later."

He nodded.

"Denki for your help."

He smiled. "Mammi must not go without a giant pumpkin." He grabbed the umbrella off the ground and opened it. Stepping close to her, he held it over both of them to shield them from what was left of the rain. It wouldn't do much good now. They were both soaked to the bone like two waterlogged cats.

"Denki," she whispered as his closeness engulfed her. She breathed in his manly scent and sighed as his breath caressed her cheek. The tarp slipped from her fingers.

He turned to stone.

Emma did her best to divert her thoughts. Holding her breath so she wouldn't be tempted to sniff at him, she thought of Adam and tried to remember what he smelled like. Not one thought came to mind.

What about his teeth? Adam had nice teeth, didn't he? She couldn't recall. What did Adam even look like?

She remembered they were standing under an umbrella before her voice failed her completely. "I am probably as wet as I'm going to get."

With an unreadable expression, he brushed a lock of soggy hair from her forehead. "Do you like Adam Wengerd?"

She swallowed hard. "I . . . I don't know. He has good teeth."

"I don't think you should date him anymore."

"You don't?" Through the fog, she latched on to one thought. Had Lizzie's plan worked? Was he jealous enough to get back together with her?

Nae, of course not. How could she dare open her heart to such a possibility?

Instead of pulling away like he absolutely, positively should have, Ben traced his finger down the side of her cheek and rubbed his thumb along her jawline. If several hailstones hadn't rolled down her back during the storm, she would have thought that maybe she shivered from something other than the cold.

"Adam can't take care of you the way you need to be taken care of," he said in a low, rumbly tone that might have made her swoon if she had been prone to fainting. A girl who saw as much blood as she did tried to avoid fainting. As much as possible.

"You're so beautiful," he whispered.

She couldn't read the emotion in his eyes as he grew breathlessly still and stared at her mouth.

Oh, no. Oh, no.

Whatever she did, she mustn't lose her composure. Ben was just performing his normal check of her injuries, making sure her eyebrows, nose, and lips were in good working condition.

Without warning, he wrapped his free hand around her waist, pulled her closer than she would ever have dared hope, and kissed her hungrily. She was glad she made that resolution not to faint. His kiss was glorious, as if heaven had emptied itself of all the angels, and they now floated over Emma's little corner of the world.

That boy she went to the bonfire with, what was his name again?

Diligently, she kissed Ben back with all the fervor of months of heartache and waiting. Her love for him multiplied sevenfold just standing there. He was so strong and kind and brave, and she couldn't see loving anyone else for as long as she lived.

Did this mean Ben still loved her, that Lizzie had been right all along? Had he just needed a push? Her heart soared to the sky, and she blessed the hailstorm that had brought them together again.

The umbrella fell from his hand, and he wrapped both arms around her until she was doubly secure in his embrace. He kissed her as if he needed to drink his fill of her lips before an impossibly long journey. She wrapped her arms around his neck and abandoned herself to the raw emotions of love and longing.

At that moment she opened her heart to him as she hadn't dared do for nearly a year. She gave it to him freely, trusting him to protect it as his own. It was no longer hers. She would let Ben do what he wanted with it.

Tears of joy ran down her face, and the saltiness mingled with their kisses, tasting sweeter because of all they'd been through together. It took her a moment to realize that his tears mixed with hers.

She pulled her face mere inches away from his. "Ben," she whispered. "Oh, Ben, I love you so much. So much."

He closed his eyes and flinched as if she had slapped him. Tears rained down his cheeks and dripped onto her face.

"What is it? How can I help you?"

His arms tightened around her in a vise-like grip. When he opened his eyes, she saw suffering of exquisite intensity.

Dread grew in her heart like mold. "Ben, what's wrong?"

"Emma, I'm so sorry."

She pulled him closer even as she felt him slipping from her grasp. "Sorry for what?"

He released her, took a step away, and pressed his hands to his face. "I should never, *never* have lost control that way."

"It's okay, Ben. I love you. I never want to be without you again." She reached for him, and he stepped back as if touching her would be deadly. Fearing a single puff of air might shatter her entire world, she held her breath and waited for him to speak.

"I can't. I can't do this to you." He swiped the back of his hand across his face. "There is no hope for you and me, Emma. You must understand that. You mustn't have any hope."

A sob would have broken from her throat if she had been able to breathe. Why did her heart still beat in her chest when she felt so dead inside?

"I want you to have a happy, long life with a husband who loves you and your children. Lots of children. I want the time we spent together to be a happy memory instead of one that causes you pain."

His words turned her to hard, cold ice. "And we must make sure that Ben gets what he wants."

"I want you to get over me."

She felt as if she would shatter into a million pieces. All those months of working so hard to be happy—trying to forget Ben Helmuth and banish him from her heart—all those months had been utterly wasted. She would never be happy again. "You don't understand, do you, Ben? You are impossible to get over."

Not caring if she tripped all over herself, she ran away from him as if her life depended on it. Ragged sobs stuck in her throat while hot tears stung her eyes and made it nearly impossible to see where she was going.

"Emma, wait! At least take the umbrella."

She didn't waste time turning back to tell him no. She'd never set foot on Huckleberry Hill again. Anna's pumpkin could rot in the sun for all she cared.

Like a cold autumn wind, she blew down the hill and never looked back.

Even weeping as she'd never wept before, she didn't fall. She didn't even stumble. Ben would have been so proud.

Chapter 13

Emma climbed the short fence between Herschberger's pasture and her family's property. She didn't even care that she scraped her leg and snagged her dress. What did anything matter anymore?

She was soaking wet. The rain had given way to a drizzle halfway home, and no traces of violent storm remained but the refreshing smell of damp grass and little puddles along the road. Usually she loved to go outside right after a rainstorm. Today she wanted to crawl into a little ball and let the world go on without her.

Her heart sank when she glanced toward the house. Lizzie and Mahlon were swinging on the swing set, going impossibly high like two first graders trying to outdo each other. Lizzie giggled, and although Mahlon had his back to Emma, he surely grinned with his whole face, the way he was accustomed to doing whenever Lizzie was around.

It seemed they couldn't get enough of each other. It was the way she and Ben used to be.

Another sob almost tore from her lips. She clapped her hand over her mouth. They mustn't see her. She wouldn't make it all the way into the house without being discovered. Should she duck into the chicken coop? Nae, she felt miserable enough without exiling herself to the chicken coop. She wanted to cry in peace without that foul smell filling her lungs.

Maybe she could slink around to the back of the woodshed and crawl through the window. Of course, she didn't know where she would sit, and the sawdust made her sneeze, but the pleasant smell of freshly cut cedar would be a nice change from flying feathers and squawking chickens.

She ran for cover behind the cherry tree. Holding her breath, she listened for any sign that Mahlon or Lizzie had seen her. She could still hear Lizzie's giggling.

It was a little farther from the tree to the shed. She poked her head around the tree. Their backs were to her. No need to fear being discovered.

Emma bolted for the shed and breathed a sigh of relief when she managed to reach its protection without making any noise. It wouldn't be a problem to open the window wide enough to climb into. It was a big window, and she'd done it before.

She propped her hands underneath the bottom half and pushed. It wouldn't budge. Not an inch. She cupped her hands around her eyes and gazed inside. Someone had fastened the latch. *Ach, du lieva*, now she'd have to sneak around the front and risk being discovered. She wanted to sit down and have a gute cry and then maybe run away forever. Was that too much to ask?

She'd have to risk it. With the way Mahlon and Lizzie were carrying on, they wouldn't notice a tornado blowing through. Emma tiptoed around the side of the shed with her gaze glued to the swing set. Unfortunately, this meant she didn't watch where she was going. She stumbled over a chicken in her path and almost lost her footing. Even though she regained her balance quietly, the chicken was not so circumspect. It beat its wings and squawked indignantly and ruined any chance for Emma to make it to the safety of the shed without being seen.

Mahlon dragged his feet on the ground to stop his swing. "Emma," he called.

She smiled as best she could and gave him a casual wave. Maybe from this far, he wouldn't see the tearstained face or the eyes as puffy as feather pillows.

Lizzie turned her head, jumped from her swing in midair, and ran at Emma. Should she turn and run the other way?

Nae. That would be a little too suspicious.

"You're home early," Lizzie said as she and Mahlon approached. "Me and Mahlon had another idea." She got close enough to see the red eyes. "Oh, dear."

Mahlon's smile disappeared. "You're soaking wet. What happened?"

Emma tried to wave away his concern. "You know. Just another wonderful day at Huckleberry Hill."

Mahlon's expression turned positively grim. "What did Ben do?"

Lizzie narrowed her eyes. "What? You think he pushed her into a mud puddle or something? Why do you blame everything on my brother? Maybe it has nothing to do with Ben."

"It always has something to do with Ben," Mahlon said.

Ben. Jah, it always and forever had everything to do with Ben.

Emma clamped her lips together so nothing would escape. She lowered her head and marched toward the house. Even Mamm's finger wagging would be more bearable than this banter between her best friend and her twin brother, who didn't care about her as much as they cared about impressing each other.

"Emma, wait," Lizzie called.

She should have run. Both of them caught up to her in no time.

Lizzie hooked her elbow and pulled her to the swing. "Sit," Lizzie said. "Talk to me."

"Swings make me dizzy," Emma said, not looking Lizzie in the eye. "I just want to go lie down."

"Let her be, Lizzie," Mahlon growled.

Lizzie propped her hands on her hips. "If you're

going to accuse Ben of being the one to make Emma cry, then I want to hear exactly what happened."

"We know what happened. Ben won't leave Emma alone."

"He can't help it if she's on Huckleberry Hill three times a week."

Mahlon squared his shoulders. "So he doesn't love Emma. Fine. But why does he have to keep rubbing it in?"

Emma lunged at Mahlon and threw her arms around his neck. Burying her face in the crook of his neck, she broke into gut-clenching sobs. Mahlon would always be on her side.

Her brother enfolded her into a crushing bear hug and let her get his shirt wet with her tears and her sopping dress.

"Oh, Emma," Lizzie said. She put her arm awkwardly around Emma's shoulder as Emma stood in Mahlon's embrace.

"He kissed me," she managed to say between sobs.

Mahlon grabbed her shoulders and nudged her to arm's length. "He what?"

Lizzie's astonishment was as complete as Mahlon's. "Just now?"

"And then he told me he would never marry a girl like me." Emma felt as if she were crumbling.

Mahlon again wrapped his arms around her and squeezed tight. "That dog," he murmured.

"But . . . I don't understand why he would do that," Lizzie said.

Mahlon's voice was tinged with a bitterness that Emma hadn't heard for weeks. "I told you, Tizzy. He wants to rub it in, to prove that he can get Emma back anytime he wants."

Lizzie caught her breath and stepped back. "Ben would never do that."

Mahlon rubbed his hand up and down Emma's arm. "Did you kiss him back, Emma?"

"Of course."

He scowled at Lizzie. "Ben thinks Emma will follow him around like a puppy, lapping up whatever crumbs he throws at her. He's back in Bonduel to gloat." He folded his arms across his chest. "And to play with my little sister's feelings."

Jah, that's how she felt. Pathetic.

"Don't talk about my brother that way."

"Quit defending him," Mahlon said. "He's a snake."

"Oh," Lizzie said, mocking him, "you called him a dog too. Any other animal names you want to throw at him?"

"How about rat? Or lizard?" His eyes could have shot darts. "Or pig? I think he's a pig."

To Emma's surprise, Lizzie looked on the verge of tears. That couldn't be. Lizzie got angry, but she never got her feelings hurt. "Well, I think *you're* a pig, Mahlon Nelson."

Emma slumped her shoulders. If only she'd been

able to make it to the safety of the shed before they had discovered her.

"I don't care what you think of me," Mahlon snapped, "as long as you stay away from me."

"I will," Lizzie said. "I'd rather chop all my hair off than ever speak to you again."

Hurt flashed in his eyes as he clenched his fists. The emotion didn't last long. Mahlon didn't often show weakness. "Tell that brother of yours to keep away from my sister."

"You tell him yourself, if you're so brave."

"Don't worry. I will," he said.

"You'll do no such thing," Emma said.

Mahlon gave her that look he always had when he scolded her. "I'll always stand up for you, Em, even if you won't stand up for yourself. And from now on, I'm steering clear of the Nelson family. Especially Lizzie Tizzy. I've had enough of her to last a lifetime."

"And I've had more than enough of you," Lizzie countered. "I've had so much of you, I want to throw up."

Mahlon folded his arms and leaned within inches of Lizzie's face. "Then why don't you go home?"

Lizzie lifted her chin. "I'm here to see Emma. I'll go home when I please."

Emma felt ill. Nothing she said could possibly make things better between them, and she was too wrapped up in her own heartache to try.

"Well then," Mahlon said, frowning so hard

Emma thought his mouth might fall off his face. He spun on his heels and stomped toward the house.

Emma held her breath as she watched him go. Would she lose Lizzie again because of Mahlon? And wouldn't it be better if she did? Being around Lizzie was a harsh reminder of Ben.

Lizzie turned her face away. "He never could keep his temper." She sounded indignant enough, but her voice shook and a single tear made a slow trail down her face.

Even though she wanted nothing more than to be alone, Emma slid her arm around Lizzie's shoulder. "Don't cry. He'll cool off in a few hours."

Lizzie sniffed and swiped the tear from her cheek. "It never would have worked between us. What girl wants such an ill-tempered husband?"

Emma gladly steered Lizzie away from the subject of her own humiliation that morning. She need never know how easily Emma had succumbed to temptation. Emma ignored the searing pain that twisted her stomach into sailor's knots. "Mahlon can get riled when he cares about something."

"I want a nice, steady husband."

"A husband who doesn't care about anything?"

"Who doesn't make me crazy."

"Crazy in love?"

"Crazy in love with Mahlon? Absolutely not." Lizzie relaxed the hard line of her mouth, shook her head, and huffed in frustration. "Oh, I don't know."

"He's been known to help farmers get their

corn in before the frost, and he still picks up Amos Eicher in his wheelchair every morning for school. He's got a gute heart."

"That doesn't mean I should marry him."

"Of course not. You should only marry him if you really want to, not because he's good-looking or spirited or has a heart of gold deep down in there somewhere. You should definitely love him first."

Lizzie blinked rapidly. "It doesn't matter, because I am never speaking to him again."

"We're supposed to forgive those who trespass against us."

"I'll forgive him. Eventually. But I won't set foot inside your house. And he can forget about ever getting another apple pie no matter how much he begs."

"It will be hard to finish our quilt if you won't come in my house," Emma said.

"You can come to my house."

Emma did her best to smile. Let Lizzie think everything was all better. "I'll come after supper tonight, and we can sew. Your machine is better anyway."

"Okay. Come over. Mamm won't mind seeing you again." Her lips twisted sheepishly, as if she wished she hadn't just said that.

"Oh." Emma felt cold and empty. "She's still mad at me because of Ben."

"She doesn't understand."

"Yes, she does." Emma's throat constricted and

she couldn't have said one more word to save her life. It was all she could do to hold back the flood of tears that threatened to overflow at the slightest nudge.

"Don't ever say that, Emma. Ben is acting like an idiot. You've done nothing wrong."

There was her nudge. The dam broke. She covered her face with her hands and bawled like a stuck pig. "I kissed him," she managed to blurt out. Might as well tell her everything. What did it matter anymore? If Lizzie knew the truth, maybe she would stop plaguing her with plans to get her back together with Ben.

"Well, that's not your fault. He kissed you. What were you supposed to do?"

"No," Emma sobbed. "No, not that." She grabbed Lizzie's hand and dragged her to the privacy of the woodshed. They dodged Dat's table saw and sat in the middle of the floor amidst the sawdust. At least it smelled fresh.

Lizzie stared at Emma, her expression a mix of sympathy and unrestrained curiosity.

Emma's voice shook uncontrollably, but she forged on. Lizzie should know the worst. "Two nights before he left me, we were sitting on the sofa and he seemed so unhappy. I wanted to cheer him up, so I leaned over and kissed him on the lips."

Lizzie's jaw dropped open. "Oh, please, Emma. That's not why he broke up with you."

"That and the fact that I can't seem to put one foot in front of the other without tripping."

"Ben wouldn't break up with you because you kissed him."

"He thinks I'm wicked."

Lizzie shook her head vigorously. "I know you, Emma. You are not wicked, and I can't believe in a million years that Ben would ever think that of you. Everybody kisses when they're dating, no matter what the bishop says. Besides, you and Ben were engaged. Kissing is expected."

Emma tried to stanch the water pouring from her eyes. "Don't you see? His kiss today was a test. He wanted to know if I would resist temptation, and I didn't. I kissed him right back."

Lizzie raised her brows and peered doubtfully at Emma. "I don't mean to sound harsh, but that is really a stupid notion."

"It's not, Lizzie. I've been replaying last summer in my mind over and over again, racking my brain, wondering what could have happened to make Ben stop loving me." She clenched her fists. "He had reason enough because of the chicken coop, but the kiss cemented his mind against me. Before he broke our engagement, he withdrew from me, as if he couldn't confide in me anymore. That's probably the time he started having doubts. My kiss was enough to push him to leave me."

Lizzie rose her knees, took Emma by the shoulders,

and pinned her with a serious gaze. "What did he do when you kissed him that first time?"

"He acted as if I'd slammed his thumb in the door, as if he was thinking, 'Emma, you've disappointed me.'"

Lizzie drew back, as if she finally decided to at least consider what Emma told her. "I can't imagine . . ." She shook her head. "I don't understand him anymore."

They embraced. Even though neither of them understood Ben, they understood each other. For the moment, that was good enough.

"Will you promise me something?" Emma asked.

"What do you want?"

"That we never talk about Ben again."

"I don't know if I can promise you that. He's my brother," Lizzie said.

"I mean, never talk about me and Ben getting back together. Never say another word about our past relationship or hope for a future one."

The corners of Lizzie's mouth sagged, and she slowly bobbed her head up and down. "Seeing how it hurt you, I should have put a stop to such talk weeks ago. I can see how it affects you. I just didn't want to believe that it was over."

"You're a gute friend, even if you are annoyingly persistent."

A sad grin pried her lips apart. "I know I'm annoying." She cleared her throat and spoke as if with great effort. "So let's talk about Adam."

Emma stifled a sigh. She didn't want to talk about Adam. "We played games with his parents last night. I think they like me okay."

Lizzie pasted on a fake smile. "He's so good-looking. About ten girls had a crush on him in primary school."

"Mahlon always reminds me what a catch Adam is."

Lizzie's eyes flashed with anger before the light seemed to go out inside her. "Will you promise me something?"

"Never talk about Mahlon?"

"Yep."

"We can't talk about Mahlon, and we can't talk about Ben, and I do not want to talk about Adam. Where does that leave us?"

"We could talk about quilting," Lizzie said.

"Or horses. Or we could talk about cows and milk."

"Or we could talk about growing peas and pumpkins."

Emma took a deep, cleansing breath. "No pumpkins."

"Jah," Lizzie said. "We can't say a word about pumpkins or chicken coops."

Emma managed a half smile. "Or apple pies. Mahlon loves your apple pies."

Lizzie's voice cracked. "I'd rather not talk about milking stools or the lake or ice cream either."

"We really can't talk about anything, can we?" Emma said.

Tears glistened in Lizzie's eyes as she shook her head.

Emma felt the stinging in her eyes too. She and Lizzie were quite a pair, both pining over young men who didn't care one whit about them. She draped her arm around Lizzie's shoulder, and neither of them said another word as they sat on the floor of the woodshed making the sawdust soggy with their tears.

Chapter 14

Ben stumbled to the toolshed. His legs reluctantly obeyed his commands. He rejoiced that he had even been able to stand this morning. All things considered, he did very well. The fear of a wheelchair had been the only thing that had motivated him to get out of bed. How close was he to losing his ability to walk? According to the doctor he'd seen last summer, it should have happened by now. Ben would be grateful for every extra day he got.

He reached out to steady himself against the wall of the toolshed. His arms worked. If he could pull himself around to the door, he'd be able to get into the shed without much problem.

Mammi's pumpkin needed fertilizer, and they hadn't seen hide nor hair of Emma for two weeks. Just thinking about her made Ben double over in pain. It was so much better that she stay away so he wouldn't be able to hurt her. Regret and guilt would plague him for the rest of his life.

How could he have lost control like that? He'd spent months steeling himself against Emma, and in one horrible moment he'd ruined everything. He thought his heart was already broken, but it had shattered into a thousand more pieces when he watched her flee down the hill.

Despair crawled down his throat and seeped into his lungs. He wanted to die. Why couldn't the good Lord take him now and be done with it? It would be so much easier on everyone.

His knees buckled, and he slumped to the ground with his back resting against the toolshed. He panted with exertion even though his exertion consisted of getting out of bed and walking outside. What to do now? He couldn't very well call for Mammi to pull him off the ground. Even if he wanted her to know about his illness, which he didn't, she wouldn't be able to lift him even if he weighed half of what he did.

He shifted to his hands and knees. Crawling was not a bad way to go, and if he lost his balance, he wouldn't have far to fall. With more effort than it should have taken, he wormed his way to the door of the toolshed, lifted the latch, and crawled into the small space. Hopefully Emma had placed the fertilizer on the floor the last time she had used it.

Straining with all his willpower, Ben pulled his entire body into the shed and let the door swing shut behind him. Lord willing, he would be able to work his way to his feet and emerge from the shed in a standing position. Mammi and Dawdi need never know his woes.

He raised his head to see if he could locate the fertilizer and groaned as he met eyes with Dawdi, who sat on a three-legged stool sharpening a hoe.

"Hello, Ben!"

Ben sat back and tried to pretend that he crawled around on his hands and knees on a regular basis. "Dawdi, what are you doing out here? You had a root canal yesterday. You're supposed to be resting."

Dawdi grinned. "Your mammi insists that I rest for your sake, but I figured what you don't know won't hurt you. I won't ever be able to enjoy that recliner again."

"But Mammi said the root canal would plow you under for at least a week."

"Not even for a few hours."

Ben cocked an eyebrow. "Were you the one who oiled the buggy and repaired the harness strap?"

"It's much easier to oil a buggy without a deviated septum."

Ben chuckled. "Did you pick the peas too?"

Dawdi took off his glasses and pulled a handkerchief out of his pocket. "I guess you caught me," he said, shrugging as if he didn't care. He wiped his spectacles, put them back on his nose, and peered at Ben as if he were in on some secret joke. "And I guess I caught you."

"Caught me?"

Dawdi motioned in the direction of Ben's legs. "How long has this been going on?"

Ben's heart sank. "Dawdi, please, you can't tell anybody. I don't want anybody to know."

"I've suspected for ages. You can't keep that kind of secret from your dawdi. I'm sharp as a tack. When my young, sturdy grandson can't even get out of bed in the morning, I know something's wrong. The question is, how long has something been wrong?"

Ben turned his face away and measured his answer. He didn't want to lie to his dawdi, but he didn't want anyone derailing his carefully laid plans. "I'm going through a bad spell, that's all."

A bad spell that would kill him soon enough.

Dawdi laid his file on the small work table, slid off his stool, and sat next to Ben on the floor. "I've been stewing about it for weeks. You've got some dread disease, don't you? That's why you called it off with Emma. That's why you left your family without hardly a word."

"Please don't ask me to explain."

"I don't expect you'd tell me if you didn't even tell your mamm or Emma. I'm far down on your list of people to tell, if you ever do." He scooted closer and put a thin but strong arm around Ben. "If you need someone to hear you out, I'm a gute listener and I keep things to myself."

Ben felt his body suddenly, inexplicably relax, as if a taut wire inside him had snapped. He managed to pull his knees to his chin and wrap his arms around them. Sighing, he leaned his forehead on his knees. The sigh turned into a moan, which splintered into a deluge of tears. He'd been captive to this burden for so long. How relieved would he feel to share it with someone else?

He choked on the brutal truth. "I'm dying, Dawdi."

Dawdi's arm tightened around him. "Slowly or soon?"

"I don't know. Soon, the doctor said. I won't be able to walk much longer."

Dawdi ruffled Ben's hair in a surprisingly comforting gesture. "I'm guessing you've known since last August."

"Last spring, everything seemed to get harder. Simple leather work at the harness shop took twice as long. I felt like I was struggling to get my hands to do what I wanted them to. Then one day I walked up the stairs, and my legs just gave out. I fell flat on my face. That's when I went to the doctor." He wiped away his pathetic tears. He hated wallowing in self-pity. "He told me I have amyotrophic lateral sclerosis, Lou Gehrig's disease."

"Who is Lou Gehrig?"

"The doctor said he was a baseball player. After he got the disease, he was forced into a wheelchair in a matter of months and was dead in two years."

"But what about a cure? Your mammi and I will sell everything if you need money to pay for it. All your onkels would do the same. I don't need Lasik that bad."

"There is no cure. When I found out, I spent a whole day praying, begging God to heal me. I promised

Him I'd do anything He wanted if He would just take this thorn from my side."

"And He said no." Dawdi said it more as a statement than a question.

Ben sniffed back the tears. "He said all things are possible to him who believes. My faith is so weak."

"Nae," Dawdi said, shaking his head vigorously. "If it's not God's will, it's not God's will. If He didn't see fit to deliver you, it's not because your faith is lacking. It's because there is a higher purpose in your trial yet."

"If there is a higher purpose, I don't understand what it is."

"Neither do I. But I know even the blessed Lord Jesus asked God to remove the bitter cup, and God said no. That 'no' meant the salvation of all mankind."

"I definitely don't have anywhere near that high a purpose."

"There is always purpose in suffering," Dawdi said, "some of which we won't understand until we get to heaven. The uncertainty can feel confusing and dismal. Our only hope for peace is through Jesus."

"I know," said Ben. "But sometimes I can't find any comfort in knowing it."

Dawdi nodded. "That's okay. So long as you know it's there for you, you can reach out and take Jesus's comfort when you're ready."

"I do. Sometimes I'm strong. But some days the thought of being an invalid frightens me."

"Are you afraid of a wheelchair?"

"If only that were the worst thing. Soon I won't be able to feed myself, then swallow, then breathe."

Dawdi looked more afflicted than Ben had ever seen him. "Oh. My boy. My heart is shattered." He gave Ben a stiff hug. "Did Emma reject you when she found out?"

"I couldn't tell her. She would have insisted on caring for me, and I couldn't bear the thought of it." Ben blinked back the tears. The hardest, most gut-wrenching thing he'd ever done was telling Emma that he wanted to break off the engagement. He'd found the thought of facing her so unbearable, he'd considered going to Florida without telling her and letting Lizzie break the news. The expression on Emma's face that day was seared into his memory. Even though he was still upright, his heart had stopped beating the moment he'd left Emma standing there trembling with emotion, trying to make sense of what he had told her.

Ben shook his head to clear it of the memory. "I wanted to be the one to take care of Emma, not make her feel obligated to take care of me."

"So you *do* love her."

"More than my own life."

Dawdi widened his eyes in astonishment. "How does your mammi do it? She knew all along."

Mammi? How had Mammi known? The realization stunned him. He had truly been blind. "She invited me to Huckleberry Hill to get me back with Emma, didn't she?"

"That was the plan."

Ben lowered his head as the tears overcame him. "I wish she hadn't. Everything is worse now."

"Because you realize you don't want to live without her."

"No," Ben said. "My life, my happiness doesn't matter. I'll be dead in a couple years anyway. But Emma . . . She's got to move on. She's got to find someone who can love her and care for her. She doesn't deserve to be stuck caring for an invalid who'll make her a widow before she's twenty-five. I won't do that to her."

"Have you asked her how she feels about that?"

Ben grimaced. "Don't you see, Dawdi? I'm not strong enough to protect her, and I don't want her to be shackled to a cripple. How long would it take before she resented my illness? How long before she hated the very sight of me?"

"That doesn't sound like the Emma I know," Dawdi said quietly. "Do you think so little of her? Don't you believe she would willingly suffer the hardship to be with you?"

Ben bowed his head. "Certainly at first she would. I doubt she's ever had a selfish thought in her life. If I told her about my condition, she would insist on staying with me, but even someone as good as Emma isn't immune to the resentment that's bound to grow. And even if resentment doesn't overtake her, think of the pain it would put her through to watch me die. In the end, whether she can see it or not, caring for me would take a heavy toll on her—a price I am not willing to let her pay. I went away to Florida for Emma's sake. I won't watch her suffer while she watches me die, and I won't allow her to sacrifice her life for mine. It's not right. She must live a full and happy life without the burden of a dying husband."

"And yet she suffers now."

Ben tried to ignore the pain that tore through him. Emma suffered greatly. "Let her remember me as I am now, young and healthy, not this shell of a man who can't even stand on his own two feet."

"You don't want Emma to see what you're going to become."

Ben trembled with emotion as pain stabbed him in the gut. "Someone will have to feed me and bathe me, Dawdi. If Emma married me, she would be the one to do it, to tend to my most personal needs."

"Emma is strong enough to bear it."

"But I'm not," Ben declared, before remembering himself and lowering his voice. Dawdi didn't need to see his descent into despair. He only let his composure disintegrate when he was by himself. "How can I bear for the woman I love to watch my body deteriorate, to watch me grow as weak and as helpless as a baby? Even just thinking about it terrifies me."

Dawdi wrapped his firm arms all the way around Ben and held on for dear life. Ben could feel the heaving of Dawdi's chest as he pressed his cheek against Ben's and their tears mingled together.

After several minutes of weeping, Dawdi pulled away and patted Ben on the shoulder. "That didn't make me feel any better," he said. "How about you?"

"I haven't felt better for months."

"Now," said Dawdi, stroking his beard. "What to do."

"There's nothing to do except send me back to Florida. I want to die with my dignity intact."

"Have you talked to God about this?"

"He won't heal me." Although for months he had tried not to be mad at God, bitterness crept into his voice. "It's wicked to ask God for things that are clearly against His will."

"Oh, no," Dawdi said firmly. "The Lord Jesus asked God to take the cup of gall from Him. We must accept what God ordains for each of us, but there is no sin in pleading. His own Son did the same."

Ben turned his face away. "I plead all the time."

"But did you get God's permission to move to Florida and separate yourself from everyone who loves you? Where have you put God in all this?"

"What else could I do? I don't want Emma or Mamm or Lizzie to waste one day caring for me."

"And who will care for you in Florida?" Dawdi said.

"The government. I've already looked into a home run by Medicare."

Dawdi shook his head. "You'd rather rely on strangers?"

"They get paid."

Dawdi grunted, rocked back and forth, and stood up. "I can only sit on the floor for so long before I go stiff as a board." Hunching over like a ninety-year-old man, he returned to his stool. "When your dat needed a barn built, he didn't rely on the government. And he couldn't have done it himself. The whole community helped, and we had that barn up in a day. There are times when we need the help of our neighbors and families, and in return, we lend them aid when they need our help. The good Lord put people in your path so they can help you. Take His gift cheerfully."

"But I can't help anyone in return."

"What does that matter? You bless other people's lives when you let them help you. How can anybody receive blessings if nobody lets them serve?"

Ben knew what Dawdi would say, but he voiced his argument anyway. "I don't want to be the one receiving charity. I want to be the one giving it."

Dawdi's eyes twinkled. "Because receiving charity requires humility, and being humble does not suit you?"

Yep, that's what he thought Dawdi would say. "I've already told you. I won't be the weak one."

"Weakness is humiliating." Dawdi rested his elbows on his knees. "When you carried Emma home after that buggy accident, what did you get in return?"

"Happiness because I could help her."

"You didn't resent having to carry her all that way in the hot sun?"

"This isn't the same, Dawdi."

"And were you glad that Emma was humiliated instead of you?"

"I know what you're trying to do, Dawdi, but this is different. I'm not going to get better. I'm never going to overcome the trial. It will be one degradation after another." He interrupted himself and raised his hands in surrender. "And you're going to ask me what better way is there to learn humility."

Dawdi chuckled, picked up the file, and continued sharpening his hoe. "You catch on mighty quick."

"By the time I die, I think I will have learned plenty of humility," Ben said. "But I don't have to drag Emma into it."

Dawdi pointed the file at Ben. "So you don't want Emma to have a say in her own life."

"I know if she chose me, she would be making the wrong choice." Ben felt less sure of his argument the more he tried to defend himself. "She doesn't understand the consequences of deciding to stay with me."

"Do you?"

Ben lowered his eyes. "I understand enough."

Dawdi turned his attention back to sharpening the hoe. "If things were reversed and Emma had

your disease, would you be relieved if she rejected
your help?" he said, almost casually, as if he were
talking about the weather.

Of course he wouldn't. The muscles in Ben's jaw
tightened until he thought he might never be able
to open his mouth again. He wanted to marry
Emma more than anything. He loved her. Taking
care of her would be the greatest joy of his life.

Even if he had to feed and wash and carry her.

Even if . . .

Let Dawdi believe what he wanted to believe
about humility and God. Ben didn't need more humility. His illness lent him his daily share of grovel-
ing, crushing humility. He needed solitude and
distance. He needed to get away from Emma and
Huckleberry Hill, to finish out his life on his terms,
not Dawdi's or Mamm's or Emma's.

Finding new strength in his legs, he pulled himself to his feet, located the fertilizer, and tromped to
the pumpkin patch without another word to Dawdi.
Only after he fertilized the pumpkin did it hit him.
He thought he wanted to live and die on his own
terms, but what about God's terms? Did God's will
make any difference to him anymore?

He knelt down and lifted his face to the sky.
"Heavenly Father, I've never thought much about
what You want for me beyond the fact that You
won't heal me. You have my heart. Will you break
Emma's as well?"

Was that what God did—afflict people with diseases and heartache and sit back to watch how they

dealt with it? Did He stand ready to smite Ben down at the least sign of unfaithfulness and doubt? Did God want Emma to suffer for something she couldn't control?

That was not the God Ben believed in. "God is love," the Apostle John had said.

If God loves me, what does He want me to learn? How does He want me to think? What does He want me to do? How will His purposes be fulfilled if I submit to the humiliation of letting Emma care for me?

More importantly, what does He want for Emma?

How would Ben ever know God's will for Emma? If he opened his heart to her, would she make the wrong decision? And would he welcome her back with open arms when he should push her away?

Dawdi had been right. He knew nothing, absolutely nothing about humility. Suddenly, Ben felt like a babe when it came to humbly seeking for God's will. His prayer changed. "Dear Father, I believe. Help Thou my unbelief."

He stood and ran his hand over Emma's giant pumpkin. It had to weigh nearly five hundred pounds by now. Like faith, pumpkins took a long time to grow. He would pray and wait and continue to pray. Eventually God would show him the way.

Chapter 15

When she saw him, she fought the impulse to run for the shelter of the trees. Instead, she did her best to ignore him altogether—or rather, pretend to ignore him. It was impossible to actually ignore Ben Helmuth. With his height, good looks, and quiet self-assurance, he commanded attention in every room he walked into, every gathering he attended. She couldn't shake him. She would just have to endure him.

Why did Ben still come to gatherings? If he found her so repulsive, Emma would have thought he'd steer clear of any place she'd be likely to show up. Didn't he know she attended every gathering within ten miles? He must know, and yet he continued to come.

Not that he did much socializing. He hung back, apart from the usual crowd of young people, and watched—didn't watch anyone in particular—just watched, as if he were the security guard. Emma found it unnerving.

She and Adam had come together, of course. The empty field would be a gute place for a bonfire. Jethro Gingerich had purchased the property a couple of months ago. It sat to the west of Shawano Lake, and Jethro boasted that he had made a wonderful-gute deal on lakefront land, even though the property didn't sit within walking distance of the lake. Still, the land had potential. Some sort of a structure had stood right where Jethro tended the fire, but other than that, the forty acres consisted of meadows and thick stands of maple and aspen trees. Emma thought it was the perfect spot for a small home and Amish farm.

Jethro and Dinah Hoover were engaged. There would be a home on the property soon enough.

An area big enough for a campfire and a circle of chairs sat in the clearing. Adam carried two lawn chairs and a grocery bag. He glanced at the fire, already blazing. "I brought two bags of marshmallows," he said. "Hopefully you don't end up burning all of them," he said, chuckling as if Emma's mishaps were the funniest thing in the world. Why did he laugh at her? Her penchant for accidents was old news.

She helped Adam set up the chairs near the fire, being careful not to pinch her fingers. She handled camp chairs well when she concentrated. To avoid Adam's teasing, she'd been concentrating very hard for the last two months.

Emma sighed inwardly. She and Adam had been spending a lot of time together, and Emma had done her utmost to make it work. She spent time with Adam's parents and siblings playing game after incessant game. She thought that if she had to play Life on the Farm one more time, she might just have to poke her own eyes out.

She baked bread and pastries for Adam and his family and always laughed at his tired jokes and undisguised sarcasm. Although she could tell her clumsiness annoyed him, he showed no signs of dumping her like Ben had done. At least he was sticking with her.

She wanted to growl. The boy she wanted wouldn't be caught dead within ten feet of her. Unfortunately, the boy she didn't want proved to be as loyal as a hound dog. Loyal but hurtfully sarcastic.

Emma slumped into one of the lawn chairs. There was a girl out there who would surely love Adam for the person he was, but not Emma. She couldn't keep up the pretense much longer. Every word Adam spoke sounded like fingernails against a chalkboard. And if he teased her one more time about burning down the chicken coop and being too scatterbrained to bake a decent loaf of bread, she might lose her temper and bite his head off.

Even though it wouldn't be dark for another three hours, Jethro had wanted to start the fire early so they could get some good coals for roasting bratwurst.

Adam laid the grocery bag in his lawn chair.

"Come on, Emma, let's go play volleyball." He laughed. "But I should have brought a helmet for you to wear."

Emma didn't even favor him with a courtesy laugh. She'd heard the helmet joke one too many times.

She and Adam stood together at the net. She didn't have to move a muscle. Adam hogged every ball that came her way.

Ben stood more than a hundred feet away with his back against a tree and his hands shoved into his pockets. Emma looked away when she thought Ben's gaze might be traveling in her direction. Under no circumstances did she want to make eye contact with Ben Helmuth. Lizzie sat in a lawn chair next to Dinah and Martha Weaver. Emma couldn't hear what they were saying, but Lizzie gestured with great animation and the three girls laughed hysterically. Emma's mouth twisted upward. No one could tell a story like Lizzie.

While Serena Kanagy tried to get a serve over the net, Emma turned her gaze in the other direction. Mahlon could have been Ben's twin, holding up another tree on the opposite side of the clearing. Mahlon made no bones about staring straight at Lizzie and scowling as if she'd insulted his entire family. Lizzie and Mahlon hadn't spoken to each other in almost a month, and Mahlon became more surly with every passing day. He often passed his time helping Emma in the vegetable patch at home, turning out to be a big help once Emma had made it clear that if he wanted to spend time with her, he must stop speaking ill of the Helmuth family.

He did a pretty good job of controlling his mouth, except she often heard him mumbling things under his breath whenever he hoed pumpkins.

Emma felt as if she were sinking. It was her fault that Mahlon and Lizzie were out of sorts with each other, and no less her fault that Ben looked so stricken all the time. How could he be happy when he really wanted to go back to Florida where some beautiful Amish girl waited for him? A girl who probably looked stunning in a swimming suit and didn't have one scar on her entire face.

Ben would never settle for a girl who did something as mundane as grow pumpkins. His Florida girl probably baked perfectly round blueberry muffins and sewed beautiful dresses with her eyes closed.

Emma swallowed the lump in her throat and reminded herself to pretend to ignore Ben—to ignore the memory of his lips pressed against hers while the rain kissed her cheeks as they stood in the pumpkin patch.

Breathe, Emma.

Anna's pumpkin probably weighed five hundred pounds by now. Or maybe, if he wanted to erase any evidence of her existence, Ben had taken an ax and chopped it into little pieces, just as he'd done with her heart.

She hadn't seen it coming, but an errant volleyball to the head knocked some sense into her.

Pretend to ignore him, remember?

Out of the corner of her eye, she saw Ben give a little jerk and push himself slightly away from the tree. Was that little movement because she'd been smacked in the head with a ball?

Adam smirked. "I can't take you anywhere, Emma."

His words stung, even though she'd heard enough of his sarcasm that she should have been numb to it. She frowned and looked away on the pretense of being on the lookout for other dangerous balls in the vicinity.

She managed to launch the next volleyball that came her way. Unfortunately, it ricocheted off her arms and caught Adam squarely in the nose. He jerked his head back in shock and covered his nose with his hand.

"Sorry," Emma said, feeling sorry that she wasn't all that sorry. His eyes teared up but she didn't see any blood, praise the Lord. She'd never hear the end of it if she broke Adam's nose. "Do you need some ice?"

He nodded, and they walked out of the volleyball game. Emma found ice in a red cooler and wrapped it in a paper towel and handed it to Adam. He winced as he gently laid it over the bridge of his nose.

"Does it hurt?" Emma said.

"Not too bad, but I don't want it to swell. I forgot

how dangerous it is to play games with you. Then again, every activity is dangerous for you."

They stood and watched the volleyball game for a few minutes. Emma didn't dare say a word for fear Adam would come up with some cutting remark that she wasn't especially eager to hear.

He pulled the ice away from his nose. "How does it look? Is it swollen?"

"A little," she said.

He reapplied the ice and fell silent. Emma squirmed in discomfort. She'd really done it this time. He wasn't even amused enough to tease her.

After a few minutes, Adam laid his towel of ice on top of the cooler and wiped his hands on his trousers. "Can we take a walk?" he said.

"Where do you want to go?"

Adam looked especially glum even though his nose appeared to be near normal size. "Let's go explore."

"Uh. Okay."

"I'll bet there's all sorts of fun hiding spots around here, but stay close to me. I don't want you getting lost again." His lips twitched. "I knew I should have brought my cowbell."

Emma was tempted to moo. She held it in rather admirably while she followed Adam down a lightly worn path into the woods beyond the fire.

They followed the trail until it disappeared, and then they marked their path by taking note of unusual trees and brilliantly bright wildflowers. They couldn't have gone more than a half mile, but it seemed to Emma that they'd walked forever.

"What are you hoping to find on our little expedition?" Emma asked as she caught her toe on a dry root and nearly fell on her face.

Adam pushed a branch aside and let it go. It whipped back and smacked her in the shoulder. Adam didn't pause in his progress.

They emerged from the thicket into a clearing that looked as if it had been used before. Emma could see buggy tracks overgrown with weeds and a small pile of weather-worn boards long abandoned, a pretty spot with wildflowers dotting the meadows and lots of blue sky overhead.

Adam stopped walking and turned to face her. "I hope you didn't mind the hike." He took her hand and studied her face with an unreadable expression in his eyes.

Was he going to propose? Did he want to hike far enough away that no one would overhear him profess his undying love?

Emma's heart did not leap with anticipation like it should have at the prospect of a marriage proposal. Her stomach felt empty as if she hadn't eaten a thing all day, and at the moment, she wanted to take a nice, long nap. What was wrong with her?

She frowned to herself when she realized that she felt completely indifferent to the idea of an engagement with Adam Wengerd.

Adam huffed out a breath of air as if preparing to do a bothersome task. "I wanted to walk far enough from the others so you aren't embarrassed if you happen to be a loud crier."

"Loud crier?"

He slipped his hands into his pockets and kicked a pebble at his feet. "Emma, I like you. I really do. You're pretty and sweet and a really nice girl, but my mamm says I have to break up with you yet."

Emma was glad that there was no wind. A light breeze could have knocked her backward. "What?"

"I mean . . . my mamm really likes you even though you've never made an edible loaf of bread. The chicken coop thing last summer was enough to make my mamm have her doubts. It made us all a little wary of you, but Mamm overlooked it since you're from a gute family and have always been so kind to us."

Emma's mouth felt as dry as sawdust. How much of a menace was she really?

Adam made no indication that he noticed she had turned to stone. "Mamm was understandably upset when you spilled rice all over that Englischer at the benefit dinner, and she held her tongue when I told her how you nearly burned down the lake with a marshmallow."

Emma longed to point out that even she couldn't have burned down the lake, but her jaw clenched so tightly she couldn't open her mouth.

"I laughed about it, but your getting lost on the day of the fireworks turned out to be the last straw. Mamm demanded I cut you off immediately. I've put off breaking it off because I hoped your little accidents would get better. Besides, I wasn't really keen to see you get hurt two summers in a row. After the blackened apple pie last week, my mamm put her foot down. She's afraid if we got married you'd burn our house down or lose one of her grandchildren."

Emma thought she might faint. The emotions swirling around in her head made her dizzy.

"And when she sees my nose, she'll volunteer to break up with you for me. I'm sorry, Emma. I can't date you anymore." He shrugged and twisted his mouth into a sheepish grin. "But I hope we can still be friends."

Why was she so shocked? Of course she knew what people thought of her. They joked about her clumsiness frequently enough. Why did she feel as if she had been swept away by an avalanche of boulders and gravel?

They hated her. They all hated her, most especially Ben Helmuth and his parents. Ben's mamm, like all other Amish mamms, wanted her son to have nothing to do with such a girl.

Emma wrapped her arms around her waist. She'd lose one of the grandchildren as sure as you're born.

Adam fiddled with the brim of his hat. "You probably want to be alone."

"Probably."

"Can you find your way back to the fire? It's a

pretty good trail, and you can follow the sound of voices."

Emma stared at Adam without really seeing him. She couldn't be sad he'd broken up with her, but his reasons for doing so stung like a swarm of wasps.

She didn't want to marry Adam. She even felt a twinge of relief that now she wouldn't have to feel obligated to tell him yes. Mamm said Adam was her last chance, but even if Adam hadn't rejected her, hopes for marriage were gone. She could never bring herself to settle for anyone less than Ben.

Why was Adam still standing there? "You don't mind, do you?" he said.

"I'll find my way back."

He bloomed into a full-blown, I'm-off-the-hook smile. "Denki, Emma. I want to invite Martha to ride home with me before anyone else has a chance to ask her." He patted her awkwardly on the shoulder. "I always thought you were the nicest girl."

He marched away without a backward glance. Emma was glad for it. At least he wouldn't see the tears that coursed down her cheeks.

She turned and strolled in the opposite direction. How tired she was of crying! If only she knew how to cut Ben from her heart. If only she could be the perfect girl who never burned the bread and never sewed through her own fingers.

What now? Ben didn't want her. Adam's mamm didn't want her. Mahlon and Lizzie despised each other. The Zimmermans had lost a chicken coop because of her. The entire community thought she was a nuisance. Except for growing pumpkins and vegetables, of what use was she to anybody? If she went away, not even Mamm would miss her. Mamm thought she was a troublesome child.

She followed the lightly worn buggy path until it ended at the center of the meadow. Dried grass and moss sprouted amongst the old boards and logs piled there. Maybe someone had planned on building something here years ago and abandoned it later. Emma walked across one of the boards on the ground as if she were poised on a tightrope. Sometimes she could keep her balance.

She didn't even have time to be surprised as she heard a sickening crack and the ground seemed to fall out from under her. She screamed as she plunged into the darkness.

Ben stood sentinel for nearly ten minutes. Emma and Adam didn't return. Even though he had come to the gathering to make sure Emma stayed safe, he'd promised himself that he'd avoid her unless there was an emergency. Was this an emergency? He had no idea, because Adam had recklessly walked Emma into the woods and away from Ben's protection.

He kept his eyes glued to the path Emma and Adam had taken into the thicket. They'd been gone a long time. If they'd walked far, no one would hear them cry for help.

He couldn't stand it anymore. Resolving to take

Adam aside and sternly lecture him about safety, he growled and stomped into the woods to find them. Lord willing, he'd locate them before they knew he was spying.

The forest floor grew thick with grass and wildflowers, but Ben could still make out a trail. He didn't know what he'd do if Adam had foolishly strayed from it. He was so focused on keeping sight of the trail that he almost ran into Adam coming the other way.

"Ben," Adam said. "What are you doing?"

"Where's Emma?"

Adam pointed. "In a clearing just through those trees over there. She wanted to be alone."

Ben furrowed his brow. "You should never leave her by herself."

Adam didn't look the least bit contrite as he thumbed his suspenders. "We broke up. She acted like she needed some time to think about it."

Ben didn't know whether to be horrified or elated. "You broke up?"

Adam put a hand on Ben's shoulder. "Hey, I appreciate you trying to get us together, but Emma isn't right for me."

Adam didn't have to tell him that. The mismatch was obvious. But how did Emma feel about it?

"She's nice and all, but every time I turn around, she's got herself into more trouble. Like I told Emma, my mamm isn't keen on the thought of me marrying someone so accident-prone. She urged me to break it off."

Adam might as well have shoved him to the ground and stomped on his chest. "You told Emma that?"

"She took it well."

Adam's unconcerned attitude only heightened Ben's sense of urgency to get to Emma. She'd be upset. Ben had always been able to reassure her that nobody thought less of her for her clumsiness.

Adam looked past him as if he were in a hurry to get away. "She's over there if you want to see for yourself."

Even with his weak legs, Ben practically ran in the direction Adam had pointed. Poor Emma. She didn't need one more reason to be upset. He halted in his tracks. What was he thinking? They hadn't spoken for weeks. He wouldn't be able to comfort her. He'd only make it worse.

He couldn't help her.

But he could at least be sure she made it back to the group safely.

He lightened his steps as he attempted to stifle any noise he made. He would sneak through the trees, find Emma, and spy on her until she hiked back to the fire. Only if she took a wrong turn would he reveal himself.

At the edge of the clearing, he found a tree thick enough to hide behind. Cautiously, he peered around it. Emma had her back to him, standing on what looked like a pile of abandoned lumber. She bent over to pick something off the ground, a wild-flower maybe. Then she spread her arms wide and balanced on a thin slat of wood. Ben's heart thumped loudly. When she didn't trip over herself, she was really quite graceful. He studied the curve of her fingers and the fluid motion of her arms as she walked the length of the board without stumbling once.

How he longed to brush his lips against those hands, to take her in his arms and kiss her to the clouds. He shook his head to before his thoughts ran away from him.

Ben heard a loud crack as a shocked cry escaped from Emma's lips. Before he registered what had happened, the wood gave way below her feet and she disappeared in a cloud of dust and splinters.

Emma! Gasping in panic, he sprinted for the spot where Emma had stood only moments before. About three-quarters of the way there, his legs gave out and he tripped. Something sharp stabbed into his hands as he tried to catch himself, and his right knee felt as if it were on fire. He tried to stand, but his numb legs wouldn't cooperate.

No, no! Not now. Not when Emma truly needed him.

Groaning in pain, he pushed himself to his hands and knees and, by sheer force of will, crawled the rest of the distance. He picked his way over the pile of lumber as quickly as his weak body would allow him, his heart pounding so loudly in his ears he could barely hear anything else.

A large and jagged hole, about four feet in diameter, gaped before him. Dread washed over him as he heard water sloshing below. An abandoned well.

"Emma!" he roared.

It was dark down there, but the rippling water reflected some sunlight, and he could just make out Emma's head bobbing above the water.

Heavenly Father, please help us.

To his relief and horror, he heard her splashing and sputtering. "Ben? Ben, help me," she screamed. Her voice echoed off the rough cement walls of the old well.

At the panic in her voice, a bolt of terror ripped through his body. Fear clamped an iron hand around his throat. He couldn't breathe, he couldn't stand, and he couldn't save her. He was going to lose it.

He took a shaky, difficult breath. "Is it deep? Can you touch the bottom?"

"No," she panted. "Nothing."

"Stay calm." One of them should. "Try to keep your head above the water."

"I can't . . . I can't see anything."

Ben squinted into the well. It must have been at least eight feet from the opening to the top of the water. He wouldn't be able to simply reach in and pull her out. He commanded his legs to move. With everything he had in him, he stood up and scanned the ground for anything he might be able to use to pull her out.

"Don't, don't leave me," she cried.

"I'll find something to pull you up with."

None of the old boards on the ground near the well were long enough. If he had strength to run, he could race to the nearest tree and rip off a long branch. But he didn't even understand how he managed to stand. He repeated his simple prayer over and over again.

Dear Lord, please help me. Help me.

"Emma, are you okay?" No answer. "Emma, answer me. Emma," he called, so frightened that tears leaked from his eyes and sweat beaded on his forehead.

He heard her take a deep, almost desperate breath. "I can't stay up. . . . I'm sinking."

"Don't you dare sink. Feel around. Is there a crack in the cement you can grab on to?"

Through the dimness, he saw her struggle to feel her way around the wall.

"It's smooth. There's nothing."

She reached for something above her head, but unable to find purchase, she slipped below the surface again.

"Don't give up," he yelled.

Her head bobbed above the water again, and Ben took a ragged breath. "Find a handhold. Keep looking."

He should have been searching for a rope or a long piece of wood, but he feared if he looked away she would sink into the black water and never come up again.

Panting heavily, she ran her hand along the wall

again. Ben willed her to find something, anything to hold on to.

"Oh!" she shouted after several breathless seconds of searching. "There's a little ledge above my head about three inches deep. Enough to hold on to."

"Good girl. Now don't let go. I'm going to find something to pull you out."

"Run for help."

"I'm not going anywhere." His legs wouldn't carry him two yards, let alone two miles. Even if he could run like the wind, he couldn't bear to tear himself away from her.

"I can hold on."

"It doesn't matter. I won't leave you."

His gaze darted around the pile of wood. Falling to his hands and knees again, he crawled to the biggest pile, moved boards and plywood out of his way to locate anything useful buried underneath. The boards got thicker and heavier as he dug, but he didn't find a rope or a ladder or even a piece of wire.

"Ben," Emma called.

"I'm here."

"There's a metal pipe sticking out of the cement above my head. It's too high to reach, but maybe if you tied something to it . . ."

Ben crawled back to the hole. "I don't see it."

Emma pointed to a curved metal pipe about three feet from the top of the well, protruding half a foot out of the cement, that he'd somehow overlooked.

"Emma, I'm going to grab on to the pipe and then swing down to get you. Do you think you can reach my hand?"

"I'll try."

It was the best he could hope for. He prayed that his arms stayed strong and that he'd be able to support his weight and Emma's hanging from a rusty piece of pipe. He flexed his hand. A deep gash, slippery with blood, traveled up his palm. He swiped his hand across his trousers to remove the blood. He'd fight through the pain for Emma's sake.

He slid on his stomach to the edge of the well and reached for the pipe with his good hand. Too far by a foot. He'd have to scoot until half his body hung over the edge. His legs were no help as he pulled himself over the edge to grip the pipe. It was flaky with rust, but it felt securely anchored in the cement. Lord willing, it would support both of them.

Clamping his fist around the pipe, he grunted as he let his body follow him into the well. He hadn't counted on momentum. Without his legs to give him support, his body swung wildly and he lost his grip. He cried out as his legs bounced against the hard cement wall and he fell head over heels. Sharp pain exploded inside his head as he plunged into the chilly water. Emma plastered herself against the wall, and he missed her by inches. He felt his feet nudge the bottom of the well before he flailed his arms to return to the surface.

Coughing and spitting water out of his mouth, he said a prayer of gratitude in his mind. If he'd fallen on Emma, he could have broken her neck.

"Ben, are you okay?"

He saw the uncertainty in her eyes. She had seen his weakness, how he hadn't been able to brace himself with his legs. He averted his eyes even as he felt himself slipping away from her. He couldn't even kick his legs to keep himself afloat.

He began to sink. With eyes widening in alarm, Emma hooked her free arm around his elbow, and with a strength that he hadn't expected, held him above the water. "I need your help, Ben. Can't you help us? We've got to get out of here."

Ben took every breath as if it might be his last. How could he bear the shame when Emma finally realized the truth? He had no other choice. If there was any chance for her at all, she had to know that he couldn't save her. "Emma, I can't move my legs."

Her eyes flashed with panic as doubt tugged at the corners of her mouth. "I don't understand. What's wrong?"

He shoved the words out of his mouth. "I'm worthless, Emma. My legs are no good. You've got to save yourself."

She frowned in puzzlement before shaking her head. "If you can't move, I'll hold you up."

"I'm too heavy."

"There's a way out. We can help each other."

Ben growled as panic threatened to paralyze him completely. Emma had always depended on him.

She needed him, and he could do absolutely nothing. "You've got to get yourself out, Emma."

"I can't."

Anger sharpened his words. "I can't save you. Stop acting like a helpless child, and get yourself out."

The whole world seemed to fall silent as her eyes met his and flashed with pain like he'd never seen before. Her sorrow tore him in half, and even though he hadn't really meant it, he didn't repent of what he'd said. He would have said anything to get her out of there.

"You think I'm a child?"

"You have to take care of yourself yet."

She bowed her head, and her tears plopped into the water like a dripping faucet. "I'm nobody without you."

"You have to be. It's too late for us."

She tightened her grip around his elbow and pressed her lips into a rigid line. "What do you want me to do?"

"Climb on my shoulders and see if you can reach the pipe. If you pull yourself up, you can run for help."

She wouldn't make it back in time to save him. With useless legs, he couldn't keep his head above water. But he could save her, and that was all he cared about.

Maybe it was better to die this way, quick and painless, rather than linger for months in a body that wouldn't do his bidding. His family would be sad, but it would spare them the suffering of losing him a little every day, waiting for him to die.

"What's wrong with your legs? Did you hit your head?"

"Get on my shoulders, Emma."

She shook her head. "My weight will push you under."

"Only for a second."

Panting, she studied his face in the dimness. "You'll drown."

"Nae, I won't. I will be okay until you get back."

"If I let go, you won't be able to pull yourself back up," Emma said. "I'm the only reason you're not at the bottom."

"That's not true. I can hold on to the ledge." He had to convince her. He refused to let her die down here with him. "Neither of us is going to get out of here if you don't go, and you know it."

Doubt traveled across her face. She looked up at the pipe that was their only option. "Don't ask me to—"

"Do it, Emma."

She blinked back her tears and lifted her chin. "Okay."

If he weren't about to drown, he would almost feel relieved.

"But you must do something for me."

"Anything," he said.

"Give me your scarf."

Scarf? He'd forgotten that Mammi had made him a lime green scarf for the party because "green is a healing color," she had said. He had slung it around his neck right before he left the house because it pleased Mammi to see him wearing her scarves, even in mid-August.

He almost smiled. "I have a scarf," he said, unwrapping it from around his neck. Praise the Lord he hadn't lost it in the fall. "Can you use it to pull yourself up?"

She still clutched the ledge with one hand and his arm with the other. With his free hand, he looped the scarf around her neck.

He blinked as something warm dripped down the side of his face. He wiped it away and then looked at his hand. Blood. He must have hit his head when he fell. "Is it bad?"

Her expression looked grim. "Not at all."

"Can you can pull yourself out of the water far enough to get on my shoulders? You might be able to loop the scarf around that pipe."

She nodded. "Take off your shirt."

"What?" he sputtered. "We don't have time—"

"Benjamin Helmuth, don't argue with me. Take off your shirt."

He stared at her. Something told him it would be pointless and foolish to argue. If she wanted his shirt, he'd give her his shirt if it would do anything to hurry her along. He wanted her safely out of the well before he lost the strength to hold himself up. His arms already shook. It was only a matter of minutes.

It proved difficult to unbutton his shirt with only

one hand, but he did it as quickly as possible, ripping the last two buttons off with a flick of his wrist. He slid one arm out of the sleeve, and she released him momentarily as he shrugged the other sleeve off his arm. Without her support, he sank immediately. As soon as the shirt came off, she snatched his arm in hers.

She slid her fingers away from the ledge. "Put your hand here," she said.

He did as he was told. His thin undershirt gave him little protection from the rough concrete wall, and the ledge would be his only support when she stood on his shoulders. He could barely keep hold of it. The cold water numbed his hands. Soon he would be completely immobile. He only had to hold on long enough for Emma to believe he was secure. No need for her to watch him die.

She took one end of the scarf and one of the shirtsleeves and tied them together with a square knot.

At the other end of the scarf, she tied a slipknot. She could slide it around the pipe and pull it tight. Despite their dire circumstances, she was thinking straight. Better than he was thinking at the moment, that was certain.

She draped the scarf and shirt around her neck. "I'm sorry," she said as she took his arm and used it to pull herself behind him. Clutching his shoulders, she nuzzled her cheek against his ear. Then she made him tremble as she brushed her lips across his jaw. He thought he had never experienced a more tender moment in his life.

"Don't let go of that ledge," she whispered. Pressing on his shoulders, she heaved herself upward, first raising her knees and then balancing to anchor her feet on his shoulders.

Ben grunted in agony and tightened his muscles, straining harder than he'd ever done in his life as her shoes dug into his shoulders. Despite his best efforts, he couldn't hold on. His fingers were wrenched from the ledge by the force of Emma's weight. Unready for the sudden force downward, he swallowed several mouthfuls of water as he went under. Emma still stood on his shoulders, pushing him farther and farther down. Would he ever come up again?

Ben didn't realize how badly he wanted to live until he sensed he was drowning. He desperately tried to kick his way to the surface, but his useless legs only served to weigh him down.

Good-bye, Emma. My last and every thought was of you.

Suddenly he felt light as a feather. She'd made it. Emma had pulled herself out of the well. He could die now.

He sensed a splash and felt a warm pair of arms clamp around his chest and hold him tight. Had Emma fallen back into the water?

Don't try to save me. Save yourself, Emma. Go and live a happy life. Let me die.

Just as his feet brushed the bottom, she dragged

him upward into the blessed air. He spewed water from his mouth and greedily gulped oxygen into his lungs. Maybe he wanted to live another day, after all.

With her arms wrapped tightly around him, Emma pulled him to the tiny ledge. "Can you hold on?"

"What are you doing? You've got to get out."

"Can you grab it before we both sink again?"

His arm felt as stiff as a cold piece of leather, but he managed to raise it high enough to hook his fingers onto the ledge.

Emma's labored breathing and his uncontrollable wheezing echoed against the concrete walls. It couldn't have been easy to pull a six-foot-plus body out of the water.

He looked up. Emma had managed to loop the scarf around the pipe. Tied securely to the right sleeve of his shirt, the scarf and shirt together reached all the way to the surface of the water. Emma gripped the end of the other sleeve in her fist to keep herself afloat.

"Pull yourself up, Emma. You've got to get out of here."

She touched her fingers to a tender spot on Ben's forehead. "I'm taking you with me."

"Emma," Ben growled.

"Don't argue. You're wasting energy." She plunged her arm into the water and found his free hand. "I need you to keep me afloat for a minute," she said, resting her elbow on his outstretched arm. He dug his fingers into the hard cement. He wouldn't lose his grip when she needed him so badly.

With her elbow hooked over his arm, her hands were free to tie the dangling shirtsleeve around his wrist.

"What are you doing?"

"For a boy who seldom says a word, you ask a lot of questions. Save your breath. You might need it."

Ben wasn't used to being the one taking orders. Frustration tightened his chest. "Emma, get out of here and go find help. Do you want us both to drown?"

To his surprise, she wrapped her arms around his neck and pulled him close. "I don't want either of us to drown," she whispered. When she pulled away from him, her eyes glistened with tears. It sent a knife right through his heart.

"That's why you've got to pull yourself out," he protested weakly.

"This sleeve will keep you from going under, but hang on to the ledge too. I don't know how tight Anna's knitting is."

With both hands, she grabbed on to her shirt-and-scarf rope and pulled. Bracing her feet against the cement wall and gripping his shirt, she slowly climbed the makeshift rope. Water from her dress rained down on Ben as he breathlessly watched her progress. Inch by inch she crawled up the wall, taking care not to move too fast and lose her footing.

Near the top, she reached for the pipe and wrapped her fingers around it, first one hand and then the other.

His breath stuck in his throat as he watched her dangling from the small pipe that was her salvation. It stuck out only three feet from the top, but how would she ever be able to pull herself the rest of the way up? "You can do it," he lied. She wouldn't be able to reach above her when she needed both hands to hold fast to the pipe.

He felt his own fingers slipping from their hold on the ledge. How long would the makeshift rope keep him up?

Her knuckles turned white, and she panted as if there weren't enough air in the entire world to fill her lungs. Her mouth drooped in exhaustion, but even from below Ben could see her eyes blaze with determination. A gut-wrenching groan bubbled from deep in her throat as she lifted her legs and kicked at a patch of cracked cement just below the pipe. Flakes of old cement plopped into the water like hail as she pounded the wall again and again.

"Hang on, Emma. You can do it."

"Look out," she yelled as she dislodged an apple-sized chunk of cement.

Ben ducked and shifted his weight to the right as the cement tumbled. The movement proved too much for his shaky arms. His fingers slipped from the ledge, and he didn't have the strength to put them back. The scarf and the shirt pulled taut and the fabric tightened around his wrist. It was a gute thing Emma had tied him to his own shirt. He wouldn't have been able to keep hold of it by his own power.

In awe, Ben watched as Emma kicked again and again, all the while anchoring herself to that pipe. How could she keep hold like that?

Another chunk of cement, this one the size of a loaf of bread, crashed into the water. Her breathing had turned ragged and wheezy, like an asthmatic in the throes of a life-threatening attack. Surely, she was absolutely spent.

"Emma," Ben whispered, barely able to keep his head above water. Emma's rope might have been securely attached, but the effort it took to bend his elbow enough to keep his head above the water was almost too much. His legs felt heavy, so heavy.

Emma shoved one foot into the hole she'd pounded out of the wall. In an amazing feat of balance, she braced the other foot on the pipe and in one swift movement catapulted herself to the surface. She expelled another scream straight from her gut as her upper body disappeared over the top and her legs followed.

She was out!

Thank You, Heavenly Father. God is good.

Ben's lifeline jerked, and he heard a ripping sound. His heart lurched. The sleeves were about to give way. No matter how well sewn they were, they couldn't bear two-hundred-plus pounds indefinitely.

But it didn't matter. Emma had gotten out.

He stared intently at the spot where Emma had disappeared. He longed for one more kiss, ached to tell her that he'd never really left her, that he loved her more than his own life.

He hung his head in exhaustion as a single tear rolled down his cheek. He'd be gone before she got back. Still, he clung to his rope, determined not to go down without a fight. He wanted to live, to see Emma's smile one more time.

With his gaze pointed heavenward, he held perfectly still. Now that she was gone, the silence of the deep well pressed on him until he thought his ears might explode. Who knew silence could be so deafening?

His tethered arm felt so tired. He let it relax, and his face slipped beneath the water. Just for a second. He must rest for only a second. When his lungs felt like they would explode in their need for air, he pulled up on his shirt and his head rose above the water. The effort sent searing pain ripping up his arm and through his shoulder. His arm might give out before his shirt did. He glanced up. Mammi's scarf held firm. She was the best knitter in the whole world.

His arm trembled so badly his entire body shook. Not much longer now. Completely drained of all energy, he relaxed his arm again and felt the profound relief to his shoulder as he slipped underwater. Holding his breath, he wondered if he would have the strength to pull himself up one more time.

"Ben!" Emma screamed. Her voice sounded muffled and strange to his ears.

He must be dying. Emma could not have returned so quickly.

A scrape and a splash. Someone yanked his arm so hard it felt as if it had been pulled from its socket. His head broke through the surface, and he gulped in as much air as he could get.

"Emma," he gasped. She was back in the water. A tortured groan died in his throat. He had no strength to voice it even though the anger and frustration boiled inside him.

Her hair had escaped from its bun. The sodden golden locks fell around her shoulders like tendrils of seaweed, but she was still the most beautiful girl in the world. Her eyes were wild as she clutched his helpless arm and studied his face. "Stay with me, Ben," she growled.

Her arm curled so tightly around his that it almost cut off his circulation. Her other elbow hooked around a weathered wooden ladder. The bottom half was invisible beneath the water and the top rails leaned against the wall of the well inches below the pipe. She must have lowered it into the well while he had been underwater.

Ben fought for breath, dizzy with relief. "How are . . . Where did you find that?"

"Buried below a tangle of bindweed. By the grace of God, it's long enough. I prayed hard."

The ladder looked to be decades old, with cracking silver wood and rusty bolts holding it together. Emma tightened her grip on his arm, and the ladder creaked in protest.

"Why did you come back? I told you to go get help," Ben said.

"And I told you I wouldn't leave you."

Using Emma's strong grip as leverage, he shifted to the left and curled his fingers around one of the rails. "When did you become so stubborn?"

"About ten minutes ago."

"When you fell in, I looked all over for a ladder. Couldn't find one."

After she made sure his grip was firm, she released his arm and let out a huge breath. "If there's one thing I know, it's how to spot something out of place in a garden. Come on. I'll help you climb up."

He bowed his head in defeat, so ashamed to admit weakness to Emma. "I don't think I can make it."

"You will make it. I'm stubborn enough for the both of us."

Maintaining her hold on the ladder, she grabbed his wrist with the sleeve still tied around it and placed his hand on the highest rung he could reach.

"We don't have much time," she said. "This ladder could disintegrate into dust any minute now."

It might not disintegrate, but Ben feared it would crack under his weight. "It's not going to hold us."

"God is with us, Ben. It's going to hold. Can you pull yourself up rung by rung?"

He grunted, straining to lift his entire body out of the water with only the strength of his arms. His spent muscles gave out before he could grasp the next rung, and it was all he could do to keep hold of the ladder at all.

Determination hardened the lines around Emma's mouth. After taking a deep breath, she disappeared into the murky water.

"Emma, don't." It terrified him to lose sight of her, even for a moment.

Below him, she nudged his legs in alignment with the ladder, then forced his foot upward, bending his knee for him. Still underwater, she propped his knee on a rung and then did the same with his other knee. Now his legs were more than dead weight, and Ben had enough leverage and strength to push himself up and reach the next rung.

Emma filled in behind him, marking progress by pushing his knees up each rung as she followed him. It was a slow, painstaking process. If he made any sudden movements or Emma leaned too near, the ladder creaked and threatened to break. How it held them even now, Ben would never know.

His hands finally reached the top rung of the ladder, three feet below solid ground. Emma pushed both of his legs up one more rung so that he knelt on the ladder, clinging to the top rung with his scraped and bleeding hands.

Leaning his forehead against the cool cement wall, he tried to catch his breath. He needed a thousand pounds of strength, but he only had a few ounces left. Behind him, Emma struggled for breath with labored rhythm. She'd already climbed out once. She had to be almost to the breaking point herself. Ben shifted his weight and the ladder creaked menacingly, as if giving a final warning.

"Push as hard as you can with your knees. There's some grass up there you might be able to grab on to."

Certain he couldn't move another inch, he mustered the last ounce of will he had left. For Emma's sake he would try. If he failed, Emma would go down with him.

Shoving his legs away from his body, he stretched his arms into the air and lunged for the top. His fingers latched on to a solid piece of wood at the surface that he gripped with all his might.

"Emma!" he cried as the ladder began to collapse beneath him.

He glanced back. Her foot found the protruding pipe, a few inches to the left, that had been their salvation more than once. She stomped on it and propelled herself out of the well before the ladder splintered into a hundred pieces and fell away.

She landed on her knees and seized Ben's arms. His legs dangled precariously into the pit. He couldn't do it. Even as Emma tried to anchor him with her grip, he felt himself slipping away.

"Don't let go," she grunted, sounding more angry than encouraging. Keeping hold of his elbows, she pulled herself to her knees to gain more leverage.

It was no use. She was nowhere near strong enough to hold on to him, and he was too out of breath to convince her how useless it was.

She lunged and hooked her arms securely around

his right upper arm. Bracing her knees against the cement at the edge of the well, she pulled, practically wrenching his arm from his shoulder socket.

A low, gut-splitting scream came from deep in her throat as slowly, inch by inch, she pulled him out. With what strength he had left, Ben clawed at the ground with his free hand. Suddenly, some of the sensation returned to his left leg, and he managed to drag it out of the well. Emma nearly laughed with relief as he braced his knee in the dirt and lent her the support she needed to pull him all the way out.

He did his best to crawl as she tugged him a few feet away from the gaping hole. Finally, far enough away from the danger, they collapsed to the ground, their lungs heaving violently in search of air.

"You saved me," he said.

"I've hefted a lot of pumpkins in my day," she whispered back.

Chapter 16

Her lungs were on fire. Every breath felt like a searing hole through her chest. She tried to sit up, to make sure Ben was okay, but she felt so weak, she didn't know if she would be able to rise ever again. Her shoulder throbbed, and when she tried to move her arm, pain tore through her like a jagged knife.

Relief flooded her, and she welcomed the rush of pain. If she had felt it earlier, she would never have been able to pull Ben from the well. She thanked the Lord with every agonizing breath she took.

"Ben?" She couldn't raise her voice above a whisper to save her life.

"Jah?"

"Just making sure you're still with me."

"Thanks to you."

After a few more groaning breaths, she gingerly rolled over and looked at him. He lay on his back, his eyes closed, with mud caking his hair and blood trickling from the wound on his forehead. Favoring her injured arm, she sat up and slid close to him. He might have looked a little worse for wear, but he was still as handsome as ever.

The hitch in her throat momentarily stopped her breath as she gazed at him. His body looked strong enough—the muscles of his chest and shoulders attested to that—but something was horribly wrong. He must be carrying some heavy burdens, probably had carried them for months, and he had chosen to carry them alone.

Nudging his head upward with her good arm, she scooted her knees over and he rested his head in her lap. He opened his eyes as she cradled his head and caressed his face.

"You have a goose egg on your eyebrow," he said weakly.

"You've got a wonderful-gute gash on your forehead," she replied, just as softly.

"Your cheek is bruised."

"You can't move your legs," she said. One of her tears splashed onto his cheek.

He frowned and closed his eyes. "Now you know."

"I don't know anything."

Wincing at the pain, he braced himself on his elbow and sat up. Raising his arm as if it weighed a hundred pounds, he tucked a lock of her tangled hair behind her ear. "I don't have much time left to live."

"What do you mean?"

"I have a terrible disease, Emma. It's called ALS

and the doctor said I've only got three or four more years at the most."

She trembled with shock and fatigue. "Are you sure?"

He gently laid his hand over hers and squeezed her fingers. "I'm sure. I'm dying, Emma, and I didn't want you to have to see it."

Every bit of strength Emma had left seeped from her limbs as dizziness overtook her. "That can't be true, Ben. I don't believe it."

He brought her fingers to his lips. "It's true. My muscles will deteriorate until I can't walk, then I'll have more trouble swallowing until I can't eat. Then I'll eventually stop breathing and die."

She yanked her hand from his grasp and tried to think. There must be some mistake. There must be some way to save him.

He bowed his head. "I'm sorry, Emma. I'm so sorry." She'd never heard such a forlorn sound.

She wasn't ready to accept an apology. There must be some way to stop this. "What did the doctor say? When did you talk to him?"

"Last summer."

A year ago?

"He said my muscles would slowly deteriorate until I couldn't walk or talk or feed myself."

A year ago?

The bile rose in her throat. She was going to be sick. "You . . . you left me."

"Jah," he whispered. "I left you."

"Why?" The question burst from her lips even

though she already knew the answer. She didn't even try to suppress the sob that followed. All these months of heartache because he didn't trust her with his pain? "You must think very little of me to believe that I would reject you because of an illness."

"Nae, Emma, I love you."

She choked on her grief. "You wanted to leave me before I had a chance to leave you."

Even though it must have been agony, he raised his hands and grasped her shoulders. She didn't even wince at the pain. "I left because I knew you wouldn't leave."

In one swift movement, he pulled her to him and brought his lips down on hers, creating a jolt of raw energy that made her heart ache.

Her Ben was dying.

The kiss left Emma struggling for breath, struggling for composure. She pulled a few inches from him. "Do you love me?" she whispered.

"Jah. More than anything."

Emma closed her eyes and savored the words she'd been aching to hear for months. She bowed her head and wept for pure joy.

"That's why I have to let you go," Ben said.

"Why?" she cried out. "I love you. I want to be with you."

"There's so little time. I don't want you to see what I'm going to become, to have to do personal, unpleasant things for me. No wife should have to do that for her husband."

She pressed her hand against his cheek. "Are you afraid I'll stop loving you?"

"It will get very bad, Emma. You don't understand. A husband should be strong for his wife. I'm the one who should take care of you."

Emma caressed the stubble on his jaw and resisted the growing urge to kiss him again. "Why does it always have to be you?"

"I want to be a gute husband."

"I may be able to find trouble without a compass, but I'm strong enough to pull you out of a well."

He fell silent and studied her face.

She put her arm around his neck and pulled herself temptingly close. "It doesn't matter if you resist, because I am never, ever letting you go again. And as we've already seen, you can't run fast enough to get away from me."

Uncertainty and fear stumbled across his features as he gazed into her eyes, trying to plumb the depths of her sincerity. "Dawdi said that God put people in my path to help me."

"I wasn't put in your path to help you," Emma said. "I am here to love you. And you are here to love me. For as long as we live."

His expression grew like a glorious, breathtaking sunrise. "You still want to be with me?"

"I don't have enough words to tell you how much."

He leaned in and kissed her until she thought she might not be able to see straight. Her pulse danced wildly, and she found herself wishing it would never end, that Ben wouldn't die, and that she could seal her heart to his forever. The tears coursed down her cheeks.

He rested his blood-encrusted forehead against hers. "Are you afraid?"

"Terrified." She traced the contour of his jawline with her finger. "But mostly I'm happy that you love me."

He cracked a smile. "Then will you marry me, even though it will be unimaginably hard?"

Jubilation raced through her veins. She could have taken to the sky like a songbird. "I already said yes a year ago. I haven't changed my mind."

He kissed her again and made her wonder how wide her happiness could spread. She felt saturated in it. After months of despair, Ben was finally hers.

"I am so mad at you right now," she said, her mouth a mere breath from his.

He pulled back in surprise. "What are you talking about?"

"We wasted an entire year because you thought you were being unselfish."

He winced as if his finger had met with a sharp knife. "I know. I wish it hadn't taken me so long to learn what God wanted to teach me."

"I'm not marrying you for your smarts," she teased.

Ben chuckled and brought on a coughing spasm that left him breathless. Pressing his hand to his gut, he grimaced and doubled over in pain. His undershirt was spotted with blood. "I think I scraped most of the skin off my chest on that ladder."

Being careful not to hurt him, Emma laid a gentle hand on his arm. "You need to lie down, and I need to go get help."

"*Now* you want to go get help. You should have gone when I asked in the first place."

"And left you to die? I will never do that."

The sun sank below the horizon, but there had been plenty of light to see by as Emma gingerly made her way through the thicket. Every muscle in her body begged for rest and shooting pains traveled from her shoulder to her arm with every step she took. Her palms stung where the skin had rubbed off from clinging to that pole in the well. Somewhere along the way, she had lost a shoe, and she shook uncontrollably with cold. Only deep concern for Ben kept her going, and it was by the grace of God that she found her way back to Jethro's fire.

Mahlon lounged in a camp chair on the opposite side of the fire. With his gaze in any direction but Lizzie's, he saw Emma first.

"Oh, no," he yelled, jumping from his chair. Taking the shortest path between Emma and himself, he took a flying leap over the fire.

Everyone turned to look. Emma heard a collective gasp, and Lizzie called her name in distress and disbelief. Soon the entire group of young folks surrounded her.

Even though they were used to Emma getting into accidents, shock registered on every face. Matted with twigs and leaves, her unkempt, kapp-less hair hung to her waist, and her sleeve had ripped at the seam, exposing a good portion of her shoulder. Every patch of exposed skin was smeared with mud or dried blood, and that goose egg on her head felt to be about the size of a baseball.

"Somebody call a doctor."

She hissed when Mahlon reached out to take her arm. "My shoulder," she said. "Don't touch my shoulder."

"What happened?" Mahlon said. "Can you sit down?"

She grabbed his elbow with her good hand. "Ben," she said.

A fierce emotion jumped into Mahlon's eyes. "It doesn't matter about Ben. We need to get you to the hospital. Freeman, grab a chair for her. Davy, do you have your cell phone?"

Somebody nudged a floppy camp chair behind her. Her knees buckled, and she suddenly found that she no longer had strength to stand. Keeping hold of Mahlon's arm, she sank into the chair. "Mahlon, Ben is hurt. He can't walk. You need to go get him."

Lizzie clutched the armrest of Emma's chair. "What happened? Where is he?"

"In the woods."

Lizzie turned her eyes to Mahlon, who gazed at her with growing concern on his face. She seemed to disintegrate into a puddle of tears as she threw her arms around Mahlon's neck. "Mahlon, you've got to help Ben."

After a brief moment of uncertainty when Mahlon must have wondered if Lizzie would smack him upside the head, he melted and enfolded Lizzie in an embrace. "Hush," he said. "It's going to be all right. I won't let anything happen to Ben."

"He's in the clearing. Adam knows where it is," Emma said, scanning faces for her ex-boyfriend.

"He left with Martha half an hour ago," Jethro said.

Adam hadn't wasted any time finding another girlfriend. Emma admired his audacity but wanted to growl in frustration all the same. She didn't know if she'd be able to find the spot again, and she wouldn't be able to walk there anyway. "Ben and I fell into an old well." She pointed in the direction she had come. "It's in a clearing."

"He's still in the well?" Lizzie squeaked in panic.

"Nae. We got out, but he's too weak to walk back."

"How far?" Mahlon said while Lizzie clung tightly to him.

"Less than a mile. Take a lantern. You won't see him."

Lizzie released Mahlon's neck. "I'm coming with you."

"No, you're not."

Lizzie narrowed her eyes. "It's my brother. You can't stop me."

Davy handed Mahlon a lantern. "You'll only slow us down, Tizzy."

Lizzie bit her bottom lip, and Emma saw the hurt in her eyes. "You don't want me to come? I'll come if I want, Mahlon Nelson, and there's nothing you can do to stop me."

Mahlon gave her an indignant huff. "We're going without you. It's better for Ben if you don't slow us down. If you can't stand not being able to order people around, stay here and boss Emma. She won't fight back."

Lizzie folded her arms and frowned ferociously. "I am not bossy."

A frown pulled at the corners of Mahlon's mouth. "We can argue about it later."

"We can argue about it never, Mahlon Nelson, because I'm never speaking to you again."

The set of Mahlon's jaw told Emma he wasn't going to say any more about it. He held up the lantern, let Jethro light it, and didn't give Lizzie a second glance. Leaning close to Emma's ear, he said, "You know I'm not real fond of Ben right now, but we'll bring him back safe and sound."

With Mahlon in the lead, the group of boys dived into the thicket, and the sound of rustling leaves faded behind them.

"I'm never, ever speaking to him again," Lizzie said as she wiped away the remnants of her tears. She reached out her hand and took Emma's. "Your hands are ice cold." Half a dozen girls stood around Emma. "Does anybody have a blanket?"

"I've got one," Lori said.

Lizzie knelt beside Emma's chair. "How bad is Ben?"

"I think he'll be okay, but he had a cut on his head."

"And you have a very big lump."

Dinah brought Emma a thermos of hot chocolate. "Can you scootch closer to the fire?"

Emma gave a slight shake of her head. She hurt too much to move a muscle. She shouldn't have sat down. She feared she'd never get up again.

"I need help here," Dinah said.

With three girls on each side and Lizzie giving orders, they carefully lifted Emma's chair and carried it near the fire. Emma held her breath as every movement to her shoulder made her dizzy with pain. But once she got closer to the fire, the crackling heat felt heavenly. She shivered down to her toes.

Lori laid a blanket over her lap, being careful not to jar her shoulder. "I have a towel and some water. Do you want me to clean off the dirt?"

"Nae," Emma said, thinking about her shoulder. "I don't think I'd be able to stand it."

Lizzie squeezed her fingers. "You fell into a well?"

"It all happened so fast. Ben jumped in to save me and then he couldn't move his legs."

Lizzie frowned. "Why not?"

"I stood on his shoulders and climbed out. It was a miracle, but I found a ladder and dragged him out. He hit his head and scraped himself up something wonderful."

"You pulled Ben out of the well by yourself?"

Emma's chest tightened at the memory. He'd been so calm, but she knew she had almost lost him. The thought made her ill. What if her strength had given out? She closed her eyes to block out that horrifying memory. Nae. Even if she'd broken every bone in her body, she wouldn't have let go.

Lizzie caught her breath. "You saved him. You've never rescued Ben before."

"I've never needed to." Ben had always been the one who rescued her.

Lizzie's eyes widened, and she stared at Emma as if waiting for her to understand something. "You didn't run away. You've always depended on Ben to snatch you out of the jaws of death and burning chicken coops." Lizzie put a hand on Emma's good shoulder. The slight movement translated to the other shoulder and made her wince. "I've never been able to convince you, Emma, but you're strong. Without Ben, without Mahlon, you're enough by yourself."

She remembered that feeling of utter helplessness when she fell into that well. "No, not strong at all."

"Who grows acres of pumpkins without a crew of farmhands to help her? Who puts her bad-tempered brother in his place without batting an eye? Who has endured months of heartache with grace and faith? Emma, you are amazing."

"You're making small things sound big," Emma said.

"Big things born of small choices." She tucked the blanket around Emma's ankles. "Emma, what kind of girl can pull my six-foot-five brother out of a well?"

"A girl who has a lot of help from God."

"What I want to know is, why couldn't Ben move his legs? Did he hurt them?"

Emma studied Lizzie's face. Was she ready for this? "He has a disease that makes his legs go weak."

Lizzie gasped. "I don't understand. He has a disease?"

"He's been hiding it for a year. He went to Florida rather than ask for help."

Lizzie's eyes widened with disbelief. "I told you he was an idiot. When I get my hands on him—"

"I just want him to be okay."

Lizzie stopped mid-sentence and frowned. "Me too." She glanced in the direction Mahlon had gone. "Mahlon purposely insulted me so I wouldn't go with them. He's so bullheaded."

"Thank goodness you're not."

They smiled at each other. Lizzie was plenty aware of her own faults.

"Even though you wanted to go, I'm glad you're here with me," Emma said. She couldn't tell Lizzie the seriousness of Ben's condition. Not when they didn't even know if Ben was safe. Ben would tell his family in his own time.

The sirens sounded as if the entire police force and three county fire departments were coming to their aid. Instead of the fleet Emma expected, two police cars, a fire engine, and an ambulance came rolling down the road.

Two men in uniform rushed toward her, but she wasn't alarmed or even particularly interested. She already had experience with paramedics and policemen. And firefighters. She'd even ridden in an ambulance once, although she didn't remember it well after the concussion.

One officer checked her pulse while simultaneously communicating with someone on the radio strapped to his shoulder. She nodded and tried to answer their questions even as her head pounded. "Please," she said, as one of the paramedics asked her to rate her pain on a scale of one to ten. Her anxiety over Ben was an eleven. "Ben is the one who's hurt. I can wait while you help him."

"Miss," said the first paramedic, still awaiting her pain score, "we've got three officers at the scene to help your friend."

Not only my friend. My fiancé. Warmth spread over her. She was going to marry Ben Helmuth, and she would cherish every minute of his love and give him every reason to be happy to be alive.

The paramedic brushed against her shoulder as he lifted his hand to inspect the blood on her cheek. She gasped in pain.

"Does that hurt?" he asked.

"Jah."

"How much?"

The paramedic waited for her to say something. What is it he wanted? Some sort of number? Whatever it was, Emma knew it had to be a big number, like a thousand million billion. She felt that happy.

But also profoundly sad. The knowledge of what was to come tempered her complete happiness, but only momentarily. God loved her. God wanted her to be happy. He would help her find the way.

And Ben still loved her. God had already helped to her find the way back to Ben. She would be greedy to want more.

Chapter 17

Mahlon brought the buggy to a stop slowly so as not to jar Emma's shoulder. Emma, on the other hand, paid no heed to her shoulder as she jumped out of the buggy as quickly as she could with her arm in a sling. She'd gone a whole twelve hours without seeing Ben. If she'd had her way, she would have come home with him and kept vigil at his bedside last night. She hated letting him out of her sight just when they'd found each other again.

She was halfway across the lawn before she realized that Mahlon still sat in the buggy. "Hurry up, Mahlon."

"I'm not going in. I'm just the driver."

"You most certainly *are* coming in. You're going to apologize to Ben for disliking him so much."

"I am not."

Emma propped her hand on her hip. "Jah, you are. Don't argue about it."

"If you make me go in there, I won't apologize.

Like as not I'll give him a piece of my mind for how he treated you."

"He's my fiancé, and he's not well. You'll hold your tongue."

Mahlon scowled until his brows touched. "Then I best not go in."

Emma twisted her lips. "You're not going to make your one-armed sister tote that big basket of goodies into the house, are you?"

Mahlon huffed his displeasure. "Fine. I'll come." He reached into the back and retrieved the basket Emma had packed that morning. "But be glad I'm not inclined to yell at Ben while he's sick."

Emma tried to ignore the stone in the pit of her stomach. If Mahlon was waiting for a full recovery, he'd never get a chance to yell at Ben again.

Anna answered the door before they knocked. They'd made plenty of noise just getting to the porch. She squealed and threw her arms around Emma. "I hear you're engaged!"

Emma all but burst with happiness as she hugged Anna back. "Jah."

Anna patted her on the cheek. "I must be honest. A shadow of a doubt crossed my mind about a month ago. You two made it hard on yourselves."

To her surprise, Ben appeared at his mammi's side sporting a bandage on his forehead and a wide, adorable grin. His legs seemed to be working fine. "I only needed to show forth a little humility."

Emma returned his smile. "And for me to show forth a few muscles."

Ben chuckled. How she loved that silky, resonant bass. Anna moved aside, and Ben took a step closer. Emma slipped her hand into Ben's, partly to be close enough to catch him if his legs buckled but mostly to hold on to him for dear life. She couldn't resist, and she didn't care who knew.

She might have heard Mahlon grunt his displeasure behind her. And she might have decided to ignore him.

"*Cum reu*," Anna said. "You are just in time to see our new arrival. It came yesterday." She hooked her elbow around Mahlon's arm when it looked as if he'd prefer to wait on the porch. "You too, Mahlon. And don't look so miserable. I've got plans."

Before Emma had a chance to even guess at what Anna meant by "plans," she caught sight of Lizzie, who sat on the sofa next to Felty.

Emma smiled, but she might as well not have been in the same county as Lizzie for as much attention as Lizzie paid her. Lizzie scowled and riveted her gaze on Mahlon.

In turn, Mahlon folded his arms across his chest and plopped himself into a chair at the table—as far from Lizzie as he could get. His reaction did not bode well for the rest of the visit.

If this was Anna's plan, Emma feared it was doomed to failure. Mahlon had said too many things he couldn't take back, and Lizzie had dug in her heels so deep she was standing in a hole.

Felty rose from the sofa. "Emma, how nice to see you. Ben says you're sticking with him."

Emma nodded. It saddened her to think that Ben could have ever doubted that.

"I told you it would work out," Anna said.

"Hi, Lizzie," Emma said, keeping her voice soft, fearing anything over a whisper would ruffle the already-ruffled feathers in the room.

Lizzie twisted her lips into what passed for a smile. "How is your shoulder?"

"Not bad. I'm trying to keep still so I won't bump into anything."

Lacing her fingers together, Lizzie shifted on the sofa as if it were the most uncomfortable seat in the world. She made small talk with Emma, but her attention still squarely focused on Mahlon. "Well, don't try to do too much too soon, even if you start to feel better."

"I won't. Mahlon did my chores this morning. He said he'd do them 'til Christmas if I need him to."

Lizzie's face turned three shades redder. Emma shouldn't have mentioned Mahlon—never mind that he sat a mere twelve feet from Lizzie. If they all pretended he wasn't in the room, it would be easier on everybody.

Ben cleared his throat and shuffled farther into the great room with Emma in tow. "Look what we bought for Dawdi."

Emma hadn't noticed it when she first came into the room, but Felty's old tattered recliner had been replaced with a new black leather one with the tags still attached.

"Ben's idea, not mine," Felty said.

"You needed a new one, Dawdi."

"I didn't. Now that you and Emma are back together, I don't know if I'll ever sit in it again. I've been neglecting my chickens."

Ben squeezed Emma's hand. "Show Emma how it reclines," he said. "I figured since Dawdi spent so much time off his feet, we should get him the latest newfangled model."

In spite of his apparent reluctance, Ben's request was all the prodding Felty needed. He was never one to resist a new gadget—as long as it was allowed under the *Ordnung*.

He sat down and seemed to disappear into the chair. "It's called the Brutus. Extra large for extra comfort." He reached down and lifted a small, flat bag that hung over one of the armrests. "This is a little holder for magazines and a TV remote."

Anna sighed. "Now, Felty."

"We'll never have a TV, but it's nice to know I've got a place for it if I ever need one." He pulled the handle and reclined as far back as the chair would take him. "A family of four could sleep in this thing."

"It's good for your back," Ben said.

"And how are you feeling, Felty?" Emma asked.

Felty laced his fingers behind his head. "Well, I got my nosed fixed, my missing tooth replaced, a root canal, and I had Lasik on my eyes last week. I feel like a new man."

Anna giggled. "Some nights I roll over and think, 'Who is this sixty-year-old man sleeping in my bed?'"

Felty rocked forward and seemed to catapult out

of the recliner. "I've decided to turn my chair over to Ben. He needs it in a worse way than I do."

A cloud darkened Ben's features. "I hope not for a while."

Emma wrapped both arms tightly around Ben's arm. "We'll take whatever time God gives us."

Ben's frown faded into shadow as he studied her face. "The Lord gives and the Lord takes away. Blessed be the name of the Lord."

"What did that doctor tell you anyway?" Felty asked. "Lizzie says he gave you seven stitches and ran all sorts of tests."

"He wants me to go back on Monday. I'm not looking forward to hearing the bad news a second time."

The more they talked about Ben's illness, the gloomier he became. Emma wanted to weep for him. How had he endured it all alone for so long? He had talked himself into believing that he was being unselfish, even though there were many people who would have gladly shared the burden with him and counted it a blessing.

She nuzzled her cheek against his arm and resolved to make him the happiest man alive. "How has my pumpkin been growing?"

"Ben has taken wonderful-gute care of it," Anna said. "I knitted a shade covering, and Ben rigged a way to hang it. The sun stays right off."

"I don't wonder that it's five hundred pounds," Ben said.

"I don't think I have enough recipes for all that pumpkin," Anna said.

"I thought the pumpkin was for Toby," Ben said, winking at his mammi.

Anna's eyes grew wide, and she shaped her lips into a silent *O*. Her eyes darted to Emma, as if she'd given away a great secret. "Ach, yes. We must take it to Toby. He'll be thrilled."

Emma smiled. She'd completely forgotten that this excitement had started because Anna claimed she wanted to grow a giant pumpkin for two-year-old Toby. Studying Anna's guilty expression, Emma knew it hadn't been about the pumpkin at all.

Thank heavens for dear Anna Helmuth. She'd brought Emma and Ben back together. Emma's heart swelled. She would never forget Anna's kindness.

Ben bit his bottom lip and gave Mahlon a half smile. "Maybe Mahlon and some of the other boys could help me load it into the wagon. We could deliver it to Toby on Monday."

"You better talk to Tyler first," Felty said. "I don't know what he'll think of a five-hundred-pound pumpkin appearing on his doorstep. It won't make no difference to Toby."

Anna clicked her tongue. "Now, Felty, Toby will love it. It will be like Christmas all over again."

"I'm busy on Monday," Mahlon grumbled.

Every eye turned to him, mostly because he hadn't uttered a word since he had come into the house.

"Busy frowning at people," Lizzie said. She leaned

back in the sofa and folded her arms around her waist.

Mahlon clenched his teeth and turned his face away from all of them. Emma was astounded that he hadn't exploded with a tart reply. Lizzie always stuck under his skin like a burr under a saddle. She admired her brother for having enough self-control to hold his tongue. Or maybe he didn't want to argue with Lizzie in front of Anna and Felty.

Anna clasped her hands, tilted her head, and gazed at Lizzie. Then she turned and regarded Mahlon. She kept a straight face, but Emma could see her eyes twinkling. "When are you planning on tying the knot?" she asked as she strolled to the kitchen and pulled a loaf of dark bread out of the fridge.

"Three weeks," Ben said, flashing a genuinely joyful smile.

Jah, she would see to it that he was wildly happy for the rest of his life. She adored that smile.

Ben cleared his throat and made another attempt with Mahlon. "Mahlon, I hoped you would help me get the dawdi house at my folks' place spiffed up a bit. The kitchen needs a new floor, and the roof has sprung a leak."

Mahlon flared his nostrils like a dragon about to belch fire.

Emma tightened her grip on Ben's arm and silently willed her brother to remain calm.

It didn't work. The flames leaped into Mahlon's eyes. "I helped you repair that roof last summer, and

I can see how well that worked out. Why would I help? You might not stick around."

"Mahlon, be quiet," Emma scolded.

Ben stiffened. "I'm not going anywhere, Mahlon. And I'm sorry for how I hurt Emma." He dropped his gaze to the floor. "You can't even begin to imagine how sorry I am."

Mahlon rose to his feet and erupted. "Really? Well, do you know what I think? I think you were so proud that you didn't even consider how badly you would hurt Emma. She was devastated. Devastated. And we were left to pick up the pieces of her heart when you hightailed it out of here."

"I'm all right, Mahlon. You don't need to be angry anymore."

Ben grew just as agitated as Mahlon, but Emma could tell he directed all his displeasure at himself. "I tried to listen to God's voice, I tried to—"

"If you weren't so proud, Emma wouldn't have spent all that time mourning for you."

Lizzie let out an unladylike snort. "If you weren't so thickheaded, you'd understand that Ben was being unselfish."

Mahlon's face twisted into a tight knot. "Unselfish? He should have had more faith than that."

Her brother's tantrum had gone on long enough. Emma refused to let him say another word against Ben. "Mahlon, stop this at once."

Lizzie stood and gestured to Emma. "I can handle this," she said as she marched toward Mahlon as if she were a wolf about to attack. "Mahlon Nelson, you are the most pigheaded, unreasonable boy I've ever met."

Mahlon met the onslaught head-on. His scowl could have popped the feathers off all of Felty's chickens. "Am I? What about you, Tizzy? You're the one who said Ben was an idiot for breaking up with Emma."

The corner of Ben's mouth quirked upward. "You said that?"

Lizzie didn't even turn to acknowledge her brother. "That's before I knew the truth."

"I still think he was an idiot for breaking it off." Mahlon narrowed his eyes. "And you do too. You're treating him with kid gloves just because he's sick."

"I am not."

"Sick or not, he's going to hear how I feel."

"You didn't even want them back together," Lizzie said, as if accusing him of stealing her horse. "You wanted her to date Adam. What a disaster that turned into."

"I didn't know he'd be a jerk."

"Adam hurt Emma just as bad as anything Ben could have done."

"That's a bunch of baloney," Mahlon protested.

Ben looked at Emma with concern. She smirked and raised an eyebrow. "Let them have it out," she whispered. "They're not satisfied until they've gotten good and riled up."

"Adam was never good enough for Emma," Lizzie said.

"Your brother fell down a well," Mahlon sputtered.

"Who falls down a well when they're trying to save somebody?"

"What about all the other times he rescued her? Remember the chicken coop? And how dare you forget the buggy accident."

Mahlon hesitated only for a second. He wasn't about to let Lizzie get the last word. "That chicken coop was a hazard. Crist Zimmerman should have chopped it to pieces years ago."

Lizzie bobbed her head up and down. "So now you think you can tell Crist how to care for his farm."

"If he needs advice, I'll give it to him."

Emma stifled a giggle. Now they were just groping for things to disagree about.

Acting like a mother who once had thirteen children constantly creating chaos right under her nose, Anna stood at the kitchen counter slicing the bread she'd pulled out of the fridge. She had a serene look on her face, as if Mahlon and Lizzie chatted about the weather. Felty, making good on his threat to never use his recliner again, parked on the sofa and watched the argument with an amused curl on his lips.

"Ben carried Emma home after that buggy accident and pulled her from the lake," Lizzie said.

"Emma saved Ben from drowning," Mahlon countered. "Why are you conveniently forgetting that?"

Anna placed two slices of bread on napkins. "Oh, my," she said. "All this noise upsets Felty's nerves."

"Why do you always blame everything on me, Banannie?"

She handed Mahlon and Lizzie each a slice of the dark, lumpy-looking bread, cupped her hands around their elbows, and nudged them toward the front door. "I want you to go out on the porch to yell at each other. And take a big bite of bread before you go. You can't win an argument on an empty stomach."

Mahlon stared at his slice as if it might bite him.

"Go ahead, both of you," Anna said. "Take a bite. You don't want to offend me, do you?"

Emma felt sorry for both of them. If Anna made the bread, it was as dry as chalk. Maybe that was her plan. If Lizzie and Mahlon both had their mouths full of dry, heavy bread, they might not be able to speak, let alone argue.

Mahlon and Lizzie each took a bite of Anna's bread, and she herded them out the door before they even had a chance to swallow. Anna shut the door and clapped her hands to dust them off. "Those two are so cute together," she said.

"What are you up to, Mammi?" Ben said.

Mischievous lights danced in her eyes. "You'll see."

Anna crouched and tiptoed to the window. Slowly lifting her head, she peeked over the top of the sill. "They're still arguing," she whispered, her eyes bright with anticipation.

"Did you poison the bread?" Felty asked, as if

such a thing happened frequently in the Helmuth house.

"Now, Felty," Anna said, not taking her eyes from the couple outside. "It's a new recipe I made up. I want to see how they like it."

"A new recipe?" Emma asked.

Anna nodded, still gazing out the window. "Jalapeño banana bread. It should be hot enough to make Lizzie cry her eyes out. Boys can't resist it when a girl cries."

"Lizzie doesn't cry," Ben said.

With her gaze still glued out the window. Anna waved dismissively at her grandson. "She will. Those jalapeños are toxic."

"I love jalapeño banana bread," Felty said.

Emma cringed. Nothing sounded less appetizing, and she'd eaten enough of Anna's cooking to know how bad it could get.

"What's happening out there, Annie Banannie?" Felty asked from his perch on the couch.

"Maybe you shouldn't spy on them, Mammi," Ben said, always concerned about doing the right thing.

"Well, dear, someone has to make sure they don't start throwing eggs at each other."

Ben's brows moved closer together. "They've got eggs?"

"They're both coughing. Mahlon is turning red. Oh, there it goes." Anna turned to Felty, and her smile could have dazzled the sunshine. "Lizzie is crying."

Only Anna could make this sound like very good news. She turned back to the window. "Mahlon is patting her on the back. His face is glowing like he's been out in the sun too long."

Ben looked at Mammi with a mixture of curiosity and guilt on his face. He pulled Emma to the sofa, and they sat next to Felty. "Maybe we should plug our ears," Ben said. "I feel like we're intruding on a personal conversation."

"Don't worry, dear," Anna assured him. "I can't hear a thing."

"Have they eaten all the bread?" Felty said.

"Lizzie tossed her piece on the grass. The chickens are picking at it." Anna jerked her face away from the window. "That was close. Mahlon almost spotted me." She stooped over so Mahlon and Lizzie wouldn't see her and shuffled to the other side of the window, where she once again peeked out. "The chickens aren't eating the bread anymore. It wonders me if they find it too spicy."

Ben chuckled and took Emma's hand. "It's like watching an exciting movie."

Anna flinched but didn't turn her gaze from the window. "Oh, my. Oh, my goodness."

Emma sat on the edge of her seat as Anna fell silent. What was happening out there? Were they throwing dirt clods at each other?

"Oh, my," Anna said again. "This plan worked out better than even I could have hoped for."

The suspense became too great. Emma pulled Ben off the sofa and over to the window. Even if he was too scrupulous to spy on his sister, Emma had to have a look. Ben could cover his eyes if he felt he must. He simply grinned at her and shrugged.

Emma giggled as Ben made a great show of sneaking up to the window, stooping low enough not to be seen. With Anna they peered over the sill, taking great pains to watch without being discovered.

Ben gasped.

Mahlon had his arms clamped around Lizzie's waist, and their lips seemed to be attached so firmly that only a crowbar could separate them.

"Jalapeño banana bread," Anna said. "It works every time."

The corners of Emma's lips curled upward. "You've done this before?"

Quite pleased with herself, Anna sighed, stood up straight, and smoothed her apron. "Once. It completely cleared out Sarah Beachy's nasal congestion."

Ben straightened to his full, impressive height and pounded his fist on the glass. The sudden noise made Emma jump. In surprise, Mahlon and Lizzie jerked away from each other and snapped their gazes to the window.

"What?" Mahlon said, looking excessively irritated and sufficiently flustered after kissing Ben's sister.

Lizzie's face glowed bright red and surely not because of the jalapeño banana bread.

Ben, grinning like a chubby cat, yelled so Mahlon could hear him. "The bishop would not approve."

Mahlon frowned as he stared at Ben through the window. Then he burst into a radiant smile. "The bishop need never know," he said, loudly enough to be heard through the window.

He took Lizzie's hand and pulled her away from the window, out of view of curious eyes from inside the house. It didn't take much imagination to guess what went on on the far end of the porch.

Felty came up behind Anna. "A little kissing never hurt nobody," he said, wrapping his arms around his wife of sixty-four years. Anna stood on her tippy-toes and laid a kiss squarely on his mouth.

Emma wondered if she should turn away. Did Anna and Felty care if other people watched them kiss?

Before she had time to decide, she felt Ben's arms around her. She turned to face him and her eyes met his.

"I won't be left out of the fun," he said.

Emma reached her arms around his neck as he tugged her toward him. Their lips met and electricity pulsed down her spine to her toes. The pain of losing him in the near future only intensified her love for him today. The urgency she felt to keep him close overwhelmed her.

She loved Ben Helmuth with her whole soul. She

would hold as tightly as she could until death forced her to let go.

Breathlessly, they parted and turned to see Anna and Felty staring at them looking as cheery as two spring daisies.

Felty shook his head. "It's contagious, Annie."

"I'm delighted," Anna said. "Two grandchildren in one day. Felty, we should start a matchmaking business. We'd get rich."

"I refuse to let them take my gallbladder, Annie. You'll have to come up with another strategy." He stroked his beard. "And you never know about Lizzie and Mahlon. I wouldn't count those eggs until those two actually take marriage vows. Mahlon might get a bee in his bonnet and call the whole thing off tomorrow."

Anna patted his hand. "Not to worry, dear. I can always make more jalapeño banana bread."

Chapter 18

Felty stood at the kitchen counter reading his paper while Anna put the finishing touches on her pudding on the stove.

"What do you know," Felty said, his paper rustling as he turned the pages. "There's a young couple in Loganville that just welcomed triplets. Rosetta, Loretta, and Floyd. And Vernon and Lori Shrock butchered their hog."

"Felty, dear. I know you said you'd never sit in that recliner again, but wouldn't you be more comfortable reading your paper over there?"

"I'm afraid if I sit down, you'll call an ambulance and have them yank out my appendix."

"Well, you don't really need your appendix."

Felty didn't stop reading. "William Graber had a blood clot in his leg. Doing better now, though."

Anna stirred her pudding, with both hands since it had turned out extra thick. "I got a letter from our granddaughter Mandy this morning. She wants to come for a visit."

"Does she? She never could resist her old dawdi."

"It seems one of her friends here in Bonduel got her heart broken in a bad way yet, and Mandy wants to be with her. To give her support, she says."

"Mandy always had a gute heart," Felty said, letting his eyes scan over the recipes in the "Cookin' with Maudie" section of the paper.

Anna heard a crack and looked down. Her wooden spoon had broken off in her pudding. She bustled to the drawer and pulled out a sturdy metal stirrer. No pudding could stand against such a spoon.

"What are you making, Banannie?"

"Jalapeño banana bread pudding. With the leftover jalapeño banana bread."

Felty smiled. "It sounds delicious. I ain't never had it before."

"Emma forgot to take a loaf home to her family, and I had a whole other loaf in the fridge. I adapted my bread pudding recipe, and it's turning out very well."

"Waste not, want not," Felty said, burying his head in the paper again.

Anna took a tiny taste of her pudding and smacked her lips. "The bishop is going to love this. He's been feeling poorly with the divertickle-itis." She took her concoction off the stove and pried it out of the saucepan. "You know, Mandy hasn't asked for our help, but I think we should match her up with someone while she's staying on Huckleberry Hill. Her parents would have a nice surprise if she brought a boy back to Ohio with her."

"Uh-huh," Felty mumbled, thoroughly engrossed in reading about Paul Lapp's hunting trip.

Anna's eyes twinkled merrily as she scooped half of the pudding into a plastic dish. "Then it's settled. She's coming next week. We'll have to get cracking if we want to find her a fiancé. For once, no particular boy is coming to mind. It won't be easy tracking someone down on such short notice."

Felty lost his hold and half of the paper slid to the floor. "Wait a minute, Annie. What did you say about Mandy?"

"Just that we are going to find her a husband."

Felty looked at his wife and sighed. "All this courting is going to give me a heart attack."

Anna smiled reassuringly at her husband. "Now, Felty. There's no need to get huffy. At least your appendix is safe."

"I'm glad to hear it."

Chapter 19

Ben slipped his hand into Emma's as they waited in the doctor's office. They sat on one side of the large wooden desk in deep green wingback chairs and perused the degrees on the wall.

Emma's arm still needed the sling. Mammi had knitted a cheery yellow covering for it so it wouldn't look so fearsome. At least Emma wouldn't be run over by a car while she wore it. The neon yellow could be seen from several miles away.

Ben couldn't relax. His jaw ached with tension and his neck felt so stiff he thought it might snap like a twig if he tried to bend it. His only comforts were the beautiful girl sitting next to him and his assurance that God would not abandon him. How could he fall when Emma and God were on his side?

Nevertheless, at times his doubts warred with his faith, and the fight grew harsh and intense. He prayed for the strength to keep fighting.

Dr. Canali entered the room wearing a white lab coat and stylish amber glasses. He was young, probably fresh out of medical school, and looked permanently grumpy, as if being cheerful took too much work.

He laid down his clipboard and sat behind his desk. "How is your head, Ben? Dr. Burningham said you ended up with seven stitches."

Ben fingered the scar on his head. "Getting better."

"There are hundreds of abandoned wells in Wisconsin. Why people don't clean up their own messes is beyond me. They ought to be fined for tearing up the landscape like that. Abandoned wells can contaminate other wells."

"My friend Jethro just bought the property. He's going to seal the well as soon as he gets the money," Ben said. At least Emma would not fall in that particular well ever again.

"Good to know," said the doctor. He picked up his clipboard and leafed through the pages, frowning and grunting when he read something he must have found interesting. "I know you didn't want to go through all those tests last week, especially since you don't have insurance. It's expensive."

"I already know what's wrong with me," Ben said. "All the tests in the world won't make the bad news any easier to take."

"But they can help us give you better treatment options and"—he glued his gaze to Ben's face and came precariously close to scowling—"sometimes correct a misdiagnosis."

Ben knew all that. To him it merely seemed like a way to part a poor sick man from his money.

"How many times have you seen a doctor since your initial diagnosis of ALS?" Dr. Canali asked.

"I haven't been back. The doctor gave me a prescription and said nothing could be done for me. Why burden the church with more medical bills?"

The doctor referred to his clipboard once more. "I requested your records from your old doctor." He huffed in irritation. "His brand of hasty medicine should have gotten his license revoked. Luckily, he's since retired and moved to California, where he won't be able to afflict any more unsuspecting Amish people." The lines deepened around his mouth, and he looked like a much older man as he leaned forward and rested his elbows on the desk. "Mr. Helmuth, he sent you home with a death sentence you didn't deserve."

Ben's head hurt trying to make sense of what the doctor was telling him.

Get on with what you have to say, and let me alone to spend the time I have left with the girl I love. I've wasted so much already.

"I have good news and bad news," Dr. Canali said, cracking a smile that looked as rare as if he only smiled two or three times a year. "Although in your case, the bad news can probably be considered good news."

Ben held his breath. He refused to let even a wisp

of optimism seep into his mind. He couldn't bear to have his hopes crushed again.

The doctor picked up a pen and made a note on one of the papers. "ALS is a serious degenerative disease. People diagnosed with ALS usually have between three to five years to live. I can imagine that you have been quite anxious about this diagnosis."

"Jah. It's been very hard."

Dr. Canali leaned toward them. "Ben, you do not have ALS, and you are not going to die anytime soon."

Ben felt as if someone suddenly sucked all the air out of his lungs. What did the doctor mean?

Emma's piercing gaze could have cut a hole in the wall. "It's cruel to joke about such things."

Dr. Canali shook his head. "I never joke. Ben does not have amyotrophic lateral sclerosis. The doctor who told you so jumped to about five conclusions with his diagnosis."

"But I have all the symptoms," Ben said, not daring to believe it.

"Early-stage ALS mimics other diseases. Doctors aren't always careful diagnosing it."

Ben shook his head. "What about the tingling and the trouble swallowing?"

The doctor referred to his notes. "The swallowing problems are a severe case of reflux, which can often be treated with a combination of medications. But we do need to talk about the other symptoms."

Emma covered her hand to her mouth. "I'm not going to lose him?"

Dr. Canali's lips curled, and he grunted softly. "You're stuck with him. For a long time."

Ben leaped to his feet and gathered Emma in his arms, being careful not to bump her injured arm. He twirled her around the room, singing one of Dawdi's livelier songs, holding her tightly so she didn't trip over her feet. She laughed as he stopped dancing and kissed her on the mouth, drinking his fill of those sweet lips, savoring this moment of pure joy with Emma Nelson.

"Okay," said the doctor, stuffing his pen into his lab coat pocket. "Don't get carried away. You haven't heard the bad news."

Bad news. Ben had forgotten there was bad news.

Emma wiped the tears from her face, straightened her kapp, and planted a kiss on Ben's cheek. "It wonders me what bad news there could be after news like that."

"There's always bad news," said the doctor. He looked like a person who always expected the worst.

Ben grabbed her hand, in plain sight of the doctor, and they sat down together.

She gave his fingers a squeeze.

"I'm ready for the bad news," he said.

The doctor nodded. "There is a reason for the symptoms you've been having. I'm ninety percent certain you have multiple sclerosis."

"Oh," Emma said, losing the light in her eyes. "I see."

Ben had furrowed his brow so much in the last

hour that his forehead ached. "I thought you said I wasn't going to die."

"MS is a disease that attacks the central nervous system. That's why you've been experiencing numbness and tingling, stiffness in the arms and legs. It can be mild or severe, but from what you've described and from the results of the tests, you most likely have relapsing/remitting MS, meaning you'll have only a few episodes a year. It's degenerative but treatable. Treatment will allow you to have an excellent quality of life."

"Expensive treatment?" Ben asked.

Dr. Canali waved his hand dismissively. "The medications are expensive. But there are dozens of aid programs to help people like you."

Ben looked at Emma. "I don't know. If I take the medication, the church will help, but money will always be tight."

She gave him that goofy smile she always got when she thought he was acting like an idiot. "Of course you'll begin treatment. Five minutes ago we thought you were dying. Who cares if we have to live on rice and fried pumpkin the rest of our lives? I don't care what it costs if it lets us be together longer."

"Much longer," said the doctor.

His heart felt as if it would leap out of his chest when he thought about all the extra time they'd been given.

God is good.

"We'll grow acres and acres of pumpkins to bring

in extra money," she said. "Each with its own knitted shade cover from your mammi."

He reached over, took her face in his hands, and kissed her with all the joy of anticipating a lifetime together with her. Was any man ever so richly blessed?

"I thought you Amish people weren't allowed to kiss," said the doctor. He cocked his eyebrow and twisted his lips into what almost looked like a grin.

"Not so," Ben said, laughing with the pure gratitude. "Why do you think we have such big families?"

Emma cuffed him on the shoulder. "Really, Ben? In front of a stranger?"

The doctor did that grunting thing again. "No need to apologize. I've heard things that would curdle your Amish milk." He swiveled around in his chair and pulled several sheets of paper from one of his files. "Now, are you ready to talk about treatment?"

"Before we do that," Ben said, "would you pray with us? I can't go one more minute without thanking God."

Dr. Canali cleared his throat and stood up. "Um, I'll wait outside while you do whatever it is you need to do."

"Nonsense," Emma said. She stood, pulled Ben with her, and reached out her good hand to the doctor. "Cum, hold hands with us."

Acting as if she'd offered to chop his hand off, Dr. Canali reluctantly took Ben's hand, and Ben held Emma's.

"Dear Heavenly Father, thank You for bringing

Dr. Canali into our lives. Thank You that he insisted that I get tests. I am grateful most of all that You have blessed me with more time. I am so grateful to have MS. And thank You for letting me fall into that well and bringing Emma back to me. Amen."

The doctor lifted his head with a sheepish expression on his face. At least he wasn't frowning. "I've never been an answer to someone's prayer before. But don't tell anybody. They'll be coming for miles for a miracle. I'm not a miracle worker. I'm just ornery."

Emma and Ben walked hand in hand out of the doctor's office into the bright late-summer sunshine. The air was fresh with the smell of recent rain. Emma had never been so deliriously happy.

"I know we barely have time to get ready for the wedding as it is, but I wish we could marry tomorrow," Emma said.

Ben shook his head. "Mahlon would accuse me of trying to sabotage his wedding. Lizzie has her heart set on a double wedding, and as eager as I am to marry you, I couldn't disappoint my little sister."

"I know. Lizzie and I have planned to have a double wedding since seventh grade."

"Mahlon's fiery temper and Lizzie's stubborn determination seem to mix like oil and water. Do you think they'll suit?" Ben said.

Emma smiled to herself. Mahlon would walk across fire for Lizzie. He'd grumble about it first, but he'd do it all the same. "Mahlon adores Lizzie. They might butt heads now and then, but they'd get bored if it were otherwise."

"Lizzie always did like getting under Mahlon's skin."

"And Mahlon loves it when Lizzie needles him, even though he'd never admit it."

They crossed the parking lot to Ben's buggy before Emma stopped walking, lifted her chin, and smiled, inviting him to kiss her. He didn't need to be asked twice. With a gentle embrace, he took her into his arms and kissed her as if they were the only two people in the world.

"Mmm," he said, without letting go. "It doesn't matter how long I live. I'll never get enough of that." He tightened his solid arms around her as apprehension darkened his features. "It will be a hard life, Emma."

"Nothing worth having ever comes easy. Heartache and struggle will only make our love stronger. And we'll be together."

"But I might not be able to rescue you when you upend the buggy or burn down a building."

"So I'll singe my eyebrows once in a while. That's not a big concern to me. I won't want for anything as long as I'm with you." She leaned up and brushed her lips across his. He trembled. "But can you truly love a girl who doesn't have eyebrows?"

He laughed softly. "I'll have to give that some thought."

She turned to climb into the buggy and stubbed

her foot on the uneven pavement. Ben reached out and caught her before she tumbled into a mud puddle.

"Are you okay? That sling throws your balance out of whack."

"What balance?" she said archly.

His eyes twinkled as he helped her right herself. "At least for today, I can still stop you from falling."

"I'll never stop falling for you," she said.

He groaned and rolled his eyes at her lame pun.

She giggled like a teenager, turned too quickly, and ran smack dab into the side of the buggy. She'd be seeing stars for days.

Please turn the page for an exciting sneak peek of

Jennifer Beckstrand's

HUCKLEBERRY HARVEST,

coming in June 2015!

The chickens gathered at Anna Helmuth's feet as she scattered scratch from her pail. "Oh, dear," she said. "I suppose I should have tossed it away from me if I wanted to keep my shoes clean."

"You're doing a fine job, Annie," her husband Felty said. "The hens are getting fat."

Anna tiptoed around the chickens as they pecked at the feed. Bitzy, the Plymouth Rock hen, put up a fuss when Anna accidentally stepped on her, but she recovered enough to squawk in disapproval before going back to her breakfast. "Did you bring the chopped carrots?" Anna asked.

Felty pulled a handful of carrot pieces from his pocket. "This is all we had."

"It will be enough." Anna took the slices from Felty's hand and tossed them into the small flock of chickens. She beaned one chicken in the head inadvertently, but surely a carrot to the head wouldn't have hurt anybody seriously. The chicken kept right on eating and didn't seem to notice. "I'm planning a special breakfast for Mandy's first day on Huckleberry Hill, and I want the eggs to be extra bright yellow."

"What special breakfast are you making for our granddaughter?"

"She's only staying a month, so I want every meal to be memorable. Tomorrow morning we're having Eggs Benedict. I've never made it before, but the picture in my recipe book looks delicious. I just have to figure out what a poached egg is, and we'll be all set."

"Do you still want to find a boy for Mandy while she's in town?"

"Jah. But don't worry. I'll see to it that any romantic goings-on will not be detrimental to your blood pressure."

"What about my ulcer?"

Anna propped a hand on her hip. "Now, Felty. You don't have an ulcer."

"I will by the time Mandy goes back to Ohio."

"We can't let Mandy leave Bonduel without a husband."

Felty stroked his salt-and-pepper beard. "It's a bit of a stretch to think Mandy will meet a boy, fall in love, get engaged, and plan a wedding in one month's time."

Anna bit her bottom lip. "Maybe we could talk her into staying an extra week."

"We better encourage the chickens to lay more eggs if we need five weeks of Eggs Benefit," Felty said.

"Now, Felty. We'll have enough time. Our biggest problem is finding the right young man for our granddaughter. Her plans for a visit took me by surprise. I haven't had the time to spy out prospective husbands like I usually do. I just don't know what boy in Bonduel would do for our Mandy."

Felty nodded. "She's a spunky sort of girl."

"Jah," Anna said, dumping the rest of the scratch from her pail onto the ground. "She needs a spunky, cheerful boy to keep her laughing."

Felty took the pail from Anna as they walked toward the house. "What do you think of Noah Mischler? He's as *gute* a boy as ever there was."

Anna furrowed her brow until the wrinkles piled on top of each other. "Noah Mischler? He's as solid as a tree."

"Is that bad?"

"*Nae.* It means he's not afraid of hard work."

"A hard worker is the most important quality for a grandson-in-law to possess."

Anna ran her hands down the front of her apron. "Don't get me wrong, Felty. I adore Noah Mischler. Saloma Miller tells me he put a new gas stove in her kitchen last April that practically makes dinner by itself. Noah is smart enough to fix anything that's broken, and he's so gute to his dat. But I don't think he and Mandy would suit. He's gloomier than three weeks of rain."

Felty rubbed the back of his neck. "Maybe he don't have much cause to smile these days."

"Mandy won't look twice at someone like him. We've got to think of somebody else."

Felty opened the door for his wife of sixty-four years and followed her into the house. "How will we ever find someone in four weeks?"

"Five weeks. We'll talk Mandy into five weeks. And I'm going to pull out my new recipe book. The way to a man's heart is through his stomach."

"In that case, Mandy won't have a lick of trouble finding a boy. Nobody knows how to cook like you do, Annie." Felty paused inside the door, looked around the great room, and thumbed his suspenders. He grinned as an idea came to him. "Annie, how would you like a new gas stove for all this cooking you're going to be doing?"

More by Bestselling Author
Hannah Howell